The Blind Wish

JINNI WARS
II

The Blind Wish

AMBER LOUGH

RANDOM HOUSE 🏠 NEW YORK

Text copyright © 2015 by Amber Lough
Jacket art copyright © 2015 by Marcela Bolivar
Interior title page and chapter opening ornaments
copyright © Azat1976/Shutterstock

All rights reserved. Published in the United States by
Random House Children's Books, a division of
Penguin Random House LLC, New York.

Random House and the colophon are registered trademarks of
Penguin Random House LLC.

Visit us on the Web! randomhouseteens.com

Educators and librarians, for a variety of teaching tools, visit us at
RHTeachersLibrarians.com

Library of Congress Cataloging-in-Publication Data
Lough, Amber.
The blind wish / Amber Lough.—First edition.
p. cm.
Summary: "Zayele and Najwa's adventure continues as the war
between jinnis and humans escalates."—Provided by publisher.
ISBN 978-0-385-36980-0 (trade)—ISBN 978-0-385-36982-4 (ebook)
[1. Genies—Fiction. 2. Princesses—Fiction. 3. Wishes—Fiction. 4. Courts and
courtiers—Fiction. 5. Baghdad (Iraq)—Fiction. 6. Iraq—Fiction.] I. Title.
PZ7.L9237Bli 2014 [Fic]—dc23 2014005756

Printed in the United States of America
10 9 8 7 6 5 4 3 2 1
First Edition

For

James, who helps me see the truth

✦   ✦   ✦

Where is the eye that can see You?
The Beloved is there, but the eyes are blind.
We are lost in our own veil,
While everywhere Your vision prevails.

So long as *Atta* is lost in Your sorrow
The people of the heart will always yearn for him!

—FARID AL-DIN ATTAR
(AD 1145–1221, AH 539–617)

ZAYELE

THE CAVERN DOMED around us and bit into the air with jagged crystal teeth. It smelled of too many people all in one place, but it was cool and misty beside the tall waterfall that gushed in through a crack. Atish, one of my few jinni friends, handed me a glass orb the size of a plum. It was hollow and clear, like the hundreds of other orbs nestled in everyone else's palms. It weighed next to nothing, and I was afraid it would float away if I breathed out too fast.

We stood along the canal that divided the Cavern into two similar hemispheres. The canal began at the waterfall, snaked through the glittering jinni city, and poured into the Lake of Fire. A web of tall gas lamps kept the city pulsing in bright, golden light. The jinn called them wishlights.

Spreading outward from the canal were the homes and buildings made by the jinn, some stacked and sloping up the curved walls. There were more jinn, more buildings, and more scents and colors here than in my human village in the mountains, and I wasn't sure I would ever become accustomed to the crowd. Today was worse than usual. I had to twist my shoulders sideways to avoid brushing up against anyone, and when that didn't work and I found myself face-in-armpit with a tall stranger, I would hold my breath and slink away as fast as I could. A few times, Shirin smiled apologetically at me, as though she understood what was troubling me but could do nothing to change it.

It was the day of the Breaking, something that happened once a year. All jinn except my twin, Najwa, who was still in the Baghdad palace, had come to the canal. As it was my first time witnessing the Breaking, Atish and Shirin guided me, like a lost child, to a row of carts where an army of old women stood handing out the glass orbs.

Atish was the newest member of the Shaitan, the elite branch of the jinni army, and Shirin was still waiting for her chance to be marked into the Corps of Physicians. Both of them had been friends with Najwa before I arrived, and had saved me when I'd made a mess of things before. *Alhamdulillah* for Najwa's friends, because without them I'd be sniffing jinni armpits all day.

"See?" Atish asked. He pointed at the dozens of children lining the canal. Some leaned out over the water, holding up their little orbs of glass. But theirs were lit from within, each a different color. One boy, taller than the rest, pulled back his arm and threw his orb into the waterfall.

The ball of light plopped into the canal and bobbed to the surface before floating downstream. Seconds later, a spray of colored orbs attacked the waterfall as the rest of the children sent theirs flying.

By twos and threes, they floated past where I stood, pressed between Atish and Shirin. Each one was still whole, still glowing, like soap bubbles in sunlight.

"How do they not break?" I asked.

"Magic," Atish said wickedly.

I snorted in response and rubbed my thumb over the slick surface of my own orb. "Show me what I'm supposed to do, oh great wise man."

He held his orb up to his nose and shut his eyes. A moment later, a faint pop came from his hands, followed by a golden flame that grew from within the orb. "Easy." He winked at me.

Beside me, Shirin groaned. "That does nothing for her, you know." She leaned in close. "You're supposed to think of something you regret, something that is keeping you from moving on. It could be something as small as lying about what you ate for breakfast, or, you know . . ."

She didn't have to finish. I knew she was referring to the wish I'd made on Najwa. When I first met Najwa, I'd been on my way to Baghdad to marry Prince Kamal. I was desperate to avoid marrying the prince, because I wanted to be with my little brother Yashar. When a jinni showed up at my window, I thought she was an answer to my prayers. I grabbed her, wished on her, and made her take my place. What I didn't know then was that I was making a Fire Wish—a wish demanded by one jinni from another. Basically, I enslaved Najwa and stole her life from her. It's hard to recover from doing something like that to anyone, especially your sister.

"But the point is," Shirin continued, "you put your bad

memory in here, where it can't get out, and then you send it to the lake."

"Why to the lake? What's supposed to happen to it there?"

"It shrivels and dies," Atish said.

"No." Shirin shook her head. "It disintegrates. It'll float out there until it comes across one of the flames. Then the flames will break the glass and absorb the weight of the memory."

"And then I won't remember it anymore?" I asked. I wasn't sure forgetting any of my mistakes was a good thing. How would I know who I was if I forgot what I had done?

"You'll remember it," she said. "But it won't drag you down anymore."

"Which raises the question," Atish said with a teeth-flashing grin, "what could *I* have done that I regret this year?"

I gulped, not sure how to respond, which annoyed me. He was teasing me, and I liked it—which annoyed me even *more*.

Shirin took my hand in hers, palm outstretched. "Just hold up the orb, like Atish did, and send the memory into the orb. It's like recording a memory in a crystal shard. Only this is more symbolic."

The jinn can store memories in crystals, which they revisit whenever they want to. It was useful, but my first experience as witness to such a memory had been morbid and shocking. I wasn't in a hurry to go through that again.

"I haven't recorded any memories. Ever."

"You just think about it, then wish it into the glass. It's not that hard. I mean, all those children did it," she said.

I nodded, and stared into the clear ball. The orbs from the

children's memories floated past, lighting my orb from behind. If they could do it, so could I.

But lighting it wasn't the hard part. I had to choose one bad memory. Why only one? I could fill up an entire box of these little balls each year.

The Fire Wish had *not* been a good idea. I should never have forced Najwa to take my place as Prince Kamal's bride. I'd been selfish, because I hadn't even considered what Najwa might want. But I hadn't known I was half-jinni, and besides, I'd fixed it. The lies I'd told pretending to be Najwa were all out in the open now, and no one hated me for them. When I'd first come to the Cavern, I'd hated and distrusted all the jinn, and now I was close friends with two. The Fire Wish had done some damage, but it wasn't holding me back.

There was one thing that still stuck in me, like a burr—my cousin Yashar's blindness. Yashar, who up until a few weeks ago I'd thought was my little brother, had been the brightest star in our village. His father had fawned over him, the women had tousled his hair, and the children had begged to hear his stories and poems. His loyalty to me ruined him. He came with me to the sand dunes, a day trip I was not supposed to take, and we were caught in a sandstorm. The sand scraped his eyes, and after weeks of pain, he was left blind. *It was my fault.* Since I'd last seen him, I'd discovered I had a twin sister, was half-jinni, and was able to grant wishes. But I still hadn't done anything to help him.

Yashar's eyes, I thought, and pushed the memory of my little cousin—wailing behind me on the camel—into the orb. A second later, there was the pop, just like with Atish's memory. Then a gold-brown flame flickered into life. It was the length of a baby's finger, and the color of Yashar's eyes before the sandstorm had scarred them white.

Shirin filled her orb and we all looked at each other. Atish's characteristic seriousness returned in the tight corners of his mouth, and he nodded. Then he and Shirin tossed their painful memories into the water and leaned over the railing until the orbs disappeared beneath the first bridge.

At that moment, the children ran past, pushing through the jinn who still clutched their unlit orbs. They moved like a herd of bejeweled deer, racing their lights along the canal.

Atish placed a hand on my shoulder and squeezed. "You can throw it in now."

"I'm not ready."

"Then let's walk down to watch the Breaking. No need to run."

I nodded and followed them down the path, sometimes waiting for a jinni in front of us to move to the side. My mind was stuck, even though my body moved. I had tried to put Yashar's screams, his agony, into the ball, but I could still hear them.

He had cried for days. I had spent most of my waking time up on the cliff, at the ledge I'd often shared with him. I didn't deserve to be there with those who were trying to heal him. I knew this not just because it was what I felt, but because of the narrowed, flashing looks I got from his father. I'd taken his oldest son into the desert and brought him back damaged and useless. That could not be forgotten. Now that I knew he'd been aware of my real mother's identity, all the sharp glances and criticisms stung more.

Without waiting another breath, I reached out over the edge of the path and threw my orb down. It landed hard on the water, splashing and pushing aside some of the other orbs. For a second, I was worried it'd break right there, before it got to the lake, but then it drifted as easily as a leaf in a stream. I followed it with my eyes until I couldn't tell it apart from the other balls of light.

I squinted at the orbs.

Shirin squeezed my hand. "Don't worry," she said. "It takes a while. And they have to be absorbed by the flames, remember?"

My stomach twisted. It didn't matter what happened with the orb, because it wouldn't change what had happened to Yashar.

2

NAJWA

IT WAS THE day of the Breaking, but I was in Baghdad and there were no grandmothers handing out glass spheres. I crouched beside the harem garden's stream, did my best to ignore the peacock scratching the gravel an arm's reach away, and cupped a jasmine blossom in my hand.

I had tested another jasmine blossom, watching it float across the garden stream and sink beneath the grate, disappearing behind the harem's wall. It would have to do. I brought the flower up to my nose, inhaled the syrupy scent, and closed my eyes.

Much had happened in the past year, and I had several regrets. I had sought out the bride from Zab, Zayele, and left the Cavern against Faisal's orders. I had lied about who I was. But worst of all, Faisal was dead because of me. He had come to save me, even though I didn't deserve his help, and Hashim had killed him. Now, the Eyes of Iblis Corps had no master. The school had no one to teach Transportation. And I no longer had someone to go to when faced with unanswerable questions.

The heaviest pain I carried was his death, but I could not

let it go. In fact, I deserved to be away from home, alone on Breaking day.

Another hurtful thought was that my real mother, Mariam, was a mystery to me. She had left her Cavern home to marry a poor human and live in the mountains. This led to her and my father's death, an unjust blaming of the jinn, and the start of the war.

I blew a shadowy image of her into the blossom and thought, *I never knew my real mother.*

The pain and loss sparked and grew into a tiny violet flame. It danced around the jasmine's stamen, and the blossom glowed, even in the brightness of midday. Discovering a memory's color was my favorite part.

I set it carefully onto the stream and gave it a push. It spun on the surface, weightless and delicate, past rounded clumps of rosebushes, the shade beneath a date palm, and a gazebo of turquoise and white marble. The blossom bent to the right, dropped down a series of shallow steps, and dove beneath the wall and out through the grate.

There was no pop, no lakefire shredding the painful memory to bits, no giggling and shrieking of small children. Just the silence that follows after a flower has been swallowed by the darkness.

The wish was real, but the Breaking didn't work.

I was still kneeling there beside the stream when Kamal returned. I hadn't heard him slip into the garden, or noticed the crunching of gravel beneath his sandals. My eyes were sewn onto the point of darkness, the little gap of air between the top of the tunnel and the surface of the stream.

"Najwa," he whispered, sinking onto his knees beside me. "What's wrong?" His hand brushed my cheek and wiped away a tear I had not felt form or fall.

I swallowed away a lump in my throat before I answered. "Today is a special day in the Cavern. I was thinking about that." I forced a smile and turned to face the prince. "Nothing's wrong."

"What kind of day?" His hand dropped from my face and joined the other to settle onto the ends of my fingers, where they brushed, softly, against my skin. My arm tingled, and I resisted the urge to pull it away.

"A day of remembering and letting go of pain," I said.

"That's wise. Atonement brings peace to the soul." His voice sounded more strained than usual. "Do you want to go home?"

I shook my head. "I promised to stay here, at least until the war is over."

He slipped his fingers off mine and picked up the pendant I wore around my neck, scraping his nail over the bit of bent silver, where the cut of moonstone had been. He had promised to replace the stone, but had been too busy to do so. "Is that the only reason you want to stay?"

I bit my lip and looked away. I wanted to tell him I was there because of him, but I was afraid.

After a second, he sighed and added, "My father is going to announce the new vizier in a few minutes."

"Then we should go." I started to push myself up off the ground, but he stopped me. There was a shadow in his eyes that should not have been there. "What is it? Am I not allowed in the Court of Honor now?"

Everything that I had been welcome to do before they'd discovered I was a jinni was slowly being taken away. The rules had not officially changed, but I was hesitant to go where I was clearly unwanted. At the mosque, some of the people shied away and hissed loud prayers of protection from jinn. The fear in their eyes kept me from taking a step inside.

It didn't matter that I'd awakened the caliph from his coma and revealed the former vizier's evil lie that had begun the war between our peoples. No one seemed to remember that my father had been human. They only remembered that my mother had been a jinni. The revelation that I was half-jinni overshadowed everything else. And to make matters worse, I wasn't an ordinary jinni. I wasn't a weaver, or a healer, or anything mundane. I was in the Eyes of Iblis Corps and had been trained to spy on humans. I had also claimed to be Zayele, the princess from Zab, and the last time I'd stood before the Court of Honor, I'd been caught in the lie.

No one but Kamal trusted me now.

He smiled. "You're allowed everywhere, of course. In time, they will get used to you. But before we are surrounded by all those old men, I want to tell you something." He bent down and picked a pebble off the ground and then tossed it into the stream. It plopped and sank immediately. "The new vizier is going to face a world of troubles. First, he needs to reach an agreement with the jinn in order to end the war once and for all. Second, he will have to find a way to tell the people about

Hashim's treason without making my father look bad. He will have to change the people's minds about jinn first, and that will take time."

I didn't know what to say to that. We needed the war to end now, and the best way for that to happen would be for the caliph to make a statement about Hashim. People's lives were at stake—it wasn't the time for worrying about reputations.

He sighed. "I know you want it all to happen immediately, but it can't. I just . . . I want you to understand all the pressures the vizier will be facing. His third challenge will be to keep you from getting angry."

I crossed my arms. "If he is working toward peace between our peoples, then why would I be angry?" I didn't think we needed to wait, but I wasn't impatient. From what I'd learned of Zayele, it seemed more like *her* to be the impatient one. I had been taught how to be watchful and still, controlling my heart rate and my impulse to quicken a situation. I had learned that people are slow to change, as well.

"There's more." He swallowed hard. "The vizier will only be allowed to speak with you in public. Otherwise, the people of Baghdad may question his loyalty. If he meets with a jinni behind closed doors, rumors will spread like the stars at twilight."

He stared into my eyes, unblinking. He was trying to tell me something else beneath all those words, something that saddened him. He pulled me up off the ground then and held me close. When I felt the stiffness of his shoulders, I knew.

"It's you. You're the new vizier."

I felt his head nod against my own. He placed his lips

against my ear and whispered, "If it weren't for the sake of all of us, I would have turned him down. Just to be with you, like this, forever." He kissed my temple softly.

"It's an honor to be chosen" was all I could say.

"I made a promise to my father that we wouldn't see each other in secret."

Tears ran down my face. "Am I such a monster?"

"No." He pulled back and held my face in his hands. His eyes were wet. "He knows you saved his life, Najwa, but he is afraid. Not of *you*, but of ignorance, and the strength of Hashim's lies. And he is an old man, slow to change."

"Hashim has great power even in death," I said bitterly.

"I am going to end all of this, as cleanly and quickly as I can. The hatred and fear must end. And it begins here, in the palace. Which is why I'm bringing you, now, to the Court of Honor. After my father appoints me as vizier, I'm going to begin showing the people how *human* you are."

I flinched. I was half-human *and* half-jinni. Neither one was stronger or better than the other. To see only half of a person's race was like looking at her shadow to see what color her eyes were.

"Kamal, I'm not going to hide who I am anymore. So if your father believes we shouldn't be seen together in private, then we'll meet only in public," I said. Had they forgotten I could make myself unseen? Or did his father not know? The thought of this strengthened me, and I took a half step back from Kamal and straightened my posture. "Then let's work on peace, together."

Finally, he smiled, and it was like daybreak. He kissed my

forehead and then guided me along the garden path to the billowing curtains in front of the harem's door. Before he pulled the curtains back, he leaned his head toward mine and said, "I know what you're planning, and it can't happen. I cannot see you. I made a promise."

I forced my face to remain smooth and calm despite my plummeting spirits.

"But I will *want* to every moment of every day," he added before sweeping the red curtain aside and stepping through the opened door.

The Court of Honor was the meeting place for the men who ruled the caliphate. Three walls surrounded the room, each a series of arches and stone, and the fourth side was left open to a large, geometric garden.

Kamal looked over his shoulder and gestured for me to stand off to the side in an alcove opposite the men's garden, in a place surrounded by a tiled arch of blue and white. From there, I was able to see and hear everyone, but I was not so close that I could cause them any discomfort. Framed by the arch, I was the jinni on display.

The caliph sat on his gilded peacock throne, a head higher than everyone, and gripped the armrests like they were his only hold on earth. He wore a robe embroidered in sapphires as rich as his throne, but the brightness only highlighted how pale he still was from his injury. He smiled weakly at me and then faced the circle of men. Kamal found a stool next to the throne and sat down on it, facing us all from beside the caliph.

The men wore black, and for some, it matched their flowing beards and the scowls creasing their foreheads. A handful looked at me questioningly while the rest made a point of ignoring my existence. One, the scholar I'd met from the House of Wisdom, gave me half a smile before turning his attention to the caliph.

The caliph cleared his throat and waved his arm in the air, pointing a gold-ringed finger at me. "Najwa of the Jinn, we welcome you to the Court of Honor." His voice had grown stronger since he'd awoken.

I bowed from my niche in the wall. "It is my pleasure, Caliph al-Mansur. My elders send their goodwill and hope for a renewed discussion regarding peace between our peoples." It was what I'd been instructed to say. Delia, the current commander of the Eyes of Iblis Corps, had drilled it into me before I'd left the Cavern. Since Faisal's death, she had stepped in until someone could be named his successor. Thinking of her only reminded me of Faisal, so I forced the pain aside.

The caliph's lips tightened, as if he didn't believe what I had said. "We know what you have personally done for the caliphate, and we all appreciate it." There was a murmur amongst the men, but the caliph silenced them with a piercing look. "I, in particular, have much to thank you for. But we have to decide what is to be told to the people of Baghdad, to the caliphate as a whole. You must understand that we cannot tell them the entire truth about Hashim."

The truth was that Hashim had killed my parents and blamed the attack on the jinn. It had started the war just as he'd planned. Why wasn't the caliph going to tell the people the truth? The only way to free the jinn of blame was the truth. My jaw tightened, and I forced myself to appear relaxed.

The caliph continued, "I regret that if we were to make a public announcement, there would be a revolt—"

Kamal lifted his head. "But, Father—"

"Not yet, Kamal." The caliph lifted his hands off the armrests and brought his fingertips together. "It troubles me as much as it does you, but the truth of the matter is that I will not make such a statement. I will not tell the people what Hashim did to all of us. Think about it, my son. I chose him as vizier. What will happen if the people think I cannot choose an honest man to be my adviser? I agree that we must end this war. There should be—there *must* be—peace. But it starts from today. We will not stir up the sands of the past.

"Najwa, I am sorry you cannot return to your people with a better story. I also regret that you cannot stay here permanently."

"Sir, is this because I am a jinni?"

The caliph nodded.

Kamal sucked in a breath and looked up at the ceiling. "But she's half-human—she had a human father."

"Any jinni blood at all makes her a jinni in the people's eyes, Kamal."

One of the scholars, the one who had been so friendly toward me, cleared his throat loudly and took a step closer to the throne.

"Yes, Jafar?" the caliph asked.

Jafar bowed. "My caliph, some members of the House of Wisdom would like to make a request." Jafar tugged on his gray beard. "Before the war, when jinn were granted access to the House of Wisdom, we had great discourse, great advancement. If it's possible, we would like a jinni or two to be allowed there again. For the benefit of scientific discovery."

There were a few disgruntled clicks of the tongue from the other men, but the caliph nodded thoughtfully. "Under supervision," he said. "And they must return to their Cavern each night."

"Yes, of course." Jafar beamed and rejoined the circle of men, who whispered amongst themselves.

The caliph studied his rings. "I am sure you are all wondering about my appointment for vizier." The whisperings died instantly. "I have chosen someone I could trust with my life, someone who would never lie to me. Someone we can *all* trust." He patted the head of one of the enameled peacocks built into the throne. "My son Kamal."

The silence that followed was as hollow as an empty cave. Kamal bowed stiffly to his father from his stool. Now that the caliph had made his appointment, it was real. Kamal would work within his position as vizier to bring peace between us, and I would have to stay at a safe, public distance.

Kamal stood up and opened his mouth. I was certain he was going to tell them I should be allowed to stay permanently in the palace, in order to mend the ties between jinn and humans, but instead his eyes widened in surprise and any such words died on his tongue.

The caliph looked up and his face immediately flushed with pride. "Ibrahim!"

Like a flock of birds in flight, we turned in unison to see Prince Ibrahim standing in a beam of sunlight at the far end of the hall. His armor glinted, his arms were crossed, and his eyes burned straight into me.

+ 3 +

ZAYELE

ATISH AND SHIRIN walked me back to the house that Najwa, Rahela, and I now shared. It was the only house in the Cavern built with humans in mind, and although I wouldn't have minded a jinni house, Rahela was much more comfortable there.

The house was tucked between long fingers of gypsum shards, with a front of malachite and alabaster. The green and white walls weren't inspiring, but they were straight, unlike in the jinni homes. The part I liked best about the house was that it wasn't out in the open, beneath the spears of crystal that hung precariously from the ceiling.

The only negative aspect of the house was that Hashim had lived in it when he was the human ambassador, and none of us wanted to go into his room. It had been cleansed after he left, but no matter how much they cleaned, no one had been able to get the feeling of Hashim out of the corners and shadows.

Atish pushed open the door and let me pass inside, where

I found my cousin Rahela sitting in front of a tall loom we had borrowed from Najwa's adoptive mother, Laira. Rahela plucked the warp like it was a harp, pausing only a second to tie a knot around it. We waited for a moment until she looked up and stopped. The silence echoed in the cold stone room.

"How was your ceremony?" she asked me. She said it in a tone my mother used all the time—both agreeable and disagreeable at the same time. Not my mother, my *aunt,* I reminded myself. It hadn't been long since I'd discovered my true mother had been killed when I was an infant, and that she'd been a jinni.

"It was interesting and pretty, I guess. It's supposed to make us all feel better," I said. "You should have come. Someone could have helped—"

"I did my prayers, like I am supposed to," she said. "That should be enough for someone of our faith."

That was what was wrong, then. I wasn't acting like a girl from our village should. I wasn't praying at the right times and I was spending all my time with jinn.

Atish and Shirin stood by the door, and both of them looked ready to run back out. I motioned for them to stay, and went to Rahela, pretending I wanted to see what she was weaving.

"Rahela, you don't have to stay here. Someone could take you back."

She plucked at the warp and continued to tie her knots. "Back where?" Pluck, knot, pluck, knot. "I have no place. I can't go home, because I failed in the one job I was ever given. *You.*"

I had failed *her,* actually, but I didn't want to irritate her more by bringing it up again.

"I'm sure if you go home, they'll understand. Or you can go to Najwa. She has no idea what humans are like, even if she thinks she does. I'm sure she needs you to help her with etiquette just like you did before."

"I don't want to go back to Baghdad. It's not safe for me there. I knew. I *knew* you'd changed places with a jinni, and I didn't tell anyone. It's not safe for Najwa either." She narrowed her eyes at Atish, the soldier in the room. "The war isn't over, and I think you've all forgotten that."

"No one has forgotten," he answered gruffly. "And I agree. Najwa isn't as safe as she thinks she is. Prince Ibrahim will return soon, and he has never liked us."

"See?" Rahela huffed. "Nowhere to go. Are you trying to get rid of me?"

"No! I just . . . you haven't seemed very happy. All you've been doing is, well, *that*." I pointed at the piles of rugs on the floor. They were hideous and had been done in a rush, but the sheer number was staggering. Rahela had been pouring all of her energy into making scrappy things that looked like nests of matted dog hair. At home, in Zab, she would spend months on one rug, and it would be intricate, patterned, and wanted. Here, she was practically throwing them aside after she finished each one. She had to know they were the ugliest things she'd ever made.

"I'm practicing," she said stiffly, "on this new machine. It's more complicated than ours, but faster. After I've learned how to use it properly, I'll make something worth keeping."

"I think you've mastered it by now," Shirin said. Rahela looked over at her and shook her head, and that was when I noticed the dark half circles beneath her eyes and the hollowing of her cheeks. She hadn't been sleeping or eating much since we'd come to the Cavern. Her fingers looked like they'd snap the next time she plucked a strong thread.

I turned to Atish. "We've got to get her home. I don't think my aunt would mind having her back, and she can explain to them all what happened. Please, teach me how to transport so I can get her there."

Everyone spoke at once.

"I'm not going back," Rahela said.

"Only a teacher can show you how to do that," Shirin said.

"Let me do it for you," Atish said.

I slumped onto the nearest chair, a carved hunk of petrified wood that was as cold as the walls. A chill spread through my legs and up my back, and I almost reached for one of the dreadful rugs to stuff beneath me. "There's something else." The idea came to me in a rush, so maybe the Breaking *had* worked after all. Maybe my little orb had just been broken by one of the flames.

"I have a bad feeling about this," Atish groaned, but there was a slight upward turn to his mouth.

"There's a reason I must go home too, although I don't want to stay there forever." Atish was about to say something, but I held up my hands, shushing him. "I have a little cousin. Yashar. Last autumn, I took him out to the desert and a sandstorm ripped his eyes apart. It was all my doing. He wouldn't have been out there if I hadn't convinced him to come. All I want to do is fix him, fix his eyes, so he can be a part of the tribe again."

"Zayele," Shirin said in a sad, earnest voice, "wounds like that, especially if they happened a while ago, are difficult to heal."

"But jinni wishes are strong! Najwa woke up the caliph from a brain sickness, and you healed a jinni's broken leg yesterday. I saw him running along the canal this morning. If you can do that, surely you can heal Yashar's eyes. They're just scarred—it's not as if he's lost them entirely."

Rahela rubbed her temples. "Yashar's situation is unfortunate, but it isn't your fault."

"Yes, it is." I pulled away from her and went to Atish. "We need to get back to the village. Not just for Rahela, not just for Yashar, but to guarantee they find out what really happened in the palace, with me, with Najwa, with Hashim. Don't you understand?"

Atish pressed his lips together. He glanced at Shirin for a second, then nodded. "I have to meet Captain Rashid in a few minutes. Maybe they will have heard back from Najwa. Maybe the village already knows what happened."

He spun around and left through the front door, shutting it behind him. I ran to the window and pressed my face against the thin glass, watching as he marched down an alley between a large, bubble-shaped building and the library. When I couldn't see him anymore, I whirled on Shirin.

"So," I asked, "how do you do the transport wish?"

4

NAJWA

IBRAHIM MARCHED DOWN the middle of the hall with his sword hanging off his hip. As he approached, the walls seemed to peel away, as if he were running a plow down the center, dividing the men in the black robes from me. The only person who didn't move away was Kamal. He placed himself in front of me and straightened his back.

As tall as Kamal was, Ibrahim towered over him. The point of his helmet looked sharp enough to kill in battle, and in fact, the braided cord that hung from the tip was edged in the dark brown of old blood. His armor was still dented and gouged from his recent battle in Basra.

He tried to push Kamal aside with the swipe of his arm, but Kamal did not budge. "Get out of my way, brother," Ibrahim growled.

"Leave her alone," Kamal said through gritted teeth.

"Ibrahim, my son, welcome back," the caliph said, talking over his sons with words smooth and soft as honey. Ibrahim turned his head toward his father but did not step away from me. "This is Najwa, our guest from the Cavern."

Ibrahim stared into my eyes and I forced myself not to look away. I had to appear calm, even though everything inside me was shaking. I squeezed my hands into fists and took a deep breath before bowing my head.

"Prince Ibrahim," I said. My voice was weaker than I'd intended, but I was pleased I'd been able to say anything at all.

"I lost sixteen men to the Shaitan at their hopeless Basra Tunnel. I do not understand, Father, why you would dishonor them—and me—by allowing one of *them* to take even one breath inside our palace."

Kamal shook his head. "Much happened while you were away, brother."

"Did we lose the war?"

"No."

"Then why is that"—he paused and gripped the hilt of his sword—"*thing* in here?"

"Ibrahim!" Kamal warned. "She saved our father's life. She is here now because there may yet be peace between us. And I—I appoint her jinni consul."

"Whatever peace the jinn offer will be a trap," Ibrahim said, seething. When he spoke to me, his words were deep and dry. "Get out of this palace before I grab hold of you and make a wish you'd rather die than grant."

"Ibrahim," the caliph said, "this is my court. We honor your return, but many things have happened."

Kamal placed his hand against Ibrahim's leather armor.

"I will take her out of the court, for her own safety, until you calm down."

Ibrahim scanned the men in the black robes. "Where's Hashim? I have news for him."

"He's dead," the caliph said. "Your brother is the new vizier."

Ibrahim stilled, breathing in through his nose loudly, and nodded. "I see. Take this jinni away, then. Don't let me ever set eyes on her again." Then he whirled away from me and went to kneel beside the caliph, careful not to scrape his long sword against the marble floor.

"Come," Kamal said. He held my elbow and ushered me across the open expanse, around a column, and down the hall. Everyone's eyes followed us, and it felt like cold water splashed across my shoulder blades.

Once we were out of the court and away from Ibrahim, I started shaking uncontrollably. Kamal wrapped an arm around me to hold me up. "What Ibrahim said . . . I'm sorry. He didn't expect to see a jinni here."

"I gathered."

"He's callous and one-minded. Of all the men in the court, he will be our greatest challenge. He will not believe that Hashim was lying, and once he hears that you came here pretending to be Zayele, it'll be difficult to prove to him how trustworthy you are." He tightened his fists and groaned in frustration. "I've been trying to stand up to him my whole life. He's bigger, stronger, and stupid, which makes him hard to defeat."

"But he isn't the caliph, and he isn't the vizier. He's just a soldier. Right?"

Kamal slowed. "Najwa, Ibrahim has many followers in the city. Every single soldier would die for him. Half the women in Baghdad seek his attention. If he doesn't change his mind about you, it will be dangerous for you to even set foot in the palace, much less stay here for any length of time."

"But you are the vizier now," I said. "You can influence the court and the people of Baghdad. You can spread the truth of what Hashim did—"

"You heard my father. The people would revolt. The caliphate would be in shambles. They aren't ready for the truth. Not yet." He set his hand on my cheek, but he was shaking. Although he meant to calm my nerves, they bubbled up.

"The jinn have waited long enough! If your people never learn the truth, must we change the minds of humans some other way?"

Kamal's face fell. "What other way is there?"

"I don't know."

"Let me get Ibrahim calmed down first."

"How long will *that* take?" I pulled away from him, realizing for the first time that he'd taken me to the Lamp. It sat innocently on its plinth, with its golden flame flickering in the layers of shadows cast in the dark hall. Faisal had relit the flame the day he'd been killed, and every time I looked at it, I thought of him.

"I don't know. He's never listened to me before, but then,

I wasn't the vizier. Maybe I can knock some sense into him. He truly cares about his soldiers. He must understand that if the war ends, so too will the battles."

"Why did you bring me to the Lamp, Kamal?"

He looked away. "To send you home."

I wanted to trust Kamal, but I knew he wasn't going to head straight back to Ibrahim and teach him to respect me. Did he want me to leave so he wouldn't be embarrassed when I saw him falter in front of his brother? "Why?" I whispered.

"To keep you safe."

"I can stay in the harem," I said.

"That's the first place he will go once he's done with Father. After he bathes," Kamal muttered. "Listen, I will send you a message through the Lamp when it's safe for you to return. Hopefully, it will only be a day or two. Then we can begin working together, jinn and humans, toward a treaty." He paused for a moment and looked up, thinking. "But until then, please go home where you'll be safe. I don't trust Ibrahim's wives not to hurt you. I don't want you to leave either, but I have to protect you. I couldn't bear it if something happened to you."

"Fine. I'll go, Kamal, but I'm worried . . . I'm worried that the moment a jinni leaves, everyone here will forget we ever wanted peace." Tears slipped out of my eyes and I wiped at them, furious I'd let them form in the first place.

"I won't forget." He pulled me into him and kissed my temple. He whispered, and his breath was cool upon my neck,

"Every second you're gone will cause me pain. Now go, and wait for my message."

He walked me to the Lamp. I wiped at my eyes again and nodded, wishing I could stay forever with his arms around me. Then I reached into the flame and let it pull me away from the hall, away from the palace, away from Kamal.

5

ZAYELE

"THIS CAN TAKE weeks to get right, so don't be disappointed if it doesn't work right away," Shirin said. We stood in the central room, which held nothing more than a few chairs, a table, and Rahela's loom. The walls were bare and smooth, and the lighting came from two sets of wishlight sconces. It was meant to feel like a human home, but it was nothing like the tent I'd grown up in. Shirin held up her fingers. "Also, there are a few rules."

I crossed my arms and shrugged. "There always are."

"First, you can't transport from one place to another within the Cavern. We can only transport to places on the surface and back again."

"Why?" I asked.

"Well, it drains your energy, so if you were transporting from, say, the library to the market all the time, you'd be exhausted. Not to mention the fact that eventually two jinn would collide. So we walk. And the second rule is that we can't transport without permission. Usually from the Master of the Eyes of Iblis Corps."

Rahela cleared her throat. "Maybe you shouldn't do it, then," she said. She had a collection of yarns laid out on her lap and was sorting the colors. I was grateful she'd moved on from gray.

"It's something I need to learn. No one needs to know," I said. I took in the room. Shirin and I were standing away from the furniture. The ceiling was not very high, but we had plenty of space. If I did it right. "You don't mind, do you?" I asked Shirin.

"No. Not if it will help you. And you promise never to tell anyone *I* showed you how," she said. She turned from where Rahela sat and breathed deeply. "Remember when Faisal was teaching you to do the invisibility wish? This is like that, but harder."

The invisibility wish had taken a few tries, but it hadn't been impossible. In fact, I'd impressed Faisal with how quickly I learned it. "I'll do my best."

Shirin relaxed her shoulders and then raised her eyebrows at me. She wanted me to relax too. "You think of the place you want to go, imagine yourself there, and then say the word."

"What word?"

"I'll tell you in a minute. First, you need to know that the hardest part is clearing your mind. You have to focus on both the experience of travel *and* the location. So, think of that spot over there." She pointed at one of the rugs Rahela had tossed aside. "I know I said we can't transport within the Cavern, but no one is over there. Besides, I don't want you disappearing somewhere between the Cavern and the surface if you mess up. Ready?" I nodded. "When you can imagine yourself in that spot, say, '*Shatamana.*'"

I relaxed my body, focused on the rug, and cleared my throat. Something tingled up my spine. It was the same feeling I'd gotten the first time I tried to ride a horse. The colors were brighter, and the scents in the room—old papers and wet wool—were stronger. I imagined drawing the air from above the rug into my lungs. I pretended I could feel the pile pushing up beneath my toes. Then when my mind was still, I said, "*Shatamana.*"

I felt the wish before anything happened. It slipped up my scalp, and a second later I was a flash of fire shooting across the room. I settled back into my body right on top of the lumpy rug.

Shirin ran over to me, picked up my hands, and flipped them over, tracing her fingers across my palms and inner wrists. "That was— Who taught you how to do that?"

"You did. Just now."

"You looked like one of the flames on the lake. When a jinni transports, the flame is usually yellow and mixed with smoke, like a candle flame. But you were bright blue. Did Faisal ever say anything to you about . . ." Her eyes sparkled. "Do you think you could try a real transport?"

"I don't see why not," I said, grinning. This wasn't as hard as she'd made it sound. "Home?"

"No," she said. She clasped her hands together and brought

the tips of her thumbs to her lips. "You need to go where there aren't any humans. I don't want us to get in trouble."

Naturally, the first place that came to mind was the one that haunted me the most. I tried to push the image out of my mind, but it wouldn't go away. "I know where to go," I said.

"Are you sure?"

"Yes."

"Oh. One more thing: There's a different wish we use to return home. *Mashila.*"

"*Mashila.* Why a different word?"

"The Cavern is protected. We don't want anyone transferring in, so we have a special word, and it's *mashila.*"

"Who else could transport in besides jinn?" I asked.

"There are rumors that there used to be other jinn who aren't from the Cavern." She shrugged. "Anyway, *mashila* will keep you from transferring somewhere like the middle of the lake, which is good."

"Understood."

"Are you sure?"

"Yes. You say '*Shatamana*' and then '*Mashila.*' I can remember that." I pressed my lips together, closed my eyes, and remembered the camel, the boulder, and the cloud of stinging sand. I tried not to think of Yashar, but he was there anyway. "*Shatamana.*"

Fire. I was breathing fire, I was breathing in myself, and it didn't hurt. Then I pushed up through the Cavern and burned through the earth.

Then the ground was below me and I landed weightlessly

onto the hard-packed sand. I set my hand on the boulder. It was hot from the sun, but I was fire and felt no pain.

A second later, my body solidified and the rock burned my palm. I gasped and pulled it against my chest. Then I turned to talk to Shirin, but she wasn't there. I was in the open desert, alone but for the chunk of fallen-down mountain that had just burned me.

The last time I had been at this spot, the sky had been angry, but today it was full of the blinding sun reflecting off each grain of sand. I raised my hand to block the glare.

The desert was quiet, but it held all the echoes from before. It was like walking through a silent nightmare, knowing someone was screaming.

I was on the surface again—only a camel ride away from home, from my tribe, from Yashar. The air was dry and seared the inside of my nose. There was an absence of scent, because here the wind blew strong. Nothing lingered, nothing stayed the same. Even the apparition of a half-jinni girl was only temporary.

The mountains pushed up from the horizon and unfolded themselves in the sun and stripping wind. There, where the range cut low, was the river I'd crossed on a dare the day Hashim had come to claim me. And no one there knew yet what had become of me.

I bent down, scooped up a handful of sand, and took one last look at the place that had taken my cousin's eyes. But those sands were long gone by now. This bit of sand was from somewhere else. This sand was innocent.

It was time to return. I closed my eyes, shut away the landscape, and could not remember the word. It started with an "M," but that was all I could remember. *Majina? Marisha?* No.

"Idiot!" I said to myself. I leaned back against the rock and rubbed my forehead, keeping an eye on the gap in the mountain range. My family was there. Why was I trying so hard to go back to the Cavern? I could walk home, tell them all that had happened with Hashim, and try to fix Yashar's blindness in secret. Eventually, someone from the Cavern would find me, and I would be able to tell them I'd ended the war all on my own. All I had to do was prove the jinn had nothing to do with the attack on my parents.

But if the last few weeks had taught me anything, it was that it wouldn't be so easy. First, my adoptive father would put me on another barge and send me downriver immediately. Second, if I didn't return, Shirin would have the entire Cavern on alert. They'd find me right at the worst moment, like when my father was slamming the barge door in my face.

No. I'd remember the word. It was swimming around in the back of my mind, waiting for just the right moment to land on my tongue.

I massaged my temples and made a mental list of every word starting with an "M." None of them sounded or felt right. I was about to move on to trying the ones that sounded the closest when I noticed a cloud of dust halfway between the mountains and where I stood in the open desert. I narrowed my eyes and tried to focus on the dark mass that was stirring up the ground. It was a group of horses, with riders, and they were heading in my direction. Fast.

Quickly, I ducked behind the boulder and crouched on the

sand. Had they seen me? I could not tell if they were men from my village, but either way, I did not want to be found alone by a group of horse riders.

I reached down and picked up a sliver of stone and gripped it in my hand. It was not much, but it was something. At the pace they were making, they would be on me in twenty, maybe ten, minutes, which meant I had ten minutes to remember the word.

A glint of steel helmets, and I knew they were not men from the village. They were soldiers or mercenaries. I squeezed the rock tight in my hand, feeling the sharp edge bite into my palm.

All I needed was one word.

They were closer. Now I could see there were eleven riders. They wore pointed helmets with thin black plumes and leather armor that must have been hot beneath the midday sun.

They reached the edge of the grassland and slowed when they hit the sand. Grateful for the extra time, I took a deep breath and rested my forehead against the boulder. One word.

Suddenly, I had it.

I took a last look at the riders and was alarmed that they looked nothing like the people of the mountains. But I wasn't about to risk staying to ask them where they'd come from.

I shut my eyes and cried, *"Mashila!"*

I dropped through the earth so quickly my stomach lurched. When I re-formed into my normal self and felt the drab rug beneath my feet and smelled the cool, stale air of the Cavern, I looked for Shirin. Her face had frozen in shock, and she sank to her knees.

"I can't believe it," she said, shaking her head.

I held up the shard of rock to her. Shirin pushed herself up off the floor and came over to me, covering her mouth with both hands.

"I went to the desert," I said, brushing a layer of sand off my knees and shins. "I'm sorry it took me a while to get back." I was not going to admit I'd almost forgotten the way home.

"Zayele, do you know what this means?" She had tears in her eyes, and I didn't like it. There was something in the way she looked at me that made me instantly nervous.

"What?" I asked.

Then we heard the door open behind us and turned to see Atish step into the house, followed by Najwa. She glanced at me for only a second before bursting into tears.

❖ 6 ❖

NAJWA

"KAMAL SENT ME home," I said. My lips were salty from the tears, and I wiped at them furiously.

"He did? Why?" Shirin asked. She was suddenly there, wrapping her arms around me.

"He said I needed to stay here until he called for me. To protect me."

"He said *what*?" Zayele screeched. "Doesn't he realize you're a jinni? You've got ways to protect yourself."

I bit my lower lip. I could not cry over this, especially in front of everyone. Taking a deep breath, I dropped my hands and looked at Shirin. "I came back because if I hadn't, Ibrahim might have killed me."

Atish hissed. "So the warrior has come home. Rashid told us this morning that Ibrahim's campaign was a failure. They'd been trying to force their way in through the Basra Tunnel." He saw me staring at him, and he looked down. "I'm sorry about Kamal."

"What did the caliph say when Prince Ibrahim returned?"

Rahela asked. She was sitting at her loom, knuckle-deep in a rainbow of yarns. This made me relax a little, because when she'd been with me in Baghdad, she'd always gone to her little loom when the moments grew intense. She had taught me more about humans while her fingers threaded through the yarn than I'd ever learned from the artifacts that had been brought to the Cavern for me to study. If only I'd been better prepared to face a soldier like Ibrahim.

"The caliph was happy to see his son," I said. I took a deep breath and let it out. "But he did tell him that I was their guest, and Kamal named me the jinni consul. When I came back and told Delia, she wasn't pleased to find that the caliph isn't willing to tell the world about Hashim."

"What's that?" Zayele asked, finally speaking. She'd been looking at me strangely. Was that how I looked at people? Were my eyes that big?

"The caliph won't make a public statement revealing the full web of Hashim's lies. He's afraid he'll lose support from the people."

Zayele snorted. "I'm not surprised."

"The caliph has always been worried about his public image," Rahela explained, "but it's not just the caliph's judgment that would be questioned. People would question the loyalty of our tribe, since Hashim was originally from Zab. It would not be good for my people either."

"The war must end," I said. "Unfortunately, Kamal believes we cannot force the truth upon the people. He wants to change their minds about jinn first, and he wants to start with his brother."

Atish crossed his arms and nodded at me. "Then I wish him the best of luck, because from what we know of Prince Ibrahim, he would rather walk around Baghdad in a dress than shake hands with a jinni."

"Atish, don't," Shirin warned.

"No, he's probably right," I said. Then I said what had been stirring in my mind ever since I left the Command. "Delia wants me to speak with the Diwan."

"Who's that?" Zayele asked.

"That's what we call our council of elders here. They need to know Kamal is the new vizier."

Rahela's eyes widened. "The *prince*? But he's so young! And what does this mean for you? If Kamal is vizier, and he's trying to change the minds of the people, how do you fit in?" Rahela's mind was quick.

"I'm the jinni consul. But we can't . . . Kamal and I may only meet when the Court of Honor is in session."

"I see," Rahela said, frowning. "But you're the consul, at least. I can't imagine anyone doing a better job."

"Thank you." I felt a blush spread across my cheeks. "But— but it means nothing if Ibrahim won't allow there to *be* a jinni consul."

"Isn't his father the caliph? And not him?" Shirin asked.

"Yes, but you haven't seen him. He's terrifying. He's as big as Rashid, but not as . . . wise. And he was so angry. He called me 'that thing.'"

"Bastard," Atish hissed.

"At least we have some good news," Zayele said. She was bouncing on her heels.

"What is it?" I asked, but my mind was stuck on what Ibrahim had called me.

She was grinning. "I can transport now."

Atish turned to her. "Already?"

"It's true," Shirin said, beaming. "But that's not the best part. She transports as *blue flame*."

"You mean— So *that's* why," he said. Then he went to Zayele and picked up her hands in his. He studied her face.

It couldn't be. My mind started ticking, like one of those clocks in the House of Wisdom, while I took in everything Shirin had said. The only jinn who could transport like that were magi.

"She's a magus?" I asked. Shirin nodded.

"I'm a what?" Zayele asked.

"A magus," Shirin said. "Some jinn are stronger than others. They can wish things most of us can't. They can *do* things most of us can't, and there's only a few left. Fewer, now that Faisal's gone."

But if Zayele was a magus, why wasn't I? Didn't we share the same blood? Wouldn't we have had the same potential?

Atish pulled Zayele into a hug. Her eyes peeked over his shoulder and stopped on mine. "What does this mean?" she asked me.

"It means ... it means your wishes can do things ours cannot."

"Then I can fix him!" she said, jumping out of Atish's arms. *Fix whom?*

"No, Zayele," Shirin said. "I don't think it's like that."

"Why not? I can go home, fix him, and be back before

anyone notices I've left." When no one responded, she paced in a circle. "I could go at night, so no one there sees me. He wouldn't even have to know. I could do it while he's sleeping. And then, when he wakes up . . ." She smiled brighter than I'd ever seen.

"Wait a minute, Zayele," Atish said. "There are rules. We can't transport whenever we want."

"But I just did it with Shirin."

"I didn't think you could actually *do* it," Shirin cut in.

Atish started to laugh.

"What is it?" Zayele asked him.

"This morning. I knew Rashid was up to something when he had us put up a sparring ring in the center of the city. They know what you are, Zayele. They already know, and they have *plans.*"

"Who does? Who has plans?" she asked. And then I knew. I knew exactly what Atish was thinking, and even though we were just friends, something pricked my heart. All those days, years ago, when we'd played at being a Dyad, where he'd fight the humans and I'd protect him with my impenetrable shield. We stopped playing when I found out I wasn't a magus, and it hadn't mattered because no one else our age was either. But then my long-lost twin suddenly came into our lives, and she . . . *she* was the magus. *She* would be Atish's other half. Rashid must have made that choice the moment they realized what she was.

The only thing I didn't know was *when* they had realized it. Was it when they first found out she wasn't me? If so, had Faisal known before he died?

Of course he knew. He must have recognized her power

the moment she made her first invisibility wish. She learned quickly. Too quickly, for someone who'd been raised by humans.

Then the thought came, unbidden and stinking of jealousy. Faisal had been in the tent when Hashim murdered my jinni mother and human father. He'd been unable to rescue both of us, barely managing to grab me before Hashim got to him. Then he gave me to his sister, Laira, to raise as her own. My twin had been left behind. What if Faisal had saved the wrong infant?

He could have brought home a magus, but instead he'd taken the quieter, weaker sister. And if he'd had Zayele all along, she and Atish would have been paired up long ago. They'd be a Dyad. They'd be nearly invincible.

I blinked them away, but the feelings wouldn't leave. I was the ordinary one, the untalented sister.

"Najwa?" Zayele asked. She had somehow made her way over to me without my noticing and was standing only a foot away. "Who has plans?"

"Rashid. The Shaitan. And probably the entire Diwan too." I caught Atish's eyes, and he nodded. "Every magus is paired up with a Shaitan. It's a good way to balance the power."

"But . . . I don't . . ."

"You won't have a choice," Shirin said softly. "A magus is too powerful to be left alone. Someone will train you. Although I don't know who that'll be. Faisal's gone. Who's left?" she asked, looking at me for an answer.

I shrugged. "There are twenty-three left, but I only know the names of a few. Hamayoun and Naveen, but they're the youngest and wouldn't be teaching you. There's Taja, who isn't that much older than us; Soraya, who is too weak now; and . . ." The last was Melchior, the jinni whose memory I'd seen when I discovered a Memory Crystal in the Baghdad palace. He had been captured by the old caliph and made a slave, forced to grant wishes each day. Hashim had freed him in exchange for a wish, but Melchior left without granting it. Hashim only wanted to help his family, his starving tribe, but Melchior didn't do it. After that, Hashim's life had been all about revenge.

"Melchior," Atish said.

"Yes," I agreed. "He was the Master of the Eyes of Iblis Corps before Faisal."

"He lives in Iblis's Palace," Atish said, nodding. "His dyad is Aga. She comes to watch us train sometimes, but she doesn't do much in the way of fighting now. I've only seen him once."

"Wait, wait," Zayele said, stopping us with a wave of her hands in the air. "So there are these jinn called maguses."

"Magi," I corrected.

"Fine. Magi. And I'm supposedly one of them, and after I'm all trained in whatever they do, I'll be paired up with a Shaitan?" Zayele's face darkened. "Is it a marriage?"

Atish's face turned as red as a ruby. "It's, um, more binding than that."

"What could be more binding than marriage?" Rahela asked.

"A Dyad," Shirin, Atish, and I all answered at once.

ZAYELE

THEY WERE STILL staring at me. Me, a jinni wizard. It was more ridiculous than the idea of being half-jinni.

That morning, I'd been worried about my future. I didn't know if they'd want me to follow in my sister's footsteps. I had been afraid they'd ask me what my talents were and I'd have to tell them: I don't have any talents. I'm only marginally good at weaving and I'm terrible when it comes to doing what's expected of me. They say I'm impulsive, but I think everyone else just takes too long to make a decision.

But it sounded like a magus wasn't expected to be normal.

"What happens to the magi when they're in school?" I asked.

Najwa blinked. "I don't know. The last time a magus went through her training, she did it all at the palace. That was Taja. Before her was Mila."

"Mila was Rashid's dyad," Atish said. "She died in battle last year."

Dyads weren't invincible, apparently. "Oh. Who is Taja's dyad?"

"Saam," Atish answered. "They're still in the Basra Tunnel."

Najwa's composure fell for a second, but I don't think anyone else noticed. They hadn't been studying her face, thinking about how their own looked the same. "They were fighting Ibrahim," she said.

I crossed my arms. "If this means I'm going to disappear into the palace, then I don't want to do it."

"They already know what you are." Atish stepped closer. He leaned in, like he was going to tell me a secret, but spoke loud enough for everyone to hear. "They will be picking your partner soon."

"Who?" I asked, both afraid and excited.

"Him, of course," Najwa said, pointing at Atish. There was bitterness in her voice, and Atish must have heard it, because he reached out to her, shaking his head.

"Najwa, I'm—"

"It's fine," she said. "It's not like we're . . . and you and her . . . it makes sense. It's better."

Atish shook his head. "I don't know that it'll be me. Rashid said there would be a competition. It could be any one of the Shaitan."

I was about to say something, but Shirin had jumped forward and wrapped her arms around both of us. "Of course you'll be chosen, Atish. It would be foolish not to pair you up, and Rashid is one of the smart ones."

Atish turned back to me, and I lost myself in his eyes. He had tipped his chin down, and his irises were pointed straight at mine, into mine. For a moment, I forgot the others. It was the same look he'd given me when I was broken and scared and lost in the tunnel. After he had left in anger and returned anyway.

I didn't know what it would mean to have him as my dyad. "You better not let it end up being some other Shaitan," I said, forcing a laugh. "Not after I've just started getting used to you."

"Come, then," Najwa said. "I've got to go speak to the Diwan at the palace. If Melchior is there, he'll want to see you."

But I couldn't go. Not yet. "Wait. Najwa, you don't know anyone from the village, but we have a cousin. I have to help him." Quickly, I told her about Yashar and how much he needed me.

She shook her head. "We can't. We can't transport without permission."

"But I just did."

"You're lucky you didn't get caught." She sighed. "Zayele, we will find a way to help your cousin. But it has to be at the right time."

"They'll never give me permission for that. No, I'm going *now*. Alone, if I have to." I braced myself for another confrontation, but it didn't come. Instead, Najwa sighed again and looked at Atish. Something passed between them—the sort of communication that comes after years of knowing someone— and I was jealous. I didn't have that with anyone other than Yashar.

"I would go with you, but I can't. They're expecting me," Najwa said. She began to pace the area, then stopped abruptly. "Atish, you need to go with her."

He nodded. "I shouldn't, but I can't let her go alone."

"I'm going too." This came from Shirin, and Najwa's eyes widened in surprise. "She's going there to heal this boy. She'll need me."

"You don't have to come," I said to them both. "It'll be easier if I go alone. They won't be expecting any jinn."

"We're not letting you out of our sight up there," Atish said. "Shirin's right. Let's go."

This entire time, Rahela had been sitting in silence, winding her fingers into the threads of her loom. When I looked at her, she shook her head.

"Don't you want to go home?" I asked.

She looked at her knuckles, at the dozens of colors wound around them. "It's not my home anymore. When I left it with you, I never intended to return. There's nothing there for me."

I went over to her and put my hands on top of hers. They were rough, but warm. "You want to stay in the Cavern? I thought you were afraid of jinn."

She looked up at me and laughed in a burst of surprise. "But, Zayele, you *left* me with one, remember?" I opened my mouth, then closed it, unable to say anything. "But I'm glad you did. I'm fine here. I've got a house all to myself, I'm not expected to do anything for anyone, and I've just started something on this," she said, gesturing with her nose at the loom.

That was when I looked, *really looked,* at what she was weaving. This was a far cry from what she'd littered the house with. The earlier rugs were like puddles of mud scattered across the stone floor, but this . . . this was a rainbow. Gasping, I let go of her hand to brush against the pattern she'd created.

It began with the field of crystals that marked where the jinn went in death, their memories preserved in the upright shards scattered across the gravel. Then came the edges of the geode that made the Cavern floor and the start of the walls. She was working from the ground up but had only just begun.

She wasn't going home. She was making one of her own.

"Oh, Rahela," I whispered. Then I looked at Najwa. "Did you see this?"

She nodded and grinned. "It's better than anything my mother would have dreamed up."

Atish cleared his throat. "We should go. I have to be back in an hour."

I stepped away from the loom, from Rahela, and said, "I'll tell Yashar all about this."

"*Insha'Allah,* he will see it one day," she said.

I took my friends' hands and closed my eyes, picturing the cliff that overlooked the fast-flowing Zab River.

"*Shatamana.*"

I was going home.

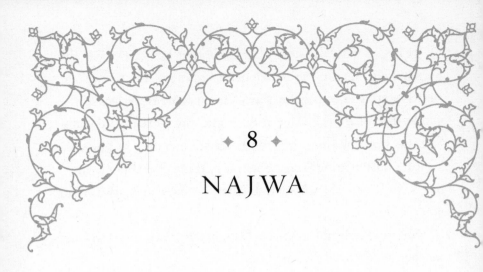

✦ 8 ✦

NAJWA

AS SOON AS they were gone, I left the house and headed to the Command, but Delia was already outside by the fountain. Delia was twice my age and did little to adorn herself. Her hair was pulled off her face with a single sapphire clip, and it fell in waves down her back. The only bit of jewelry she wore was a single band on her forefinger. The rest of her was straight, unafraid, and as alert as always. When she saw me approach, she stepped away from the fountain and nodded her head once.

"Ready?" she asked. I stepped beside her and tried to match her steady, smooth gait.

"As ready as I can be," I said. I didn't feel ready, but it didn't matter.

Delia knew everything about me, but the only thing I knew about her was that she had been close to Faisal. Maybe closer than I had. But our one similarity was not something I wanted to talk about.

I needed to ask her about Zayele. If Rashid knew something, certainly Delia had heard of it first. I waited until we'd crossed the canal and were heading down the empty street that brushed the edge of the city.

"Delia," I said, as quietly as I could manage, "there's something about Zayele. I was hoping you could explain it."

She kept her eyes straight ahead, saying nothing for a moment. "I was wondering when you'd put the pieces together." She sounded so much like Faisal it hurt. "She's a magus. Faisal alerted those who needed to know before he was killed. They'll begin her training soon, and then they will decide on a Shaitan for her."

"I'm surprised they haven't already decided," I said. We neared the lake wall and took the steps leading to the top. We would have to walk along the wall to reach the palace's gate. As we made our way, I saw the colored balls from the Breaking. So some had not yet found their flames. For a brief moment, I longed for a ball so I could cast off my own, knowing that the one I'd set in the palace harem didn't count.

Delia slowed. "Why do you say that?"

"Because Atish is the best choice. And Rashid has been pulling him aside for extra training the past two days."

"He is a good choice, but I would be surprised if he was the only one being tested for that role. Being chosen for a Dyad is the highest honor, and I'm sure there are others vying for the position."

She was right, of course. But who would compete against Atish?

We walked the rest of the way in silence, and then took the steps down to the palace gate. It was made of twisted red iron, letting anyone passing by peer in to see Iblis's doors. I had come this close a few times, years ago, but I'd never been inside. Delia rested her palm against a plate of black glass set into the wall, and the gate swung open on its own, propelled by a wish from when it had first been made.

She glanced at me once before hurrying inside and leaving me to follow. As soon as I'd entered the grounds, the gate latched behind me with a groan and a clink. "When jinn approach the Diwan, all faces must be seen at once," Delia said.

The Diwan was the jinni version of the human Court of Honor, but while the caliph resided over the Court of Honor, there was no single man or woman taking charge over the proceedings in the Diwan. Even so, alliances were made and favorites were followed, and many members would try to convince the others to agree to their terms.

The palace doors were made of gold and they too swung open when we approached. I had to take a quick step to stay in line with Delia.

Naturally, I'd heard what the great hall would be like, but when I looked up, I let out a slow breath. I was amazed. None of the stories had described it accurately. The inside was far bigger than it had seemed from outside, and the air was filled with the scent of flowers. Hundreds of copper pots hung suspended from chains clipped into the stone ceiling, and from these pots dripped flowers that I did not recognize. A few petals were falling through the air just as we passed beneath them, and I watched them land silently, delicately. The floor was stone, but the sifting petals had softened it over the ages.

Because I'd heard it would be there, I looked to the

right-hand wall. There, nestled in a frame of turquoise and silver, was the angel's feather. It wasn't truly a feather, but the impression of one. The angel had dropped the feather onto the ground, where it had singed the earth and turned to ash. Iblis had dug up the impression and dragged it with him when he fled the surface, and he had built his palace around it.

While I was awed by the flowers and the angel's feather, it was the tree that made me pause. In the very center of the hall, beneath a beam of white sunlight, was a gnarled tree twice as tall as any jinni. Wide leaves feathered the branches and soft, topaz-colored apricots dotted the greenery. What was a tree doing down here? How did it bear fruit? How did the sunlight make its way down here? And most importantly, why had I never heard of this tree?

It was a moment before I realized Delia was saying something. "Come, don't stare at the tree. They're over there, watching."

I looked past the tree to where she had pointed. In the back of the great hall, a pair of red curtains cascaded from the ceiling and flanked a shallow set of stairs. At the top of the stairs, and in the glow of dozens of wishlights, sat the eight members of the Diwan on their wide, cushioned benches.

One of them, a woman in the flowing black robes of a Shaitan general, waved us over. "Welcome, Delia and Najwa. Come sit at the table."

I walked over the layer of fallen petals and through the scented air, past the apricot tree, and up the stairs beside Delia. Because I had to stay beside her, I had to move at her pace, which was quick. The faces of the Diwan all turned toward us, their eyes watchful and their mouths straight as blades. The closer we got, the narrower their eyes became.

The Shaitan general motioned for us to sit on the only empty bench surrounding the low rectangular table. Like a puppet, I sank down at the same time as Delia onto the padding and tucked my ankles beneath me. Then the woman spoke again: "You're right on time. Delia, does the Corps have anything to report?"

Delia bowed her head. "Yes, Aga." *Aga.* This was the woman Atish had mentioned. She was Melchior's dyad. A leather belt wound around her narrow waist and held her sheathed dagger, which pressed tight against her hip. One long, gray braid draped over her shoulder, its tip bronzed and filed into a point. Her muscular shoulders were bare and revealed her lion mark, as is the custom of the Shaitan. She was the embodiment of litheness and strength, and I was instantly conscious of my softer, weaker body. My only mark was the small blue eye of an owl on my hand.

I scanned the others' faces and found a man staring straight at me. I gulped, and tried to feign a smile at the man with gray eyes. He did not smile in return. His brows rose, as if he was challenging me, and I could not pull away to look for his mark. But I didn't need to. I had seen through those eyes before. I had *been* him, even though it had been just a memory.

Melchior, the jinni who had spurned Hashim's request when he freed him from the caliph's prison. The jinni who had, essentially, planted the seed for the war between the caliphate and the jinn.

Delia turned to face me. "Najwa, the Diwan would like your account of what happened in the palace."

I told them about Kamal's appointment and Ibrahim's return. Then, when I was done, everyone began speaking at once.

"Ibrahim must be assassinated," the woman to my left said.

"You cannot ever return," the man beside her said to me.

"No. She must go back and watch," another man said to the first.

But I was paying close attention to Melchior. For some reason, I wanted most to know what his response was.

"So he chose Kamal as vizier," he said to himself. He leaned back on the bench, pressed his palms onto his thighs, and nodded. "A wise choice."

"Melchior," Aga said, giving me a jolt at the mention of his name, "Ibrahim must be dealt with."

Melchior sighed. "Yes, but I do not think an assassination is the answer." Relieved, I nodded in agreement, and he raised an eyebrow at me. "You think so too, child?"

"Sir, she is a member of the Corps," Delia interjected.

"Quite right. But she is also a child." Then, to me, he said, "Have you accepted the position as jinni consul?"

"I do not believe it was presented to me as a question, but I would accept. If the Diwan wishes, of course."

Melchior's mouth twitched. "You're far more agreeable than I'd expected."

"Sir, the Corps would like to know when our new master will be named," Delia said.

Aga looked around the table at the other jinn, all of whom

nodded. Then she swished her hand at the table. A second later, a ring of small cups appeared, steaming and full of tea. She picked hers up and the rest of us followed. I brought the cup to my lips, where it burned. "Sip, and we will speak," Aga said.

"No need," Melchior said, setting his cup down on the table. It was already empty. "We have a magus to train, the Corps is without a master, and the warrior prince has returned to Baghdad. It all points to one thing."

"Melchior," Aga warned.

"Faisal was my replacement. Now that he is dead, I will come out of my retirement and resume command."

This statement sent the Diwan into another round of outbursts, starting first with Delia. "But you've retired!" she said.

"Yes, but I am not dead. You are too inexperienced to take on the command, as I know you wish to do. Besides, you're not a magus, and I think it's best—"

"Enough, Melchior," Aga said. She tapped at the hilt of her dagger, and all of us fell silent. "Delia, in this case, I agree with Melchior. But he will not conduct the day-to-day operations. You will do this, as you did under Faisal. And there will be an understanding, Melchior, that Delia will be training to replace you."

Melchior snapped his fingers at the cup and refilled his tea. Then he held up his cup to Delia. "A partnership, then. Now, where is your sister?" he said to me. "I must begin training her as soon as possible, because as we all know, the death of Hashim was not, after all, the death of the war."

Melchior was the reason the war had begun in the first place.

He should have been there, instead of Faisal, to face Hashim in Baghdad. He should have seen the man he'd created with his neglect.

All of this I kept bottled inside me. With a forced smile, I bowed to Melchior and left the Diwan, shuffling through the layers of petals that had fallen to the ground. None of them had browned at the edges like real petals do. It struck me, just before I stepped over the threshold, that nothing in Iblis's Palace changed. Not even the hearts of old men.

ZAYELE

WE EMERGED A little higher than the village, on one of the plateaus atop the gorge. I knew we weren't likely to see anyone there, and after I shook off the feeling I got when I turned into a flame, I made sure the others had made the journey.

Atish was staring at me openmouthed.

"What?" I asked. His skin was more golden in the late-afternoon sunlight, and I used this opportunity to look at him.

He snapped his mouth shut. "Nothing."

Shirin shoved his shoulder. "I told you she transported like that. Pure sapphire."

They were talking about the magus part. "How can you see my flames when I can't see yours?"

"You could have seen ours if you looked," Shirin said, "but you were focused on what you were doing. It's a good thing."

"Right." I cleared my throat. "So, we are on a plateau, where we take the animals to graze sometimes. The river is down there," I said, pointing to the edge of the plateau. It was a cliff, really. "And the village is downriver, about ten minutes away."

Shirin frowned. "Why'd you have us show up so far away?"

"It was smart," Atish said curtly. "Let's go." He gestured for us to approach the cliff. When we got to the edge, my breath caught in my throat. There was the river, just as I'd left it. Just as gray-blue, just as flooded, and probably just as cold. The rope bridge still strung across, damp from spraying water. It probably hadn't been touched since that day I'd been dared to cross it.

"That's a long way down," Shirin said.

I looked downriver, making sure no one would see us peering over the cliff. But there was no one. In fact, the riverbank was emptier than it usually was this time of year. "I'll show you how to get down," I said.

I took them along the goat path. Each step I took filled me with an increasing sense of excitement. I was going to help him. I was finally going to do something right.

By the time we were down by the river, I couldn't hold myself back. I was ready to run. "Come on," I said, looking back at them over my shoulder. Shirin was twenty feet behind, eyeing the river with caution, but Atish was right behind me.

He trotted up to me. "How long do your wishes last?"

"What?"

"I'm asking because we have to turn ourselves invisible soon, and we don't have the endurance someone like Najwa has. We cannot afford to be seen."

"I don't know how long. Long enough?"

"Wait, Zayele," Shirin huffed. When she caught up with

us, I realized how out of place we looked. Emeralds dotted her uncovered hair, and Atish's Shaitan mark reflected the sunlight like polished armor. And I had completely forgotten to wear a hijab.

"Save the wish for now" was all I said. We hadn't gone far when I saw a figure crouched beside the river, kneeling on the gravel between two piles of wet laundry: Yashar.

His turban was stained with rust-colored mud, his sleeves were wet to the elbows, and his shoulders were shaking. Everything I had planned on saying left my mind in an instant as I stumbled down the embankment, sending rocks scattering into the river.

Yashar lifted his head. "Who is that?" he asked. He was washing the women's underclothes, which no man would normally touch, young or old. His eyes were covered by a dirty strip of cloth that wound around his head and was tucked beneath his turban. Why had they given him this chore? Why had they covered his eyes?

"It's me," I said as softly as I could.

"Zayele? No, it's not you."

I pushed some clothing over and knelt beside him. "Yashar, it's me," I said, laying a hand on his forearm. He shook his head.

"No."

"You don't want it to be me?" I asked, smiling now. "I'm back."

He dropped a pair of undergarments and the current dragged them away. Then he put his other hand on top of mine. His hands were shaking. "Zayele," he croaked.

I pulled him into me, pushing his face into my shoulder and holding him there. "What did they do to you?" My throat constricted, and I knew I was about to cry.

"Why are you back?" he asked.

"I'm . . . I came to help you."

He pulled a strip of cloth off the wide rock he had been rubbing it against. It peeled away with a rough, gripping sound. "You found me a job there?" he asked.

"No. I'm going to heal you."

"Zayele," he began, pulling away from me. "You can't heal me. It just . . . it just happened. It wasn't your fault."

"But it *is* my fault," I snapped. "Please, let me heal you."

Shirin had started to come down to us, and the rocks clattered. Yashar jerked out of my arms and turned himself to face her. "Who—"

"It's my friend Shirin."

"That's not a Baghdad name," Yashar said.

"Hello, Yashar," Shirin said. Her voice was like honey tea, and I could see it soothing him. As she scrambled over the gravel and picked her way around the laundry, she kept talking. "Zayele and I are going to try to heal your eyes."

"Who are you?" he asked again.

"Yashar," I began, "after I left, I found out some things about myself." I hesitated. What would he do when he found out? I hadn't considered this at all until now, and I suddenly realized that it mattered. I couldn't tell him. Not until I'd healed him.

I had to do it now. I had to make a wish that I knew no words for.

"Shirin, what do I do?"

She frowned. "Yashar, can you see anything when you have this strip removed?"

"Only a bit of light and color. But they don't want to see my eyes anymore. They say they aren't nice to look at."

"Would you mind if I took it off and had a look?" Shirin asked. Yashar shrugged.

I saw in an instant that Shirin was not like me at all. She didn't grimace or flinch as she unwound the cloth, peeling off the grimy top layer to reveal the pure, soft layer wound over his eyes. His irises were thickly scarred, and the color of milk, and I watched as Shirin's expression went from concern to disappointment. "I'm so sorry," she said, her voice cracking. "You can't alter the healing after it's done."

"But it *never* healed!" I said.

"It's fine, Zayele," Yashar said. "I'm used to it now. I can do almost anything, even though no one believes me. I'm not *just* a blind person."

"No! We came here to do this. And I know I can." I glanced up at Atish, who was busy scanning the riverbank for others. I reached out and put my hands over Yashar's eyes. I would be able to do it. I was a magus. I had powers Shirin didn't have. I closed my eyes, took a deep breath, and thought of how Yashar had been before the sandstorm. How he'd always been out in front when we raced, how excited he'd been when describing a particular butterfly he'd seen, how he'd always known what everyone was feeling, just by looking at their faces. Everyone had loved him for that. But then I'd brought him to a sandstorm and ruined his life.

"I wish for you to be able to see again, Yashar."

The wish bubbled up inside my chest and flooded into my palms. Without warning, I remembered the darkness of the tunnel I had been lost in, in the Cavern. I'd been blind like Yashar there, in the dark, and had been terribly, terribly afraid. I did not want him to be alone in the dark. I did not want him to be afraid, ever again. Then the wish, as real and heavy as jeweled rings on my fingers, throbbed, and I let it go.

The wish released with a bolt of fire, leaving my fingertips tingling. I let them drop off his face, and opened my eyes.

Yashar shuddered in terror, peeled away from me, and screamed. And screamed. And screamed.

Then a circle of darkness rushed in, clouding everything, and I fell.

I woke with a pounding in my head, and I wanted to press on my temple to relieve some of the pain, but my arms wouldn't budge from my sides. I creaked open my eyes and saw a headboard of clear crystal shooting straight up from above my pillow and poking through a low charcoal ceiling. I could tell by the oily-rich smell that I was in the Cavern again.

I had been laid out on a bed and wrapped tightly in thin wool, with my arms tucked in. I tried to pull them out, but someone hadn't wanted me to use my arms. *Ever,* judging by how tightly I was swaddled. For a brief moment, I worried I was wrapped in a *kafan* and readied for burial, but there were other beds beside me, some with people lying on them.

"You might be a powerful jinni now, but you still do foolish things, Zayele." Rahela was sitting on a stool beside me, tapping her foot.

"What?" I croaked.

"You take these risks, without thinking of anyone else."

I tried to sit up, but I was cocooned, and strained against the swaddling. "What do you mean?"

A boy's voice cried out on the bed beside me, and my stomach lurched. It was Yashar, lying on his side, facing me. He had drawn his knees to his chest and was shaking his head side to side. A band of sweat had soaked through the top of the wrappings on his eyes, and his skin was the color of wet clay.

"Yashar," I said, but he kept shaking his head. Could he not hear me? "Yashar, it's Zayele." Again, he didn't respond.

"*He* is what I mean," Rahela said. Her voice was a mixture of disappointment and sadness. "You did something to him, without his consent."

"He sleeps." A woman came to stand between our beds and looked down at me with a severe frown. "Although this is not the kind of sleep one *wants*." She wore a long gown with a matching emerald scarf tied over her head. Her hairline peeked out, revealing thick, wavy hair with a streak of silver. But it was her nose—straight as an arrowhead and pointing down at me—that caught my attention.

"Is he all right? Where have you taken us? Why am I dressed up like the dead?"

She crossed her arms. "As I said, he sleeps. I'm Razeena, head physician. You are wrapped exactly as one who fights off her healers *needs* to be wrapped. I let Shirin handle you, but you scratched her so badly that *she* needed attending." She paused, inhaling sharply through her nose. "Of course, she should have restrained you to begin with." Then she bent over and pulled on the end of a strip of cloth. When my arms were free, I pushed myself up onto my elbows.

"What happened to me?" I asked. I watched as Rahela got up off her stool and went to wipe a folded cloth over Yashar's forehead.

"You tried to heal a *human,* and you are *not* a healer. You may think that since you're a magus you have unlimited powers, but this is not the case. You depleted your wishpower, which always causes a jinni to lose consciousness. And then, while you were dreaming, you clawed at us like a crayfish. If I had been here when they carried you in, I would have turned you away."

This woman was not who I would have chosen if I'd had my choice of physicians. I swallowed and looked away from her. "Can Yashar . . . see?" I asked.

She shook her head. "His eyes are still heavily scarred. But your wish did something to him. We've all been waiting for you to tell us what that was."

My worries for Yashar were like the cracking, spreading glaze on a pot. "Who has been waiting?" I asked.

Rahela paused with her wiping. "Shirin and Atish, plus me."

"Now, tell me what it is you wished," Razeena demanded.

Faisal had asked me the same question once. That time, I had made a wish without knowing I had any of my own powers. Without knowing what a Fire Wish was. I had been forgiven because I'd been ignorant. But this time, I knew what I was doing. It just hadn't turned out the way I'd planned. And, contrary to what Rahela said, I wasn't thinking of myself—I was helping *someone else*. Wasn't that the definition of thinking of others?

"I wished for him to be able to see. That's all."

Razeena's irises filled with greenish flames that matched the snake mark wrapping around her wrist. "You were told it was not possible, but you did it anyway," she hissed. "A magus should *never* try to do the work of a physician!"

I blinked, waiting for her to say more, but she pressed her lips together till they were white. Then she bent over Yashar and placed a hand on his forehead. His whimpers faded, as did his shaking. She took the cloth from Rahela, who had given up on her own method of care.

"If my wish didn't work, then why is he like this?" I asked.

Her reply was deep and hollow. "Your wish *did* work. We just don't know what sort of 'sight' he has been given. Whatever it is, it is nightmarish. He cannot stand to be awake, and I have had to keep him unconscious. Otherwise, he screams."

"When his eyes are open, are they . . . ?"

"Your cousin here, Rahela, assured me they are exactly the same," she finished. She had said "cousin" like someone says "mucus." "Whatever you were feeling or thinking when you made this wish affected him. He cannot see like you or I, but he sees something. He will wake soon. I hope your presence will comfort him."

She turned and left us, trailing her long green skirt behind her. I watched it slip across the stone floor. The air in her wake felt warm, if that was possible.

I pulled the rest of the blankets off me and went to kneel

beside Yashar. "Yashar," I whispered. "Please wake up. It's me, Zayele."

"Zayele, he needs to rest," Rahela warned.

He stirred a little. His fists were clenched tight and his body was rigid, and I squeezed his shoulder, gently, hoping to reach him wherever his mind had gone.

"Yashar, I'm sorry I did this to you, but you are in a safe place. Please, Yashar, wake up."

He reached out and gripped my sleeve and I startled in surprise. "Zayele?" he croaked.

"Yes! It's me," I said. Tears sprang from my eyes, falling onto his cheek. "How do you feel?"

"Zayele, I'm afraid."

"Shh. You're safe here," I said.

"Where am I?"

"You're in a safe place. They will take care of you here. They're all healers."

His breathing was too shallow and quick. "Jinni healers?"

Rahela reached out and took one of his hands. "I'm here too. I didn't want you to be alone."

"Yashar," I said, using the voice our mother had used whenever she needed to catch our attention, "I am right here. You are safe. Breathe slowly."

He sucked in a deep breath and gasped, and I lifted him into my arms, squeezing him tightly. When his shaking settled a little, I pressed my face into the side of his and whispered, telling him again, "You're safe."

"They're everywhere. I can see them everywhere."

"What's everywhere, Yashar? What can you see?"

Sweat beaded on his pale brow. "Frightening things."

"What frightening things?" Rahela asked, alarmed.

"I can see them all, Zayele. They come whenever a jinni comes close."

"Are you sure you aren't seeing the jinn?"

"Do they look different from you?"

"No."

He shivered again. "They're not jinn then. They're . . . monsters."

"If there were monsters here, I'd be able to see them too," I said, trying to bring some rationality to this conversation.

"There is one swirling around you," he said with a shudder. "It's sharp and twisty."

"What do you see, Yashar?"

"I don't know," he whispered. "Zayele, leave me *alone!*" He pushed me away, and I scrambled up from the bed. "That thing twisting around you is scaring me!"

❖ 10 ❖

NAJWA

DELIA AND I left Iblis's Palace for the Command and walked in silence along the lake wall. When we made our turn at the fountain, I saw Atish running toward us. His steps were long and quick, and he reached us before I had time to wonder what the problem was.

"Najwa," he huffed, "you have to come."

"What happened?" I asked. "Is Zayele hurt?"

"No, she's fine. But the wish . . ." He eyed Delia warily, but she stared him down.

"You better tell me now, Shaitan, because I'll hear about it anyway," she snapped.

"We found the boy right away," he said in a rush of words. "Shirin tried to tell her the wish wouldn't work, but she's so stubborn. She wouldn't listen."

"Just tell me what *happened*. Are they safe? Is she here?"

"They're *both* here. In the hospital."

I didn't wait for more. I ran toward the hospital, stumbled once over the cobblestones, swerved around a pack of children, and pushed open the hospital's double doors before any of the physicians could stop me.

Atish was behind me the entire way, silent as a warhorse, and he stood beside me while we blinked and waited for our eyes to adjust to the darkness of the hospital.

The main room was filled with beds lined up against the far wall like the teeth of a comb. Each bed was made of blue marble and a smoky quartz headboard that reached up to the ceiling. Wishlights hung suspended in clumps of three above each bed, illuminating them in weak, golden rays. Most of the beds were empty, but a few contained the ill or wounded. It was to these beds that we ran, scouring for any sign of Zayele.

First, we saw Rahela. She was standing next to a bed in the center of the room. Then we saw Zayele, bent over the curled form of a boy. Her face was contorted, as if she was in great pain, and her lips moved slowly, like she was singing. All of this changed when she caught sight of us.

She blinked away the pained expression and tucked a stray hair behind her ear.

"Yashar is awake," she said. Her voice was strained.

"He is?" I started for her, but she shook her head in alarm, and I stopped, mid-stride. "Is he . . . is he any better?"

"If seeing shadowy monsters is better, then yes," she said bitterly. Then she whispered something to him that made him stir.

"I'm sorry it didn't work." I didn't know what else to say.

"Yashar is safe here," Rahela said, more for him to hear than for us.

Yashar pushed himself up into a sitting position and faced

me. He kept his face still, giving me a chance to study him. I tried not to look away from his scarred eyes, forcing myself to take all of him in, because if he was Zayele's cousin, then he was mine also.

Yashar's hands shook from where they lay on his thighs, and he curled them into fists. "There's something dark swooping around you, around and around."

I fought off the urge to brush at the air. A line of goose bumps built up on the back of my neck.

"Is it there now?" I said. My voice shook, betraying me. "What do you think you're seeing, Yashar?"

"Yashar, you don't have to look at it," Zayele said, sending me a glare. "Stop bothering him. He's living in a nightmare."

"I'm sorry," I said.

Atish came up beside Yashar, on the opposite side, and crossed his arms. "You're a strong boy," he said, "and you've got us here to keep you safe."

Yashar turned to face Atish and his hair cascaded over his eyes. "You've got something following you too," he said to Atish. "All of you. I know you're coming because I see these scary shadows coming with you." Then he pulled his knees into his chest and tucked his nose between them. Atish looked at me sheepishly.

"What is it?" Zayele whispered to Yashar.

Yashar pointed behind me, and I turned. Razeena and Shirin were shuffling across the hospital's expansive floor. As I watched them approach, I couldn't help but wonder what sort of shadows they carried with them.

Whatever they were, they frightened Yashar far more

than mine had. Maybe he somehow knew Razeena was coming. The head physician wasn't the most pleasant of jinn. Zayele straightened her back and lifted her chin, as if daring the oncoming women to move any closer.

"The boy is awake?" Razeena asked when they reached me.

I turned, bowed, and nodded my head. "He is, but he is still . . . troubled."

"He's awake," Zayele said. "But he is afraid of you. He isn't used to jinn."

"That's ridiculous. I am a healer, and if I'd wanted him dead, he would be so already," Razeena snapped. "Shirin, since you carried him here, maybe he will tolerate you."

"Yes, of course," Shirin said before stepping cautiously to the bed. "Yashar, it's Shirin. I was at the river, remember? I'm Zayele's friend, and a healer." She paused. When he didn't show any signs of distress, she took another step. "Would you like something to drink?"

Yashar nodded. Shirin smiled at him and said to Razeena, "Would you get him some juice?"

Razeena huffed. "Yes, I will get it. You stay here. Clearly, I disturb him." Then, as quickly as she had come, she was gone.

"I'm sorry you're afraid of Razeena," Shirin said to Yashar. "She acts that way because she is always tired. But she is a kind person. You will see." I raised my brows. I'd never thought of Razeena as kind. Intelligent and hardworking, maybe, but not kind or gentle in the way Shirin was.

Zayele shook her head. "He isn't afraid of Razeena. It's whatever I've just cursed him with. All these monstrous visions."

"Visions?" Shirin asked.

We had to be cautious. If Razeena discovered that Yashar could see something dark swirling around jinn, she'd have half of the elders in here, prodding him, dissecting him. I cleared my throat, caught Zayele's attention, and shook my head. Her eyes widened slightly, and she nodded.

"He has no idea what jinn look like, so he's imagining things," Zayele said.

"Oh, I see," Shirin said. "So he's not actually seeing something."

"He sees *something*," I said, "but I don't think it's a good idea to let Razeena know yet. Besides, maybe Zayele can undo it like she did the Fire Wish."

"The Fire Wish?" asked Yashar. He lifted his head a little off his knees, so that his chin rested there. He was like a rabbit, ready to jump back into his hole if needed.

The Fire Wish had left a scar in my lungs, and each time I breathed in too deeply, I could feel the air dragging over it. Whenever someone mentioned the Fire Wish, I breathed in just enough to sense the ragged bit in my lungs. I did this now, and then let the breath out, slowly. No one knew about this, because I didn't want Zayele to feel even worse about what she had done to me.

Zayele's brows creased deeply. "When Rahela and I were on our way to Baghdad, on the canal boat, I saw a jinni—Najwa—and caught her. I made a wish so she'd take my place. I had to get back home to you, and I thought the wish would send me there."

"Why did you want to go home to me? I was doing fine."

"But you were blind!" Zayele fiddled with the edge of Yashar's blanket. "Anyway, after the wish was made, Najwa took my place and went to Baghdad with Rahela, and I ended up here, in the Cavern. We each had to pretend to be the other."

"Zayele wasn't very good at that," Atish added, grinning.

Yashar turned to Atish. "Why didn't anyone know right away? Don't jinn look different?"

Shirin patted Yashar's leg. "Humans and jinn look the same. The only thing different is how we dress and do our hair. And Najwa and Zayele . . . well, they're twins. Sisters. Separated at birth."

"Not at birth," I said, finally finding my voice. "At our parents' death."

A wrinkle creased between Yashar's eyes. "But our parents aren't dead, Zayele."

"Yours are still alive," Rahela said. "But Zayele and Najwa's parents are not. Their mother was a jinni, and their father was Evindar, your father's brother. You're cousins."

Zayele squeezed his shoulder and half-smiled. "But you'll always be my little brother."

"You're my cousin too," I said, but no one was listening to me. Everyone was watching Yashar.

Finally, his quivering lips peeled back and he croaked, "Why did you do this to me, Zayele? It was better when I couldn't see anything at all. It was better when you had left for Baghdad."

Zayele cupped his face in her hand and wiped a tear with her thumb. "I wanted to heal you. I didn't want you to be blind anymore. I'll fix this. I promise."

"No. You'll only make it worse," he said. He pushed her away and then slid down into the blanket and straightened his legs. He was like a vein of gold lying in silence within stone—thin, fragile, and almost glowing. "Shirin," he said, "can you make me sleep again? I don't want to see the monsters anymore." The desperation caught in his voice, and Shirin looked up at me, confused. I nodded.

"Of course," she said. She laid a hand gently across his brow and whispered a wish.

The tension in his body released like a song, and he sank further into the bed. The creases around his eyes smoothed out, and his mouth softened. A moment later, Shirin picked up her hand.

One task was over. The next was equally stressful. "Zayele," I said, and she snapped out of a lost gaze. "I have to take you to meet Melchior."

"Where?"

"Iblis's Palace. He is waiting."

ZAYELE

THEY CALLED IT Iblis's Palace, but no one named Iblis lived there now. It sprawled along the far end of the Lake of Fire, right up against the Cavern's crystal wall. The fence surrounding it was made of iron strips a hand's width apart, tiled with thousands upon thousands of multicolored scales.

"Are those jewels?" I asked Najwa, gesturing at the fence ahead of us. We had taken the lake wall path and were closer to the palace now than I'd ever been before.

She shook her head. "Just stones. But they've been wished upon."

Iblis's Palace grew from behind the steel-and-tile fence like a rosebush. It scaled the Cavern wall, finding nooks and crevices in the gypsum shards. The palace was wide at the base, where its walls were made of dark marble and granite, but tapered into a series of five obsidian minarets, each taller and sharper than the one before, until the very last, which was built against the crystal wall. I craned my neck to see the top. A small curved window peeked out on the side.

The palace reminded me of the base of a frozen waterfall, except it was darker, harder, and tall as a canyon cliff.

"How high are we going?" I asked.

"Just the first floor."

"What's up in the minarets?"

Najwa shrugged. "I'm not sure. I've only been in the main hall, and I haven't had permission to go anywhere else." She stopped and gripped a railing, then took a set of steps leading down the lake wall to a gate of scrolling, intricate ironwork. As we walked, I dragged my fingertips along the fence. The stones were smooth and slippery as snakeskin.

"What's Melchior like?" I asked. She had been about to set her hand on a black square set into the fence beside the gate, and she hesitated.

"He's a little frightening. I didn't know that when I was inside his memory," she said. "In the Memory Crystal, he was angry, but he was also worried. Not for his own safety, but for his family. Mostly, though, he was very, very tired. The caliph was making him grant huge wishes daily. So I was imagining him to be feeble. Or weak. But he is not. He's powerful."

I smiled. "Then he may be able to help Yashar."

Najwa took me into the palace, where we waded through ankle-deep sweet pea petals, passed a curious apricot tree, and climbed a set of stairs leading up to the Diwan's dais. There, a jinni stood and gestured for us to approach, smiling. His warmth was unsettling, making the hair rise on the back of my neck. To his left sat a jinni who looked like she'd seen too much sun in her youth and would cut off your tongue if you mentioned it. They had to be Melchior and Aga, the powerful Dyad couple. The third jinni, the one on his right, was about twenty, with short-cropped hair threaded with turquoise beads, straight brows, and a thin nose. Like the older warrior woman, she carried a Shaitan dagger at her belt. I had no idea who she was.

Melchior slapped his hands against his knees. "Welcome, Najwa and Zayele. Now all we need to do is figure out which one of you is which." Then he laughed. It was not the laugh of a happy soul.

"Najwa said you wanted to see me," I said.

Melchior nodded. "Ah, so you're Zayele, our half-human magus. I am Melchior, the one who trains the magi."

"*One* of the trainers," Aga corrected him.

"Yes." He gestured at the other jinni. "This is Taja. She and Aga will also train you, especially when it comes time to be bonded with your dyad."

"My dyad." My legs began to feel jumpy.

"Naturally," Melchior said. "Taja will join us whenever we need an example, as she is one of the more recently trained magi. There will only be the two of you for most training sessions, because the other new magi are elsewhere. Magi are a minority, as you will find."

"Thank Iblis," Aga said. Her eyes were shining.

I crossed my arms. "What if I don't want to train to be a magus?"

"You don't train to *be* a magus," Melchior said, lowering his eyelids until only his dark, endless pupils showed. "You are *born* one. You train so that you don't get someone killed with an unfocused, hastily made wish."

"I'm not unfocused."

"Melchior, are you sure about her?" Taja leaned away, like we were something diseased. "She *is* half-human."

Melchior picked up a scroll that had been lying on the table in front of him. He unrolled it and read out loud, although he was really reciting it. His eyes were locked on mine. "'Zayele brought us a human of her relation. It appears he has been wished upon, by her, with negative effects. None of my attempts have proved useful. Unfortunately, Zayele would not say what she had wished. Signed, Razeena, Head Physician.'"

"That's not true," I countered. "I told her everything. I just don't know why it didn't work like I'd planned."

Melchior rolled the parchment back up and tapped it against the armrest of his divan. "So it seems you have a level of power but do not know how to use it. Uncontrolled. Unfocused. *Untrained.*" I stared at him and nearly bit off my tongue. "Any sensible person would agree to my training so that she does not disrupt anyone else's life."

"In Zayele's defense—" Najwa began, but he cut her off.

"There will be no defense! She is not on trial. Zayele is here to report to training, like any good jinni. Have no fear, I will look after your sister." Najwa and I looked at each other, and in her eyes I saw a flicker of concern. "You have your own duties to attend to."

"Yes, sir," she said quietly. "Can you undo the wish she made on Yashar? The things he sees frighten him."

He had been about to wave us away, but he froze. "What things?"

"We don't know. But they are scaring him, and they seem to come and go with any jinni."

He and Aga both stood up at once. She nodded at him and said in her rich voice, "I'll have him brought here."

"Wait!" I shouted, panicking. "Why are you so interested *now*? Why bring him here?"

"Because, child," Aga growled, "it seems you've done it again. This boy needs our help. Quickly." She whipped her gray braid over her shoulder and trotted toward the entrance, adjusting her belt while she moved.

"Can't they help him in the hospital?" Najwa asked.

Melchior crossed his arms. "If she made a wish to change him, there is nothing they can do to return him to his previous state. I, however, might know how to help him."

"What wish was it?" Taja asked, but he ignored her question. Instead, Melchior had locked eyes with me.

I resisted the urge to look away. "I want to be here when you help him."

"He is my concern now. Yours is to train. Taja, you will be taking over the exercises." When Taja opened her mouth, he waved his hand in the air at her. "You will do just as I did for you. No more, and no less."

He took one last sweeping look at us, and then went to a door and disappeared behind it. I ran up to the door just after it closed, but couldn't pull it open. I whirled on Taja.

"Where is he going? Where will they put Yashar?"

Taja shrugged. "I don't know. But whatever you did, it surprised him. What did you wish anyway?"

"Nothing," I grumbled, then I pulled on Najwa's arm. "Come. We have to get to Yashar first."

"You can't just leave," Taja said, stepping in front of us. "Melchior told us to get started immediately."

I gritted my teeth. "I am not going to stay here when someone is off to steal Yashar!"

"You are a student. You don't have a choice in the matter."

"Zayele, I can go for you," Najwa said. "You stay here."

"Are you really going to stop me, Taja?" I asked.

Taja's nostrils flared, but she shook her head. "Be here first thing in the morning, or I'll suggest to Melchior that he train you himself." There was something mischievous in her eyes, but I didn't have time to think about it. I dragged Najwa down the steps and over the fallen sweet pea petals.

We were too late. When we got there, we found Shirin pushing open the hospitals doors, her soft mouth tipped down at the corners. After she told us what had happened, I ran home, suddenly needing Rahela. She was the only other person who cared about Yashar and would understand.

I was half-asleep on the pile of pillows in our main room when I felt someone's hand on my cheek.

"You don't want to come with us?" It was Atish's voice, so I opened my eyes.

"No," I said.

"You've never had honeyed dumplings before, and the best ones are only served today," he said. "Also, you'll miss the fight."

I raised a brow. "What fight?"

He grinned. "Rashid has started the competition for your dyad, and one of the first events is tonight."

Najwa groaned in the background. "Atish, you can't be serious."

"But I am."

"You're going to *fight* over me?" I asked. I pushed myself up off the floor. "That's . . . but why? Why can't Rashid just pick someone and be done with it? I thought it was going to be *you*."

Atish rubbed his scalp and looked away. "It will be, don't worry. I just have to win every event. Or most of them."

"You don't sound very confident." I thought about being partnered with someone else, some other Shaitan that I didn't know, for the rest of my life. What if I hated him? What if he was rude, or stupid, or disgusting?

"I'm confident," he said. He pulled me onto my feet and held me close. "I just need you to be there for me." His mouth was only inches from mine, and I couldn't look away from it. "But first, we need to get some of those honeyed dumplings."

He let me go and smiled, flashing his teeth. He knew I had been staring at his mouth, and my face flushed hot with embarrassment. "Sounds delicious" was all I could say. I took one glance at Najwa and Shirin, who were whispering with each other and stopped just long enough to give me a look when Atish ushered me out the door.

"Aren't they coming?" I asked him when we were outside. Then I gasped. The whole Cavern had been transformed.

Where there had been clear gypsum shards poking down from the ceiling before, there were a thousand blue, green, and gold crystals lit from within. The ground was sparkling in dappled colored light. White-hot sparks burst from the streetlamps, popping and dancing around the glass casings.

Drumbeats, quick and strong, came from the center of the Cavern. Atish took my hand, grinned, and nodded at the sounds. "That's where the fight will be. And the food."

"Is that all you Shaitan care about?" I asked, matching his grin. Guiltily, I thought of Yashar, locked up in the palace, not knowing what all those sounds were. Not getting any of the food.

"Believe me, you wouldn't think of anything else either if you knew what you were about to eat," he said. He nearly dragged me along the route to the Cavern's center. I took another glance at the crystals glowing above us, and trotted beside him.

Someone had wished a crushed mica layer on top of the cobblestones, and it glittered beneath the feet of hundreds of jinn. Children, all wearing white tunics embroidered with tiny silver disks, joined hands and wove themselves between the adults. In contrast, the adults wore darker, richer tunics in jewel tones. In the corner of my eye, I saw Najwa's adopted mother, Laira, laughing beside a circle of women. Her tunic was jade and gold, and hemmed with a ribbon of gold beads. She caught me looking at her and stopped just long enough to nod once at me in recognition. Then she turned back to her friends. That was all I'd ever get from her.

Atish was right about the food. The smell was heavy and

sweet, and I'd never felt hungrier. I was dizzy from the sounds and swirling lights, and it took me a moment to realize he was holding up a small, bronze-colored ball of dough.

"Taste this and you'll never go back to Zab." Atish held it under my nose and I nearly swooned at the syrupy scent. I put it in my mouth and thought of the Greek story of Persephone. The moment the roll melted on my tongue, I forgot her plight and thought only of the smile spreading outward from my tongue. I moaned in delight, and grabbed for another.

"These are delicious," I said, not caring that I was speaking around the sweet globs. "Honey?"

He nodded and stuffed two at once into his mouth.

A horn blew from nearby, long and haunting, then ended with a series of trills. Everyone turned toward the sound, which echoed with murmurs from the jinn. Atish swallowed and wiped his mouth with the back of his hand.

"They're calling us." He took my hand again and pulled me away from the food cart and in the direction of the horn. The jinn parted, allowing us through, whenever they saw the golden lion on his upper arm. Wherever he was taking me, it had something to do with the Shaitan.

We stopped when we reached a group of soldiers, all with the Shaitan mark gleaming on their upper arms. A handful of them were women with long, bronze-tipped braids, but most were men. They surrounded a circular pit lined with jagged volcanic rock. The center was combed white sand and one man stood in the very middle of it. Rashid, Captain of the Shaitan. He looked past his soldiers and caught my eye.

"Zayele, welcome." He bowed and I stood frozen, not sure

if I should bow in return or wave. "We are honored to have you watch our first contest." To the Shaitan, he said, "Regular sparring rules apply. First sign of blood ends the match. The final victor rises to the top of the chart and has the best chance at being the next soldier to take part in the Dyad tradition."

Atish squeezed my hand and then let go. My palm was suddenly cold, and I wiped it against my thigh while Atish walked up to the circle of black rocks. He tugged on his vest and nodded at Rashid. "I request a chance to fight for the position."

"Anyone else?" Rashid asked the group. Seventeen men stepped forward to join Atish. Like Atish, they were all built like cats, with quick muscles and a graceful stance. One of the women came to my side. Her face was furrowed with a frown that began between her eyes and ended at her tense jaw. When she noticed I was staring, she clicked her tongue.

"If you were lucky, they'd let you partner with a woman." When I didn't respond, she huffed and stalked off. If Dyads were usually male-female pairs, it wasn't my fault. Would I have been more comfortable watching women fight each other to be with me? I doubt it would have made a difference. Rashid clapped loudly then, and my thoughts returned to the circle of white sand.

Atish stood in the center, facing a soldier with an array of ugly scars scratched onto his forearm. He was narrow-eyed and his cheeks were fleshy. When he sneered at Atish, I prayed silently that he would not win the fight. They unbuckled their scabbards and tossed them to the empty hands surrounding the ring.

The fight began without any warning. The round-faced

soldier rubbed his palms together and then flicked his wrist at Atish. A ball of hot light shot out toward Atish, but he leaped out of the way. While the soldier stepped sideways to wait for his wishpower to return, Atish jumped forward and pummeled him in the face. The soldier stumbled into the others and Atish pulled him back into the circle and set him on his feet.

A stream of blood dribbled from the soldier's nose. The fight was over. Atish bent forward and exhaled deeply. "I'm sorry, Rohan," he said. "I just can't afford to lose."

Rohan covered his nose and grinned. "It was a good tactic. I wasn't expecting it."

"Next," Rashid called out. His face had hardened, like bread left out in the sun.

Atish waited out the next few fights, but he did not come to stand beside me. I stood alone and forced myself not to wince while the men bloodied each other. I had found a way to keep my face expressionless when Atish hopped back into the circle and winked at me.

"Atish and Samir," Rashid said. He crossed his forearms and nodded at each Shaitan. Samir was slightly taller than Atish, with wider shoulders. His eyebrows were thick and overshadowed dark, deep-set eyes. When he lowered his chin and locked his gaze on Atish, he looked like a ram readying to leap against his competitor.

Atish's jaw tightened and his nostrils flared. There was something about Samir that put him on edge, while the other Shaitan had not. As soon as Rashid said, "Go," Atish launched himself at Samir. He hurled into him, but Samir had lowered his body and, without even a grunt, grabbed Atish and threw him over his shoulder. Atish hit the ground and the sand exploded into the air. Samir turned, wiped the dust from his eyes, and flicked his wrist. A jet of white fire shot toward Atish.

Atish rolled to the side before the fire hit him, and jumped onto his feet. Samir lifted his hand—his wishpower was strong enough for another attack—but Atish was ready. He pushed his palm at Samir and shouted a word I didn't understand. This time, there wasn't any fire. The air cracked and Samir flew backward into the onlookers.

The Shaitan crowded around Samir, but he did not rise. Atish sank to his knees and let out a long, exhausted sigh before turning toward Rashid. Rashid's arms were still crossed, but he nodded approvingly at Atish, with one brow raised.

"I don't think Samir realized Atish was his equal," someone muttered to my right.

"He's not Samir's equal," another Shaitan snickered. "He's better."

My chest swelled with pride. Atish had won the fight. As alarming as it was that they were fighting over me, I was proud—and relieved—that Atish was as good as he was. Maybe, just maybe, he would be my dyad.

Atish rubbed at his face and then got up off the sand and came to me. He was glowing with adrenaline and sweat. "That was lucky."

"Lucky? You *surprised* him. That's skill."

He laughed softly. "No. Samir is better at hand-to-hand than I am. I just happened to be faster that time."

"You've fought him before?"

"Lots of times. He taught me everything I know."

"Did you ever win against him?"

"Not till today." He grinned and leaned in close to my ear. "I'd never had anything like *you* at stake before."

Goose bumps trickled down my neck and I smiled before pulling away from him. "Well." I knew I should say something else, but my mind was spinning and I couldn't come up with a single additional word. All I could think of was the way his breath had felt against my ear and the heat in his eyes before he had leaned in.

✦ 12 ✦

NAJWA

I SLIPPED AWAY when everyone went to stand along the lake wall to wait for the last orb to break. I had never missed this moment before, because when the flames broke the last of the glass orbs, the air over the lake would erupt in dancing, swirling sparks. They'd fall, light as ash, and settle on the water's surface like a glowing, multicolored blanket. When I was younger, I'd wait for them to flow closer, where I could stare past the sparks and pretend the lake had turned to liquid diamond.

But I would not be there tonight. More than anything, I needed to visit Faisal's Memory Crystal. I had too many questions, and to be honest, I didn't have the heart to see beauty rain down in the Cavern.

The market stalls were emptying, and no one paid any attention to me while I snuck past them. I checked behind me twice, to make sure no one was watching, and then I ran across the open expanse of the central courtyard to the golden domed building that contained all I needed to know.

The dome was shaped like an upside-down acorn and grew straight up from the ground. The roof sloped softly until it reached the golden spear with a shard of plain, clear quartz affixed to the end. Rich gold foil covered every outer surface, except for the simple door of wood. Even the door handle, a ring the size of my fist, was made of gold.

I wrapped my fingers around the cold ring and twisted it. The door began to open, pulling away from me as if the air within was sucking it in. I let go and watched it swing forward, cutting into the darkness. No one should be inside, I thought, because everyone was at the Last Breaking.

"*Narush*," I whispered. A moment later, a series of flames ignited down a chain of sconces, lighting the path to the cold world beneath the Cavern. A narrow gilded staircase led the way, and I gripped the railing as I descended.

The air grew cooler and drier with each lamp I passed, and although it was not so very cold, I shivered. The last time I'd been on these steps was for Faisal's funeral, a few weeks ago. Nearly half the jinn in the Cavern had been there, but I'd felt as alone then as I did now.

When I reached the base of the staircase, my foot crunched in the gravel. The floor was made of crushed volcanic rock, and every so often, a spear of colored crystal as tall and wide as a man jutted up from the rocks. When I was small, I used to think we turned into those crystals when we died. At my first funeral, I saw the memories pulled from the body and set into an empty crystal, where they floated around like wisps of smoke. My adoptive mother, Laira, added her memories of the deceased into the crystal, and it was then that I realized we were transferred—the parts of us that mattered—into something that would not decay.

The chamber was full of upright crystals in every color. During that first funeral, I had thought that array of colored crystals was what a rainbow looked like. Faisal had spoken to me of them, and I had not understood then how they were really connected in a ribbon and spread across the sky. But then, I didn't know what a sky looked like either.

I crunched over the gravel, threading my way between crystals of jinn I did not know. Finally, I reached the green crystal that contained the memories of Faisal. While Mariam's was a curiosity, Faisal's was a shard in my heart. I still half expected him to stop by the fountain and interrupt my break from school with something he'd found on the surface. But now he would never do that. He would never admonish me for not doing my best. He would never do any of these things, because now he was dead, and all that remained were his memories, locked up and swirling like smoke within the crystal.

His stood beside my mother's in a row composed entirely of fallen Dyads. A stone sat on the ground between the two crystals, with the front edge sliced off. The smooth surface was engraved with their names.

Dyads were together even in death.

I had come here for help from Faisal, but now that my mother was within reach, I stood mesmerized by the coils of yellow and gold swirling within her crystal. What had she been like? Why had she left the Cavern and married a human? What made her so brave?

Would she have wanted me to grow up in the Cavern, away from my sister?

Faisal's crystal stood silent beside Mariam's as though it agreed I should take a look inside the golden memories first. I took a step closer to her crystal and pressed my palms against the surface. Tendrils of yellow smoke licked the quartz behind my splayed fingers, but I could not feel them.

"Mariam." My voice scratched at the air. "Mother. What would you tell me now if you were still alive?" I knew she could not listen. The crystal was cold and hard, and had never contained life. It was a museum housing her memories, inviting me with its curlicues of golden smoke.

My eyes glazed over, my mind felt pulled to the right, then the left, and I slipped into Mariam and her life from long ago.

A beam of daylight poured down in a single stream and illuminated the main hall of Iblis's Palace. It drenched my hands in a pure white light and reflected off a ring on one of my fingers.

I didn't wear rings. I tried to clear my head by shaking it, but it wouldn't move. I wasn't in control of my body, and there was someone else there. *Mariam*. I was reliving one of her memories. Swiftly, her mind wrapped around mine, and I was her. Her body was mine.

I squeezed my fist, holding the light within my hand, and then drew it to my chest, as though I'd been able to capture the sunbeam. Like an unopened gift, it was still and promising, its musk and blossoms tightly woven, still hidden from the world.

This was something I understood well, and I loosened my fingers, letting out an imaginary bit of captured light.

"Mariam. Welcome home," my father said. I looked up and saw him standing beside the impression of the angel's feather. I—Mariam—gulped away any sign of surprise and smiled.

No. Her father cannot be Melchior. That would mean . . .

"I just returned."

Melchior is my grandfather.

"And? Is your wanderlust under control now?"

He still did not understand. I didn't go to the mountains because I wanted to travel. I didn't dance in the snow because I wanted to feel my toes numbing from the chill. I hadn't learned the tribe's songs because I felt the need to sing. All these things were wonderful, of course, but they were not why I had stayed in Zab.

"Yes, Father." I glanced at the floor between us. How was I going to tell him? I had come back for just this purpose, but now that I faced him, I felt weak and my breath was uneven. These were things he would notice.

"Why don't you report back to the Shaitan and let them know you're ready for the next stage in your training?" He began to head toward a door, then paused and turned back to face me. "By the way, where's Faisal? I haven't seen him in days."

"Um . . ." The words caught in my throat. When I last saw him, Faisal had been as pale as a branch scraped to the quick.

Then he transported away, and I did not know where to find him. "He hasn't been here?"

Father frowned. "Did you have an argument? Was he displeased with the humans up there?"

"He wasn't . . . he didn't . . ." I could not finish. Any more, and I'd be saying too much.

"Mariam, I understand how complicated relationships can be in a Dyad. When your mother was alive, she was quite jealous of my connection with Aga." His mouth thinned, and he forced smile. "Are you two in love?"

I balked. "Of course not."

"That seems like a rather quick decision. You never know what could happen, after a few years together."

"Father, I do not love him. I cannot love him."

"Why are you so certain? Is there someone else?"

Everything we'd said had led to this. Swallowing back my fears, I nodded and suppressed an urge to lie. Lying would seem easier, but it would not last long with my father.

"Who is it?"

"Evindar." Half of me sang with his name on my lips, and half of me trembled, belying all of my Shaitan training.

Father whipped his whole body around to face me. "That is a human name, Mariam." It was more of an accusation than a statement of fact. I cringed.

Don't tell him. He never understands. Never.

"Yes." I had expected him to be angry, but he was quiet. Almost too quiet. I stole a glance and saw he was looking over my shoulder at the apricot tree.

"Did you ever eat one of the fruits?" he asked me.

I blinked. "I . . . I don't think so. Why?"

"Because eating from the poisoned tree is the only thing I can think of that would explain your treasonous heart." He said each word delicately, as though he were talking to a child frightened of the dark. Then he pressed a palm to his chest. "The thought of you with a human man hurts my soul, Mariam."

"But, Father, you don't know him!"

His face flushed in anger. "You are going to have to make a decision, daughter of mine. You can either be the Shaitan you've been trained to be, or you can betray me and never return. I suggest you think about it."

My breath froze in my lungs. This was not a choice! I couldn't choose between Evindar and my family. Was this what Faisal had meant when he said Evindar would be the end of our Dyad?

I woke up gasping for air and shivering from cold. I slid down to the gravel and tugged on my shawl. My head was buzzing, an effect of the Memory Crystals, and I had to blink several times before I could see clearly.

Mariam's father was *Melchior*. Why hadn't he told me when I saw him earlier? Was this a secret?

It was a long time before I got up off the rocks and made it to the staircase. I could not shake the feeling of dread Mariam had felt when she was faced with having to choose between her lover and her father.

If she had not chosen Evindar, I would not exist.

ZAYELE

TAJA MARCHED DOWN a dark corridor and stopped at an iron gate set into a gap in the wall. The bars were thin and taut, like stitches holding the palace together. When she pressed on the black square that made them open, I sucked in a breath—I was worried the walls would fall apart. Taja cocked an eyebrow at me and I shrugged before going out the gate.

"The black square is interesting."

She smirked. "It's just a key."

We entered a courtyard that was tucked away between the palace and the Cavern wall, where the gypsum had not been left in its usual state. The long, pointed shards were filed down and carved into various shapes. I recognized a snake, a rabbit, and a lion. One crystal had kept its sticklike shape but was covered in round owl eyes. It was eerie.

A thin iron railing swept away from the wall, curving outward from the courtyard, and met up on the other end with the side of the palace. Between the railing, the palace, and the crystal shards was a plain, triangular courtyard containing nothing but creamy stone tiles, two obsidian benches facing each other, and a line of tiny potted trees along the palace's wall. Behind the iron railing was the last point of the Lake of Fire. The lake wall did not continue this far, and without its width and stone, the flames flickered tauntingly at foot level through the railing's bars. One swept up the side of the Cavern and disappeared in one of the untouched crystals' shadows.

"This is where we will train."

"Is this only for the magi?" I asked.

Taja nodded. "That black key will only work for us. You included. You must not bring anyone who isn't a magus here, understand?"

"Yes."

"Good. Now it's time for the first lesson." Taja frowned and pointed at the benches. "Sit there, facing the wall."

I sat, pulled on my dress to straighten it, and waited for more instruction. Taja paced in front of me, swishing her caftan back and forth over the stone floor while rubbing her forehead with the tips of her fingers. "The first thing I need to do is explain the role of the magi in the Cavern. We aren't a separate group, like the Shaitan. We don't have any particular talents like the others, such as reading minds—"

"There are jinn who can read minds?" I blurted out.

She rolled her eyes. "Of course. They're in the Mark of the Law, and they're not supposed to read your mind without permission. You can tell them by their mark. It's a bat. Anyway, there are jinn who can heal and jinn who can make themselves invisible for long stretches of time, like your sister. But the magi have nothing specific that defines us outside of the others, other than the fact that we can do a little of everything they can do. We're great adapters, and so we can blend in with any talent, learn their trade, and sometimes even outperform them. Most magi end up in the Eyes of Iblis Corps because it's dynamic and challenging."

"Are you in the Corps?"

She stretched her neck to one side. "No, it's too calm for me. I'm in the Shaitan, with my dyad."

"Do you have to do something other than be a dyad?"

"You can't just 'be.' That'd be a dull life. You'll find out soon enough." She shook her head and turned toward the Lake of Fire. "I must admit I did not expect this assignment, and I don't know what it will mean for you as a magus if half your blood is human. Maybe it makes no difference." She walked over to the railing and held her hand over the lake. A moment later, one of the blue flames flickered near her fingers, like she had beckoned it. It flowed through her hand before crashing against the crystal wall and dissipating.

I went to the railing and leaned against it, careful to keep my distance from her. "What did you learn at your first lesson? Was Melchior your teacher?"

"No. Well, yes, but he was only one of them. I was also taught by a few other magi and Aga, Melchior's dyad. Aga will teach you too, but not now. She will be there when you're ready to pair up with a Shaitan. But first, you must learn to control your power." She smiled and closed her eyes. "You have to learn to quiet your mind on command. It's the only way to make your wishes clear, direct."

I winced. "Is that why my wish on Yashar didn't work?"

"I'm not allowed to discuss him with you." She spun toward me and I saw determination in her eyes. "To be a magus is a great responsibility. We are the ones who keep the Cavern alive."

"How do we do that?"

"That's something you'll learn in your final lesson. First, see the ceiling's midpoint?" I followed her finger to where it pointed at the very top of the Cavern. The crystals knitted together like charcoal webbing, which made them difficult to differentiate. Only the tips made their way out of the shadows.

"Yes."

"In the crevices, you'll find a nursery. Your task is to find out what sort of stone is embedded in the top of the dome without waking any of the babies."

I squinted up at the ceiling. "What in the world would live up there?"

"Bats, of course." She grinned.

"I'm glad we're starting with an easy lesson," I said, groaning. The ceiling was at least a hundred feet high, and although there were crystals I could use as handholds, once the ceiling curled inward, they'd be too slick to keep me up. And all that just to reach into a sleeping horde of bats. "Is this what you had to do for your first lesson?"

"It's not as difficult as it looks. Remember, you're not limited to your human weaknesses."

I could *wish* my way there.

"I should mention that you can't fly there, and you can't transport within the Cavern. Someone tried that once, and they ended up impaled on one of the shards," she said dryly.

"This keeps getting more and more interesting." I pulled up my sleeves, rolled back my shoulders, and studied the shadowy darkness above. "And this is something only a magus can do?"

"No one else has tried, but I'm sure they'd fail. It takes our unique . . . adaptability, as I mentioned earlier. The best way to understand that is to complete this lesson." She walked over to the bench and sat down, spread her skirt out over her ankles, and gestured at the ceiling. "Go on," she urged.

I almost rolled my eyes at her before going to the wall and grabbing on to the bottom crystal. It was the color of salt and as long as I was tall. I pulled myself up onto it and then onto the next one, climbing the crystals like they were giant, slippery tree branches. Each time I made it onto a crystal, I had to stretch, pull, and hike my skirt up to my knees to get to the next one. When my arms and back were burning and my fingers were slick with sweat, I sank down into a crouch on a smoky quartz shard to rest and think. My resting place wasn't level, and I had to hold on to keep myself from sliding forward. Carefully, I leaned over to my right to look down. Taja was on the bench still, but she was tiny. If I slipped, I'd land either at her feet or on the iron fence that lined the Lake of Fire.

There had to be a better way. Somehow, Taja had managed this. She was a fighter, but this had nothing to do with strength or the ability to climb. I knew this now that I was halfway there. The crystal above me was pointed *down at the ground.* Unless I turned into a spider, there'd be no way to get myself to the bat nursery.

My stomach fluttered. Maybe that was it. I couldn't transport, but I could change things, maybe even myself. I needed to focus, like Taja had said, and make the right wish.

My feet slipped forward an inch, and I let them drape over the side so that I could grip the crystal with the back of my knees. I leaned back on my palms, took a deep breath, and closed my eyes.

Darkness and silence surrounded me like I was inside one of the Breaking's glass balls. It only took a second before I remembered seeing a bird climb the cliffs at home. I knew this type of bird well because I had raised one. When I was eight, I found a wallcreeper hopping beneath a shrub. Her foot was broken, probably from a fight with a cat, and I picked her up off the ground, splinted her leg with my mother's help, and brought her crickets to eat. After a few weeks, I took her back to the base of the cliff and set her free. She didn't chirp or sing when she hopped up the side of the cliff, and within moments, she was higher than I could ever climb. This bird was what I needed to become.

I slowed my breathing and visualized her little gray head, her dark, swept-back wings, and the crimson feathers that peeked out beneath. She had tiny little feet that were strong and sure. They could grip rock, even if it was slick like glass. They'd find the smallest cracks in the crystal and cling on easily.

Carefully, I crafted my wish as though it were clay. I shaped it into a wallcreeper and put myself inside. *Change*, I wished.

My skin tightened, and I screamed, but my scream wasn't

human. In a heartbeat, my body folded into itself and I sprouted feathers. My lips hardened and pushed forward.

I screamed again, and the call went out far into the empty air.

In pain, I lurched forward and rolled toward the end of the crystal. My vision was brighter and clearer than ever before, and I saw Taja's eyes widen before my feet—my claws—gripped the edge. They gripped it easily, as though I'd spent my whole life on vertical walls.

"Zayele! Are you all right?" Taja called from below. I twisted my head and tried to spit out words, but my tongue was too stiff. Taja raised an eyebrow and then laughed. "That is not what I expected! Go, but don't wake up those bats!"

I snapped my beak shut and hopped up the crystals like I weighed nothing. Once, I spread my wings out just to see the blood-red feathers and took a long lunge to the next crystal, which hung down like a bottomless pillar. It wasn't flying, exactly.

I'm the only jinni ever who turned into a bird and didn't get to fly.

A few minutes later, I reached the nursery. Hoping I wouldn't wake the babies, I hopped from open space to open space, which was hard to find because the bats were packed in tight. But there was one place they weren't hanging from— right in the center, a golden spike pierced through the huddling mass. It didn't go much farther than their wrinkly ears, but I was able to spot it. It was sharp as a knife, and just looking at it somehow pinched my little bird heart with awe.

I spread my wings and fluttered over their heads to the golden point. My claws curled around it. It was cold as ice, which I hadn't expected from something made of gold. Suddenly, bats exploded from their perch, their wings stirring up clouds of foul-smelling air. They swooped around me, nudging me away from the babies with their noses. Now that the ceiling was left mostly bare, I was able to get a better look at the golden spike. The base fanned out in a perfect circle, and the edge was engraved with Arabic script that repeated the name of one of Allah's daughters, over and over.

When I returned to the magi's garden, Taja was bent over one of the potted plants, picking at the leaves. I chirped, and before she could turn around, I wished myself back into my normal form. It hurt, but it was quick.

"I'm back."

She glanced upward. "You woke the bats."

I shrugged. "No bat was harmed during my test."

She harrumphed, but I noticed a gleam in her eye. "What did you see up there?"

"I saw her name. It was—"

"Yes, I know," she said, cutting me off. She went to the door. "See you here tomorrow." Then she pressed her hand against the black key. The bars slid into the wall, and she stepped into the darkness.

That was it. She didn't explain the name. She was gone.

I left feeling uneasy, and it wasn't until I was walking along the lake wall that I realized what I felt was disappointment. I wanted to know where I fit in this crystal-studded Cavern, and no one was giving me any answers.

A pair of middle-aged jinn passed me then, and while I

stepped aside, I scanned them for marks. The man on the left had a bat embroidered on the sleeve of his shoulder—a mind reader! The other man had a spider marked onto his forearm. I hadn't met anyone else with these marks yet, and in a moment of daring, I made a decision: I was going to talk to them. Strangers. Jinn. Men. Reminding myself that it wasn't frowned upon here, I called out, "Excuse me."

The men stopped and turned around. The man with the spider mark smiled, but the other one looked wary.

"I'm trying to learn more about the jinni marks. Can you tell me what yours mean?"

The friendlier man nodded, shaking his shoulder-length hair into his face. The strands were thick with jewels and multi-colored feathers. "Yes, you're the human girl. Za-something." He gestured for me to finish.

"Zayele. I'm *half*-human."

He smiled widely. "My mistake. I'm Abdas, and this is Firuz." Firuz bowed his head, which didn't have any of the adornment that Abdas's had. His hair was the straightest, blackest hair I'd ever seen, and it was combed forward, down to his flat black eyebrows.

"Faisal mentioned you." Firuz had a shockingly deep voice that rumbled like far-off thunder. "You're Najwa's sister."

"Yes."

"You look just like her," the other man said.

I wanted to say something about that being pretty obvious, but instead, I said to Firuz, "You're a mind reader?"

He brushed his shoulder. "I'm in service to Iblis."

"Like the Eyes of Iblis Corps?" I asked.

"Not at all. I serve the Law of Iblis, not the Eyes." Something in the way his mouth hardened made me not want to question him further.

"They make sure we don't run around messing everything up," Abdas added. He spun to face his friend and put his fingers on his chin and winked at me. "But if you ask me, Firuz does some strange things."

"We keep the peace," Firuz said. He narrowed his eyes at Abdas, who smiled widely in return.

Abdas stepped back and bowed his head. "I'm a weaver, like Najwa's mother, Laira. In fact, she was one of my teachers."

Now my question had been answered, and we all fell into an uncomfortable silence. I glanced at the flames on the lake, and then back at Abdas. "My cousin Rahela is weaving something now. Laira gave her a loom."

"Really?" His eyes were black as obsidian, and just as shiny. "She's the human staying with you, isn't she?"

"She is. She left Zab with me and was with Najwa in Baghdad. She probably saved Najwa's life when she had to pretend she was me." I blinked, not sure why I wanted to tell them that. The words had suddenly come, unbidden. Was it something the mind reader did to me?

Abdas bowed his head. "Well then, I'd love to come by and see her weaving technique. I've always wanted to learn the human patterns."

Firuz's cheek twitched, as if he was trying hard not to smile. "Come on," he said. "We've got to go."

"Right. It was nice to meet you, finally," Abdas said. "Maybe I will come, if your cousin doesn't mind having yet another jinni nearby."

I had no idea what Rahela would do if a man suddenly walked in and asked her about weaving. I suppressed a laugh and nodded. "I'm sure she will appreciate the visit."

We went our separate ways, and this time, I felt less disappointed. I had learned two new things. There was a system of law here, led by a corps of jinn who could read minds. And the spider mark meant you were a weaver.

A flame from the lake slipped up the wall and came close to my foot. Laughing now, I hopped over it and kept going, running along the wall like the children did. Like Najwa must have, when we were younger and I was busy learning to embroider my false father's clothes.

✦ 14 ✦

NAJWA

AFTER WAKING THE next day, I went directly to the Eyes of Iblis Command. While the woman at the desk slipped the copper disk on the peg to designate my presence in the Command, I tried not to think about Melchior. I tried not to feel the ache my mother had felt when told to choose between her family and the man she loved.

I passed through the great red and gold hall that housed the Lamp, and then to the room with the Eye of Iblis. The Eye was a wall of thinly sliced white crystal squares. They were tiled in such a way that any image projected from a Corps member's mark could be displayed either across the entire wall or on a single square. All a member of the Corps had to do was press on their owl eye mark, and what he or she saw would be sent to the Eye. It was the best way to capture images, because the Eye caught details the jinni might not remember or understand. Our motto was "The more Eyes, the more we See."

When I entered the room, Delia was studying the wall of white crystal, waiting for someone to send her information.

There, she controlled the chaotic flow of traffic as the Eyes brought her their information and images from above. A group of jinn were bent over a table in the center of the room. One was drawing a line across a flattened bit of parchment. One by one, they stopped watching her and looked up at me.

Delia turned away from the Eye of Iblis. "Ah, Najwa. You've arrived. Just who we need now. We are working on a project that will help us detail who supports Kamal. And who doesn't." She joined the cadre of jinn at the table and trailed her finger over a series of ovals dotting the parchment and connected by a web of lines. Each oval contained a sketch of a human's face, and the lines connecting the faces showed their relationships to one another. "This is all we know of the men in the Court of Honor. As you can see, it isn't much."

The sketches were roughly the same, and only a few bore names beneath them. In the center of the paper were two larger ovals set above the line of men, and in these were two alarmingly accurate sketches of Kamal and Ibrahim. One of the smaller ovals was linked to Ibrahim's with a set of pins and a red cord. It tied them together, like blood.

"Who is that?" I asked.

"That is Badr al-Din, second in command of the caliph's army and fiercely loyal to Prince Ibrahim. Once we know who supports whom, we can aid you better when you return as consul."

I swallowed. "I have new orders to return tomorrow. But not as consul."

Delia blinked, and in the moment before her eyes reopened,

I could see the stress, the disappointment that she was trying to wipe away. "Melchior has given you orders to return."

"Yes, ma'am."

"I suppose he means for you to watch these men, then, and help us with this."

"I believe so." I glanced at the other Corps members. Some were openly watching this discussion, while others stared intensely at the table. I knew a few of them were irritated that I had been the first into the palace, and now I was being given the assignment they all craved. This, I realized, was what Kamal was going through. Some men would be pleased with the caliph's decision, but others—particularly those who had hoped to be the next vizier—would not. I shook away the thoughts of Kamal and leaned forward, pressing my palms into the table. "Delia, there's another thing."

"Yes?"

I felt everyone's eyes on me, and did not like it. "It's about Melchior. And . . . my mother."

"I will be right back," Delia said to the room, cutting me off. She grabbed me by the elbow, led me out of the room, and did not let go until we had gone into a smaller, empty room. Her eyes were narrow slits, and her reddish-gold eyelids weighed heavily over the darkness of her irises. "We cannot discuss the Master of the Corps in front of so many people," she explained. "Now, tell me what is troubling you."

I winced. "Last night, I visited my mother's Memory Crystal."

"We all wondered when you'd get to that."

"She . . . she's Melchior's daughter."

Faisal would have taken me into his arms, or he would have offered me something sweet to eat. He always treated difficult news with compassion or sweets. But Delia was not Faisal. She stared me straight in the face and blinked before nodding. "Yes, although he'd like to forget it."

"This means he's my grandfather."

"And Zayele's," she added.

My throat was thick. "Why hasn't he said something?"

"I don't think there's been any time." We both knew that wasn't true. It was a statement to keep me from saying any more on the topic. "Regardless of the fact that he is your grandfather, you must obey his orders. I understand you made a promise to Kamal, but some things cannot wait. If Melchior thinks you need to return, then you must." She sighed and reached out for my wrists, wrapping her fingers around them gently. I looked down, surprised by her sudden show of affection. "Sometimes, even bright young men don't know when they've stepped into something very, very deep. Go back tomorrow, but don't get in his way. And remember to record as much as you can. We need faces, names, and allegiances. We need to know what is going on so we know what to do. If this war is ever to end, we need this. Faisal would have asked you to do the same, I believe."

I did not want her telling me what Faisal would have said, because he was gone. It didn't matter what he would have wanted, because he was *gone*.

I needed to get away. The air was too warm and too old.

And Delia was too close to me. If I stayed, she'd see that rotting part of me.

"I will go back."

She smiled, but it didn't reach her eyes. She clasped my shoulder and squeezed it, like Faisal used to do, and said, "Iblis be with you. And keep your eye on Badr al-Din."

+ 15 +

ZAYELE

RAHELA SAT ON the bench beside me, mindlessly tugging on the yarn while I told her about my first day of training. I had a bowl of olive oil on my lap and was dipping my bread into it, swirling it around. I hadn't eaten much.

She selected a sparkling gray skein and threaded it onto the loom. "I think it's good that Melchior is not the one teaching you," she said.

"Why?"

"Because he does not sound like a nice man."

"But he's only having Taja train me because he's with Yashar." I shuddered. "I don't even know if Yashar is all right. No one will tell me anything."

We heard the door handle turn and looked up just as Najwa came in the room. She looked as gray as the wool Rahela had wrapped around her fingers.

"What's wrong?" I asked her.

She shrugged and went to the cushions, sinking onto them in defeat. Rahela and I watched her for a minute. She pulled a cushion to her lap, shaking her head. Then she glanced up and I saw fire in her eyes.

"Zayele, I have something important to tell you."

My stomach dropped. Something must have happened to Yashar. "What is it?" I managed to say. "Is he hurt?"

She must have known who I was worried about, because she said, "It's not about Yashar. I haven't heard anything about him."

"Oh."

"Remember the Memory Crystal Faisal showed you? The one with our mother's memories?"

Mariam, lying in a pool of blood and reaching out toward the infant me. Hashim, slicing the air before my father, Evindar. Mariam, dancing in an orange grove in full bloom.

"Yes," I croaked. Visiting my mother's memories had been too realistic. Recalling them was like remembering my own life.

"Well, I went to the funeral grounds and found her Funeral Crystal. It was right beside Faisal's."

"You went below the Cavern?" Rahela asked. "By yourself?"

"Yes. I had to go. I went last night, when everyone was busy with the festival. Anyway, I went into one of her memories."

"What did you see?" I asked. I was afraid she'd tell me now that Mariam wasn't our mother after all. Everything seemed to change rapidly lately, and I was afraid that Mariam would be taken from me before I'd even gotten used to the idea of her.

"I found out who her father was, and who banished her from the Cavern." This was not going to be good news. I could tell by the dark look in her eyes. She tugged on the cushion's orange fringe. "Mariam's father is . . . Melchior."

I laughed. "No."

"Ah," Rahela said, with a hint of revelation. "That makes more sense."

"How?" I asked, and Najwa blushed. "I mean, how can that be? Why wouldn't he have told us? He must know."

"I'm sure he knows. And I'm sure he has a reason not to tell us."

"But—but he's so . . . *no*. He *can't* be our grandfather."

"I'm afraid he is," Najwa said. She rubbed at the space between her brows before looking back at me. "Do you know what this means?"

"That our grandfather is a magus? Wait. Is Aga our grandmother?"

"No. His wife died a long time ago." She laughed in a huff. "Zayele, he is the jinni who was imprisoned in the palace long ago. He was freed by Hashim, and when he didn't grant Hashim's wish, it set Hashim off. I know this because when I was stuck in the Baghdad palace, I found the Memory Crystal. I saw it happen. Anyway, later, when Hashim discovered our mother, *Melchior's daughter,* living with his very own tribe, he . . ."

"So in a way, Melchior began the war," I said.

"He is not the only one responsible," Rahela warned. "Hashim had a choice. The caliph had a choice. Your mother had a choice."

"Yes, but Melchior started it all!" Najwa cried. "He could have helped Hashim. Maybe if he'd done something kind for him, to show him we weren't monsters, Hashim would have lived his life differently. Maybe he would have liked us, instead of working his way into our trust only to betray it later."

I set down my food and stood up. "I can't believe this."

"It's all true," Najwa said. "I witnessed Mariam's memory of telling Melchior she was in love with our father, Evindar. He told her to either give him up or never return."

"No, I mean I can't believe he didn't *tell* us. There's a reason for it, and it's probably not a nice one."

There was a knock at the door. I had been pacing anyway, so I went to the door and opened it to find Atish standing in the doorway.

"Want to go for a walk?" he asked me. He was happy about something, but his smile faded. "What's wrong?"

"I'll tell you soon enough," I said. Suddenly, I wanted to get out of the house, away from the sickening news that still hung in the air. I looked back at Najwa. "Do you want to come with us?"

She shook her head, but her eyes were on Atish. "No, I need to rest."

"Are you going back to see . . . more?" I asked her, knowing she'd understand what I meant.

She leaned back on her hands. "I hadn't thought about it. Maybe."

"*Insha'Allah*," I said to her. To Atish, I said, "Let's go."

We shut the door behind us and headed out into the Cavern. He reached for my hand, but I didn't feel like being touched at that moment. I shook my head, apologized, and then noticed that his arms and torso were speckled with bruises and scrapes.

"What happened?" I had to stop myself from reaching out and brushing the wounds.

He lifted up an arm to inspect it and then shrugged. "Training."

"What were you doing? Feeding lions?"

He chuckled. "No. Just some special things for the Dyad competition."

I cringed, noticing how some of the scrapes were singed on the edges. This was because of me. "How are you doing? Were you fighting Samir—"

"Oh, don't worry about him. He's fine," he said.

We walked behind the houses and along the Cavern's wall of crystal spears. Surrounding each long shard were smaller ones. This area was easier for climbing than the one by the magi's garden. Atish gave me a sly smile and then reached up to the nearest crystal, set a foot against the smaller points, and pulled himself up the wall. He reached a large blue and green shard that overshadowed the rest and climbed up onto it. It was wide enough that his entire body disappeared from view.

Atish's head appeared from over the edge of the crystal. "Are you coming?"

I wondered for a moment what he would do if I turned into a wallcreeper and hopped up, and chuckled to myself. Then I climbed until I was level with the large crystal he had settled onto. He was lying on his back with his arms resting behind his head and his legs stretched out before him, one ankle crossed over the other.

"Took you long enough," he teased.

I rolled my eyes at him. "My arms are worn out."

"From that little climb?"

"I did a bit of climbing earlier, for my first magus lesson." I pulled myself onto the crystal's smooth, slippery surface. It was wide enough for two, and the thought made my cheeks flush. I crawled over to the end point and looked down. The Cavern sprawled beneath me, curving out in a circle from where I hung above it. The waterfall was to my right, and straight ahead in the distance was the Lake of Fire. To my left rose the towers of Iblis's Palace, and after a quick glance to see if Yashar was at any of the windows, I turned away.

"This is quite a spot."

"I know. No one can see us." He gestured for me to come to him, and I did, carefully. I crept over to him, conscious of the heat of his body and the grin on his face. I knelt beside him, and forced myself to look away from his golden eyes and instead at the scratches and scorch marks on his skin.

"What did you do to get all these?" I trailed a finger lightly over his forearm, where a long, red welt stretched from elbow to wrist. As I did, the hairs on his arm rose, and I pulled back.

"Training." He leaned close, as though he was going to kiss me, and then cleared his throat and looked down at the stone. "So, this crystal we're on is called tourmaline. It's not usually this big, but I caught some boys wishing on it this morning. They were trying to make a secret hideaway high up the wall and hidden in plain sight. Anyway, they ran off and I found myself all alone. And no one wants to be alone in a secret place."

I started to feel warm all over and inched closer. "Want to know what had me upset earlier?"

"Always." Again, his lips were close. Too close.

"Melchior is my grandfather."

Atish made a sound halfway between a cough and a squeal. *"What?"*

"It's true. He is my mother's father. He's the man who exiled her. He's the jinni who made Hashim so angry that he spent his whole life getting even. He started the war. He ruined my life. And Najwa's. And everyone else's who died in the war."

"Zayele, no one is that powerful. Not even a magus like Melchior."

"But he's ruined so many lives. And he's my grandfather. And he's here, in the Cavern, holding Yashar hostage."

He exhaled slowly and gazed over the expanse of the Cavern. "I'm not certain, but I doubt you have too much to worry about. Melchior won't hurt him, because he may prove to be valuable."

I dragged my fingernails quietly against the crystal. "A human who sees something no one else can see . . ."

"Like I said, *valuable.*" He picked up my hand, pulled the sleeve back, and rubbed his thumb over the soft skin of my wrist. "What you need is a strategy."

"Right. I need to get him to trust me so he'll let me get close to Yashar." I tried to ignore the tingling I felt beneath his fingers. "First, I need to surprise him with how quickly I can learn my lessons, and then I need to convince him I'm a loyal jinni. After that, I'll get to Yashar and take him out of here."

He lifted my wrist and brought it to his mouth. A soft moan escaped from my lips, and his eyes brightened at the sound. "Do you realize you're forcing me to be an accomplice?

Are you sure you want me to know everything that goes on in your half-human brain?"

I pulled my arm back to my side and rubbed briskly at the tingling. "You'll have to know everything about me soon enough."

"And why is that?"

"Because *you're* going to be my dyad. Or else."

"Or else what?" He reached for my wrist again but I slapped softly at his hand and he shook it, feigning pain.

"Or you'll never get to kiss me again." I twisted my torso toward him and pressed my hands against his chest, leaning in close to his face. His eyes were inches from mine and they were aimed on my mouth. "Someone needs to properly motivate you, or I might end up with Samir for the rest of my life." At the moment, the thought of spending all of my time with Atish sounded more like a gift than a prison sentence. I had to hold myself back from leaning closer and kissing him.

"Trust me, I'm motivated," he said huskily.

Then he kissed me anyway, the fool.

✦ 16 ✦

NAJWA

I SAW THE first one beside a pale pink crystal. He was crumpled against it, chin tucked into his chest, with a mass of beaded braids falling over his face. He didn't move except to breathe, which lifted his head slightly.

He would have looked like any other jinni jumping into a Memory Crystal if it weren't for his sallow cheeks, the crusty edges of his sleeve hems, and nails long enough to curl over the tips of his fingers. A bowl sat beside him with a white residue indicating the water had not been consumed but instead had evaporated.

In one of his hands, he clutched a small wooden soldier that had long ago lost any traces of paint.

Carefully, I stepped around him, crunching as quietly as I could on the black gravel path. He was one of the Haunted, those jinn who wasted their lives away down here. It was sad that so many were lost, unable to live their own lives. Unable to break free of the memories. They hadn't been here before, when everyone was at the Breaking festival.

I would never be like them. I was only here to see Faisal. There was so much he meant to tell me before he died, and the only way he could teach me now was through the recordings of his life. I wasn't here to mourn him. At least, not primarily. I was here to learn from him.

Did that man by the pink crystal have any other family, or was the child he mourned all he had left to cling to? I dug my fingernails into my palms. They would never be as long as that man's. I wasn't the sort of person who let herself waste away in the shadows of the Cavern.

Quickly, I found my way to Faisal's and Mariam's crystals, passing two other Haunted jinn and a few who looked like they only came here once a year. Those jinn had faces that glowed, and they carried a basket of leftover pies from the festival.

Faisal's crystal was taller than he had been in life. I stared at it, wishing I could feel the smoke that swirled inside. I had seen thin, wispy clouds like this in Baghdad, and I hadn't been able to run my fingers through those either. Both were mesmerizing, and I could not look away.

Without meaning to, I found myself kneeling before Faisal's crystal with my nose and palms pressed against it. It was as cold as Mariam's had been, but where hers had been foreign, his was familiar. I knew Faisal better than I knew my own mother.

"Tell me what to do, Faisal," I whispered. My words were absorbed by the green swirls within. "My sister is a magus, and I am not. I'm not even that good at being an Eye in the Corps. Or a . . . a consul. And the one person alive who I feel happy with doesn't want me there with him." I swallowed away a hardness in my throat and knocked my forehead onto the crystal. "Faisal, I miss you."

When I closed my eyes, I felt his presence and I was pulled in.

My head was full of haze, and after a moment, I realized I was in Faisal's memories. I was seeing the world through his eyes. He blinked, and I felt my mind shrink like a grape in the sun. I became Faisal, and his memory was my memory. His thoughts were my own.

My arms—Faisal's arms—were thick and strong. I flexed them out in front and tightened my fists. *Why haven't the magi chosen a path for me?*

I would do well in the Shaitan. Or even the regular army. Everyone else had been selected for specific training, and I was left with nothing to do after the group lessons were over for the day.

Today, I managed to convince the captain to let me train with the soldiers by claiming a need to "test my strength." It was ridiculous, and I could tell she thought so too, but she allowed me to line up with the students who were training to enter the Shaitan.

The captain walked down the line of students. She was a fit, older woman with basalt-straight hair and eyes that could sharpen a dagger. We stood and allowed her cold gaze to pick over every infraction in our clothing or manner of attention. When she stopped in front of me, I stared at the empty space behind her. I desperately, hungrily wanted to impress her and I could not afford to lose my composure.

"Faisal, you're putting my other students to shame," she said. Her voice was dry, but friendly. "We'll have to see if you'd fit in with us. From what I've heard, the reason you haven't been chosen for any marked path is that everyone is fighting over you." I blinked. What was she talking about? No one seemed to even notice I existed, except for the Transportation instructor. "You didn't know?" she asked.

"No, ma'am."

"Interesting," she said. Then she continued down the line, leaving me to settle my own mind. I was wanted? By whom?

After she was done, Captain Aga split us into pairs, partnering me with the one girl I had hoped to avoid. Mariam knew I couldn't keep my eyes off her, and now she would think I was only here to be with her. The truth was, I had avoided asking to train with the Shaitan because I didn't want to be near her. She unsettled me. I couldn't understand why I naturally tracked her whenever she entered a room. I tried to ignore Mariam, but I couldn't.

As I expected, Mariam raised a brow at me before gesturing with her head where we were to stand. "Fighting over you, huh?" she asked.

"I think she was just kidding."

"Aga doesn't do that." She strapped on a set of leather pads, covering her arms, chest, and thighs until she looked like an overstuffed lizard. She tossed me a set of pads, and I did the same.

"Well, maybe she's wrong then, because no one has shown any interest in me." I cringed, knowing I sounded desperate.

"Faisal, they don't tell us *anything*. I had no idea I was going to be a Shaitan. I thought my father would insist I join the Eyes, like him, or something equally dull, like ... building things. But here I am, about to pummel a jinni who doesn't know how to strap on his chest pads." I looked up just as a bolt of fire hit me in the shoulder. I stumbled a few steps back, caught my balance, and turned to glare at her.

"I wasn't ready."

"But Aga already blew her whistle. Didn't you hear?" Mariam was grinning.

"How do you do that?" I asked her.

She shrugged. "Just something Shaitan can do. If you can do it, then I guess that means you get to stay with us. I'm sure we're always open to having a magus in our midst." She was teasing, but it stung anyway. I was the odd one, the one jinni in our year who would always be separated, and I'd done nothing to deserve it.

She spent the rest of the lesson talking me through fireballs, but I wasn't able to get anything more than a spark, and once, I made the air shimmer, which did nothing but make everyone laugh at me. When we were leaving, Mariam bumped her shoulder into mine.

"I hope Aga gets to keep you. Knowing her, she probably will." Then Mariam ran off with the other students, leaving me standing alone and covered in goose bumps in front of the Shaitan gate.

I found myself—just me now, without any of Faisal's mind forcing me out—huddled in a ball. My knee was pressing into my chest, my chin was tucked, and it was hard to breathe. Gasping for air, I pushed off the ground and leaned my back against the emerald crystal.

Faisal hadn't always been so sure of himself. It was strange to think of him as a student, before he joined the Eyes of Iblis Corps, and before he became Mariam's dyad. He hadn't known where he belonged. He hadn't known anyone cared about him.

I took another deep breath and left him behind, smiling at myself. On the way out, I made sure to look away from the Haunted. They were to be pitied, surely, but I could not understand how they let themselves rot.

At the top of the stairs, just before I emerged onto the Cavern floor, I looked down at the burial chamber and decided I had had enough memories for now.

ZAYELE

WHEN I ARRIVED in Iblis's Palace for my second day of magus training, I was ready to take on whatever Taja threw my way. I entered the palace, ignored the flowers and the giant feather impression on the wall, and marched down the corridor to the iron gate that led to the magi-only training area.

I pressed my hand hard against the black glass plate, and when it began to slide into the wall, I pressed my lips together, took in a deep breath, and stepped out into the little garden. Taja was already there.

"Welcome back," she said, raising one eyebrow at me. The gate scraped the ground behind me and latched with a firm click.

"What's my task today?" I said, making sure to keep my voice level. In truth, I was excited to learn more, but I didn't want her to know. I had turned myself into a wallcreeper again the night before, after everyone had fallen asleep. It wasn't just to prove to myself that I could do it on command; it was also because it was fun to hop up the wall sideways, weighing no more than an apricot.

"Today you have to be focused and alert," she replied.

"Is that what Melchior's teaching Yashar? Or is he skipping that part and going straight to torture?"

"Melchior is not unfair. He knows Yashar is young, even if he is human. You have changed his capabilities, and now he's our responsibility. It is because of this that Melchior had to bring him here. He's safe, and he's being taught how to handle his . . . alteration."

I wanted to take a few steps and shake her into telling me more, but I wasn't brave enough. She was grinning as she gestured at a table. "This was my favorite lesson. It's similar to some of the training the Shaitan do." The table held a lump of reddish-brown clay, a corked pot, and a long, metallic box.

"A pottery lesson?" I guessed.

"Why would a magus ever need to make a pot? Anyway, for this lesson, you have to make a horse out of that clay. This is easy—*if* you can keep your mind agile and focused."

"Why would a magus ever need to make a clay horse?" I asked, smirking at Taja.

Taja rolled her eyes. "I will show you how it's done. Then you can try it."

She moved to the center of the garden, away from the crystals and benches. Then she pointed at the objects on the table and hissed something in the older jinni language. A moment later, the objects rose into the air and moved toward Taja. They became a twisting ring of items, with Taja at the center, the clay held between her hands.

Two alarming things happened at once. First, the box opened up to reveal a quiver of flaming arrows, and second, the jar upended, the cork dropped to the ground, and several dozen hornets crawled out and began to swarm around their orbiting ceramic home. Taja kept an eye on the objects spinning around her while her fingers worked the clay, pushing and pulling it into something that was quickly starting to look like a horse. She was close to being done when one of the hornets flew a little too close. She pointed at it with her smallest finger and it dropped to the ground, legs bent and stiff. Then she whispered to the clay and it glowed red-hot for a breath or two before she looked up and held it out to me.

"There," she said. "Now you try."

I took the horse from her, and the moment my fingers wrapped around it, it melted back into formless clay.

"Good luck," she said before walking out of the circle. She timed it so that she could fit right between the hornets and the arrows without getting stung or burned.

I tried to keep an eye on the hornets and the flaming arrows while I kneaded the clay, but it didn't take me long to realize I couldn't make a horse. I'd never made anything but bowls out of clay before. How could I make a horse without looking down at my hands?

I pulled the clay into two pieces and rolled one into a ball, then stuck it on the other, which I began to pull on to make what could, in some other world, be thought of as horse legs. I was starting to get it, and I smiled at myself.

"Have you thought about the name?" she asked. I flicked my eyes at her and saw that hers were trained on the arrows. "Oh, I forgot to tell you: The objects will stay put if your mind is focused. If it wanders, they will attack."

"Right," I said, and started to mold the horse again, this time without taking my eyes off the hornets. Holding up one hand to ward off any flying objects, I rolled the clay over my thigh and then began to shape the body.

As I kept an eye on the swarm of hornets spinning past, I imagined a horse's body and tried to make it with my fingers. Why couldn't I wish the clay into the right shape? Would she even know if—

One of the arrows lifted up out of the box. Yellow and black flames sprouted from the arrowhead. It aimed straight at my hands, and I froze. How could I focus on the clay with something like that pointing at me? The arrow pulled back, as if caught on an invisible bowstring, and let loose.

Without thinking, I held up the half-formed lump of clay to stop the arrow's approach. With a swish, the arrow embedded itself into the clay, which then caught on fire and began cracking in my hands. Its work done, the arrow fell to the floor and another one began to lift itself out of the box.

The clay was turning to powder. Quickly, I squished it together and spat on it, trying to get the clay back into something resembling, well, clay. From what I'd learned so far, the arrows only aimed for the clay. If I spun around quickly, they wouldn't have time to aim.

I was at the storm's center, but I was not calm. My heart was thumping in my chest now; I was eager to get this horse made and scatter the rest of the objects. The horse was coming along, and the remaining two arrows stayed in their box. The hornets, however, were starting to leave their ceramic hive. A few ventured away from the pot, some staying outside the circle but others coming alarmingly close to the center. I wasn't focusing hard enough.

I pulled out the legs, not caring at all that they were more wormlike than leglike. I smoothed out the neckline, cementing the head to the body, and began pulling out little bits for the ears. And then three hornets took off from their hive and flew toward me, fast as falcons. I pulled the horse up against my chest and pointed at the hornets. What had Taja wished earlier, when that first hornet came after her?

I didn't have time to think. When the hornets were almost within arm's length and as loud as a river, I closed my eyes. I could not think of them. I could not let myself hear them. I could only think of the clay in my fingers.

While my pulse beat fast at my temples, I finished the horse. Or what might, in some places, be considered a horse. Now I had to seal it with fire.

I wished again, pressing the energy into the clay. I wanted it to stay together, without cracking, and I wanted it to glisten. It flared brightly, but it didn't hurt my hands. A moment later, I turned to face Taja and held up my horse.

The head fell off and smashed into pieces around my toes. I swallowed. "When I'm done with training, do I get to show my sister all the little things I've made?" It was a bit much, but the twitch at the corner of her mouth was worth it.

"If you can make it through the rest of your training," she

said simply. Then she waved a hand at the arrows and they dropped to the ground. The hornets returned to their pot and crawled inside.

I set the headless horse on the ground beside the other, powdered fragments and stood back up. "Did I fail?" Part of me wouldn't have minded being released from the magi, but with the sting of failure came something else. Determination, maybe. I wanted to stay in, and finish the training. I wanted the challenge.

"Of course not," she said. "You passed, although I don't think anyone would call that much of a horse."

I was drained. The exercise hadn't taken much time, but it had sucked out whatever energy I'd had before I'd come in. I sank onto the nearest bench, which was across from where Taja sat.

"It's difficult to focus the mind when it's under stress. It takes years of training to do it well. I sometimes have a hard time, and I've been training for nine years."

Nine years? "How old are you?"

"Twenty-four. I was fifteen when Melchior came to my house and told my mother I had to leave with him, right then and there."

"Did you ever get to see your family after he took you away?"

"Sometimes. But some days, I was so tired that I'd sleep right here, on the ground. It was never the same again, at home. My mother and father hadn't known I was a magus, even though I'd left hints that whole year for them to find. Even now, I don't know if they just didn't notice them or if they didn't want to think about it."

"But why? Isn't being a magus a good thing?"

She gave me a lopsided grin. "Oh, it depends."

"On what?"

"On whether you make it through the training. And if you do, how long you can last out there, with your dyad. We're the first targets in every battle, you know. The caliph's army knows about us. They can pick us out in minutes, so minutes are all we have to do our job." A frown slipped over her lips. She must have been thinking of another magus who died recently, like Faisal.

"What *is* our job?"

She stood up in one swift, flowing movement. "We protect the Cavern and everyone in it. We hold up the shields. There's more to it than that, but for now, I think we should find something to eat." Then she went to the gate and leaned into the glass key, watching me with one eyebrow raised. All of the sadness in her face was gone, and by the time I got to the gate and we were making our way through the palace, I wasn't sure it had been there in the first place.

❖ 18 ❖

NAJWA

I WAS SITTING at the end of the pier, eating my midday meal and watching the Lake of Fire lap beneath my feet. I had come to be alone, to think through what I would do when I reached the palace. As a child, I had never been allowed to sit at the end of the pier all alone, and this was the first time I'd ever tried. It was daring, for me.

Then I remembered how I had defied Faisal's rules and transported to the surface just to see a princess I'd heard about. That had been daring. This was ... I swallowed hard and pressed my hand against my chest. It ached in the hollow space between my breasts, and I could not tell if the pain came from missing Faisal or missing Kamal. Or was it something different altogether? Was I sad because of the twisted knot my grandfather had made? If it hadn't been for him, the war might not have ever begun. But if it weren't for the war, I might not have met Kamal.

I sighed and took another bite of bread.

"Excuse me," someone said. I looked over my shoulder and saw a man gesturing at the boat tied to the pier. "I didn't want to come up unannounced and surprise you."

"Oh, of course." I shifted to the side so he could get to the rope. I tried not to watch him, but I couldn't help it. He was interesting. His forehead was wide and creased with many lines, but the rest of his face was smooth. His hair was thick and combed straight down to his level eyebrows. His prominent nose matched the largeness of his eyes and lips, which were serious. He wore a black wool tunic that ended at clean, sandaled feet.

When he finished untying the boat, he looked up at me. "I'm sorry I disturbed your thoughts."

"No, no, I'm fine. I mean, it's fine. I wasn't thinking about anything important anyway."

He frowned. "No one thinks of unimportant things at the end of this pier."

"What do you mean?" I shifted on the wooden planks.

"This is a place of introspection." The boat began to drift away and he tugged on the rope to keep it near. "It is for me, at any rate."

"Well, I was about to go anyway." I stood and brushed the crumbs off my thighs. "I enjoyed meeting you."

"And I, you. I am Firuz, and I assume you're Najwa, one of our half-humans." I nodded, frowning. "I met your sister earlier. You two are quite . . . interesting."

"Why?"

"We haven't had identical twins in the Cavern since the time of Iblis. Everyone claims it's because our human nature is dwindling, but I think it has more to do with the way the jinni tribes divided." He tugged on the rope again.

"What do you mean, divided? Aren't we all here?"

He nodded. "Possibly. But there was once a group of jinn who did not agree with the way things were, and there was a scramble for power. They lost and were exiled."

I felt my eyes go wide. "The Forgotten?"

We had few stories in the Cavern, which was one of the reasons I loved studying humans—they had hundreds of them. But there was one story that had always fascinated me, and that was about the Forgotten. Long ago, sometime after Iblis had died but before we separated the jinn into trades like the Shaitan, the physicians, and the Eyes of Iblis, a group of powerful jinn tried to gain control over everyone in the Cavern. A fight ensued, and a small crowd of jinn, all magi, were exiled from the Cavern. After they left, the trades and marks began, and the Dyads were formed in the hope that no magi would ever try to steal control again.

No one had ever told me what became of the Forgotten, and I'd intended to find out one day. So when Firuz mentioned them, my mind flooded with ideas, theories, and fears.

He shrugged. "If they're alive. They could be living in the sea for all we know. We haven't heard a word about them since they left, but we keep our traditions. That is why we have a special word we use to enter the Cavern. We can't have just any jinni popping in for a visit." He smiled wistfully and then climbed into his boat. "It has been nice to meet you, Najwa. I'm sure we'll speak again."

I nodded absent-mindedly. There were other jinn out

there. Where had they gone? What were they doing at this very moment?

"Wait!" I called out to him. He had begun to row away, but he paused and looked at me expectantly. "How do you know all this?"

"I am interested in knowing everything. It's a habit." He gripped the oars and bowed his head at me. "I will be seeing you again soon, I hope." Then he pulled his hands to his chest and the boat skimmed over the water.

I stood for a long time, watching him row across the lake and listening to the water lap against the pier. I had a feeling he knew more about the Forgotten than he was willing to share.

✦ 19 ✦

ZAYELE

THE AFTERNOONS WERE reserved for practice, Taja told me, so after the meal, I made my way back to the magi-only corner of the Cavern and tried to focus my mind. I settled down on one of the benches, this time facing the palace instead of the wall, and closed my eyes.

A magus was in complete control of her mind, Taja said. I had to be physically strong also, but most of all, I needed to be able to make wishes that were exact. No more vagueness or imperfections. No more impulsive flashes of power. I needed focus and a quiet mind.

Rahela would have laughed if she'd heard Taja telling me I needed to develop a quiet mind. She had been trying to tame me since the day I began to crawl out of the tent. Nothing anyone had tried had worked. I was busy, and I thought of too many things at once. How would I ever be able to focus when the world around me was so distracting?

At that thought, I opened my eyes and looked up. One of

the minarets loomed over the practice area, and one of its windows faced this side of the Cavern. I squinted and saw that the window was open, and someone was standing there, looking down.

I flushed, realizing that whoever it was had been watching me. I looked away, and then back up again. This time, I dared the person to keep watching. Maybe, I hoped, he or she would go away and leave me alone.

Then I saw who it was. *Yashar.*

I felt two things at once: relief, because he was well enough to stand on his own, and frustration, because now that I knew his room was right above the training area, I'd never be able to focus.

I waved before I remembered he wouldn't be able to see me.

"Yashar! It's Zayele. I'm down here!" He didn't move. "If you can hear me, wave your arm!" I waited. He lifted his arm as though he was going to wave it, but then he shut the window.

I knew he had heard me. He must have, because I'd heard the latch click shut.

I held my face in my hands. I had only wanted to help. Didn't he understand?

Hurt that he had shut me out, I went to the table and picked up a fresh lump of clay. Then I went to the open area, used the words Taja had taught me, and made the jar of hornets spin around me. Just the hornets for now, she'd told me.

I practiced the rest of the afternoon and suffered half a

dozen attacks from the hornets. By the time I left the pal-ace, I had welts all over my hands and had nearly bit through my lip.

I was going to find a way to get to Yashar. I just didn't know how I was going to do it yet.

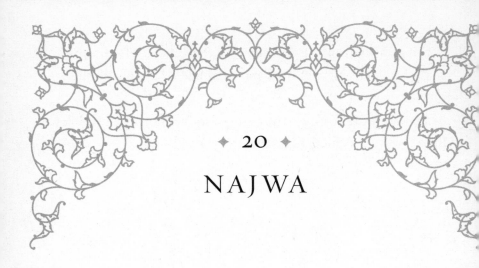

20

NAJWA

MY FIRST BREATH back in Baghdad was heavy with jasmine. It was dusk, and the blossoms had released their scent, calling for moths and anything else that flittered in the dark.

I had transported straight into Kamal's private garden. It had three stone walls dividing it from the other private gardens, and a curtain that separated it from his bedroom. I froze beside the lemon tree and listened for any noises, any implication that there might be someone inside.

When I heard nothing, I slipped across the paving stones to the curtain hanging heavy and dry along the latticed doorway.

There was no need yet to wish myself invisible. That wish only worked once in an hour or so, and I needed to conserve it. Besides, no one was there. I had hoped Kamal would be in his room so I could catch a glimpse of him, but the only creature in the room was his yellow cat, Hamza. He lifted his eyelids just long enough to see who had entered, then closed them and curled tighter into a ball on Kamal's bed.

A moonbeam cut across the floor, and I walked along the edge of it. It divided my slipper into two colors—blue-gray and charcoal—and I had the feeling I was walking between more than moonlight and shadows.

When I reached the inner door, I pressed my palm into the carved frame, feeling the ridges beneath my fingertips. I was all in shadow now, with nothing to light my way. Somewhere else in the palace, Kamal would be in the bright, clear light of a lamp. There was nothing about him that had to lurk in the dark; he didn't have to slink down corridors, hiding from sight.

I swallowed and whispered, *"Shahtabi."* The moment the invisibility wish passed through me, I pulled open the door and slipped into the corridor, where I stood for a moment, blinking away the brightness of a flame that stared me down from the other side.

As soon as I could see clearly, I pattered down the corridor. I checked the harem and the laboratory, but neither Kamal nor Ibrahim was there. Finally, I found a guard of six men posted outside the dining hall. Half of them still had dirt encrusted in the edges of their armor. They had to belong to Ibrahim.

They guarded the entrance to the dining hall, but the door itself was wide open. The smells—of roasted lamb, saffron rice, and minted cucumber—wafted through the opening, and I sucked them in. The food in the Cavern was fine, but this was something else. I rushed between the guards, happy that I was invisible, and stopped at the first set of malachite pillars that held up the plaster-and-gold ceiling. There in the very center of the dining hall were two long, low tables surrounded by dozens of pillows. Each table was laid out with platters of steaming food. A peacock wandered the hall freely, as though he too belonged with these glittering, posturing men.

Kamal sat centered at one table, between half of the men from the Court of Honor. Ibrahim sat in the middle of the opposite table, flanked by his officers and a few men in the court robes. Several women of the harem had seated themselves throughout, covered in veils and dresses that hid their legs. One of the women, with soft hands and a chartreuse veil, sat a little too close to Kamal, but he did not seem to notice. He and the rest of the men at his table sat pensive, watching the men at the other table with guarded interest. The soldiers exploded in laughter and jeering, elbowing each other the way people did when they had shared both horror and honor.

Quickly, I pressed the eye mark on my right hand. The Corps needed to analyze who was sitting with whom, and how the two groups of men were divided.

I walked over to the potted palm behind Kamal and crouched behind it, just in case my wish wore off. He took a bite of the lamb, wiped his fingers, and nodded at his brother.

"It's good to have you back," he said, raising his voice so he'd be heard at the other table. "When you were gone, I had to eat all of this myself."

Ibrahim took a sip from his cup and blinked at Kamal from over the brim. Then he set the cup on the table, slowly and deliberately, and leaned onto one elbow. "I see the extra meat made you soft."

"And the lack of it made you hard," Kamal said.

Ibrahim shrugged. "I consider that a good trait in a man. Take Toqto'a, for example." He pointed at a man at the end of his table with a braid as long as a woman's. A scar ran across the bridge of his nose, and his eyes were deep-set and black as oil. The man bowed his head at Kamal, but did not smile. "He is as hard as a man can be. In fact, he is one of my strongest and most reliable soldiers. I allow him to eat at my table even though he's just a sword for hire."

I pressed my mark, making sure the Corps would get a good look at this man. He was oddly different from the other humans. He wore a leather tunic embroidered in an alphabet I couldn't identify, and his dirty skin was more golden than olive. I had never seen a human like him before, and I could not place his origin. Someone in the Cavern must know where he was from.

"I didn't know we hired soldiers," Kamal said.

Ibrahim took a long drink before answering him. "We don't, but I do. Toqto'a knows much about fighting from horseback, and he has been teaching my officers, who will in turn teach their men. Soon, our army will be invincible." He glanced sidelong at Toqto'a. "Though our soldiers don't eat as much."

Toqto'a lifted a rib and saluted Ibrahim. "It is my pleasure to eat all that your kingdom can provide."

Several men at both tables laughed at this, and the tension eased.

"Toqto'a, if you don't mind," Kamal said, "where are you from, originally?"

"Far to the east, past the mountains."

"I didn't realize we had an agreement with the king there." Kamal smiled.

"I am . . . on my own."

Ibrahim growled. "He's the best horseman I've ever seen, and he has saved my life more than once. Now, let's talk about that jinni of yours. Your little *pet*."

"Don't ever call Najwa that again."

My skin was crawling, and it took me a second to recognize that the sensation was coming from the waning of the invisibility wish. Quickly, I tiptoed out of the dining hall and made my way toward Kamal's room. I shut the door behind me just as the invisibility faded.

Hamza looked up from the bed and meowed.

"You're the pet, not me." The cat's ear twitched.

I went out to the garden and slumped onto the bench. The scent of jasmine had thickened in the air, and so had the stars in the sky. My chest ached just as it had in the Cavern, and I knew why. Kamal was so close, but I could not talk to him. I had to stand beneath the stars alone, and without him there to tell me their names, they were nothing but twinkling dots in the sky, as numerous and nameless as diamonds.

+ 21 +

ZAYELE

IT WAS LATER that night when Atish showed up at the door
again. Najwa was still gone, Rahela was out looking for something in the market, and I was alone.

"Do you want to come in?" I asked. He stayed in the doorway, looking uncomfortable. "What?"

"You need to see Yashar, and I'm going to help you. Come
on, before I change my mind." His words came out in a rush,
like one of his fireballs. He pulled me out of the house into the
light of one of the wishlamps.

"Thank you." I picked up his hands in mine and looked at
them. They were larger and more golden than mine, but they
fit. "I'm not going to leave him there, though. I am going to
take him far, far away."

"Then we need to get going." His voice sounded strange,
and I looked up just in time to see a blush receding from his
cheeks.

I told him where I'd seen Yashar, and he told me how we

were going to get into Iblis's Palace, past the guards, and up the minaret.

The palace was a different place at night. With the wishlamps dimmed throughout the Cavern, the top half of the palace disappeared into biting shadows. Yashar's minaret was somewhere in the darkness, lost to the night, but I was not going to let the darkness make me afraid.

We hid in the bushes until we were certain no one was out front, and then turned ourselves invisible. I held Atish's hand so I wouldn't lose him, and then pressed my hand against the glass square.

It didn't open the gate.

"Maybe it only works during the day," I said.

"I think it's because we said 'Shahtabi' too soon."

"What are we going to do now?" I didn't know how long the wish would last, and we couldn't afford to spend all our time waiting for someone to open the door.

"We're going to climb over." He picked me up by the waist and lifted me up against the gate. I grabbed the top, scrambling to get a footing. Then he shoved, and I almost fell over the top. I grabbed the cold iron and helped myself down.

"How are you going to get over?" I asked.

He grunted, the iron moaned, and then the gravel beside me crunched beneath his weight. Then his hands were on my shoulders and I jumped. He laughed quietly.

We slipped in through the doors, which were fortunately unlocked, and I heard a faint whistle from his lips.

"We don't have time to admire the pretty flowers, Atish,"

I teased, and I pulled him across the great hall and to the corridor I thought would lead to the stairs.

"Do you know which way to go?" he whispered.

"No."

We wandered for the next few minutes, and I began to panic. Soon we'd be fully visible, and we had to get to Yashar's room before the guards could see us.

Finally, we found a circling set of stairs at the back of the palace. "This has to be it," I said. "Come on."

We ran as quietly as we could. The stairs were narrow, and I prayed no one was coming down, because it wouldn't matter if I was invisible or not—there would be nowhere to hide.

When we reached the top and found the door, it was unguarded.

"This doesn't feel right," Atish whispered in my ear. "He should be guarded."

I didn't wait. I couldn't wait. Yashar was right behind that door, and I didn't even bother to knock.

I pressed the door open and stopped. Yashar sat in the center of a stone room on a three-legged stool, facing us. He had his head hanging down, but he lifted it, slowly.

"Hello, Zayele."

I ran to his side and fell on my knees. "I'm so sorry you're here, Yashar. You're all alone. And it's so . . . bare." The walls were gray stone, and the single bed was as sad as a lonely lamb in a field of rocks.

"A blind man doesn't need decoration."

"Yashar," I chided, "don't talk like that. You're not *blind*. You're just . . . scarred. Also you're not a man yet."

"That's something you never understood," he said.

"What? That you're not a man?"

"That I'm blind, and there's nothing that can change it."

"But you can see something. Light. And whatever it is you see now. Now that I . . ."

He reached down and gripped the sides of his stool. "Do you want to know what it is I see, Zayele?" He didn't sound like an eleven-year-old boy anymore, and hot tears came to me unbidden.

"What?" I croaked, wiping at my cheeks.

"Those shadows you made me see? We think they mean something."

"Like what?" Atish asked.

"Who's 'we'?" I asked at the same time.

"Melchior and I. He's my tutor. He's going to help me figure out what it all means."

I swallowed back a sudden bitter taste in my mouth. "Yashar," I began.

Yashar held up a hand. "He told me you'd come soon. They've had the guards gone for the whole day. He said if a boy came with you, I was supposed to tell him."

"Yashar—"

"But I won't." He dropped his head again, and my heart broke for him. "I don't want you to get in trouble. Again. So go, please."

"Are you—"

"I like it here. I'm protected from the other jinn, and I get to see you, in a way, when you're down there in your garden."

I didn't have the heart to tell him it wasn't much of a

garden. "Yashar, I'm sorry I changed you. I wish I could have done better. When I'm finished with my training, when I'm better at focusing, I will try again."

"No. Don't ever wish on me again. Please."

Atish touched my elbow. "We should go."

"What will you do now?" I asked Yashar.

"Melchior is training me, and someday I will help him."

"With the magi?"

He shook his head. "With the Shaitan. Now go. The guards are coming back soon."

Atish tugged me out of the room, and we ran down the stairs, down the corridor, and halfway across the petal-covered great hall before I heard someone say, "We knew you'd come."

It was Melchior.

✦ 22 ✦

NAJWA

I WAS STILL sitting on the bench, watching the moon climb higher in the sky, when Kamal returned to his room. I caught my breath and sat perfectly still. I didn't know whether I should transport back or stay in this fragrant garden, waiting for him to find me.

His footsteps stopped at the curtain, and he sighed. "If you're there, don't say anything. Just stay and share these stars with me." The curtain rustled, but it didn't retract. "Not that they're all that bright tonight. The moon is full, which over-powers them. But they're there, just as they're there while the sun is up." He paused for a long time, but I didn't move a muscle. "I've been staying inside at night, just in case you're out there in my garden."

Heat spread through my chest and down my arms. He had been talking to me, just in case I was there.

"I'm starting to really regret the promise I made to my father about not seeing you. I miss you. Ibrahim is a very poor substitution." His fingers wrapped around the edge of the curtain. "But I cannot go back on my word."

I sighed, and it was too loud.

"Najwa? Are you really there?"

For a moment, I let the question hang in the air. Should I let him know? Would he be angry I'd returned before he asked me to?

"It's me."

His knuckles tightened on the curtain. "This is the most frustrating moment of my life."

"I'm sorry I came back already," I began. The air was suddenly too sweet, too heavy. "But I had to. I was ordered to."

"I'm glad you're here, but don't they understand it's not yet safe for you?"

"They're more worried about Ibrahim than they are about any danger to me."

Kamal sighed, long and shallow. "Ibrahim has always been like that. He isn't very adaptable, and he doesn't like it whenever someone . . . I don't know, *changes* things. And that's exactly what has happened since he returned. He needs time to adjust. And until then, he's like a rabid jackal."

I stood up and went to the curtain and pushed against it until I found his arm. He stiffened. "Kamal, did you tell your father that you wouldn't *see* me?"

"Yes." His hands reached around the sides and trailed down my back, sending goose bumps all over my skin. "I shouldn't have ever agreed to that foolish idea."

"Did you say you wouldn't talk to me?"

"No."

"Shahtabi," I whispered, quiet enough that he couldn't hear. When it was done, I pulled aside the curtain.

"No, Najwa," he warned, clamping his eyes shut.

"You still can't see me."

A mischievous grin slid up the side of his mouth and he opened his eyes. "I see. I mean, I understand. I guess I didn't promise I wouldn't touch you," he said quietly.

"We don't have long, because I've already made this wish tonight. I'm a little weak, and I have to save my wishpower to get home. Still, we have a little while before the wish fades."

"If I don't close my eyes, my brain doesn't know what to think, because it keeps telling me that you aren't there. But you are. You're right . . . here," he said, pulling me close. I nestled my nose in the crook of his neck and breathed him in. He smelled like the feast still, all mint, garlic, and game.

His lips pressed on the top of my head. "I should be angry with you, you know." I nodded. His face scratched my cheek. "But I can't be. I'm glad you're back, even if I can't see you."

I lifted my chin, aching for him to kiss me. He kissed my cheek, and then took my face in his hands and pressed his lips against mine. I was almost lost in it, when I remembered.

"Kamal, I'm . . . I'm here on orders. I have to return with something to tell them."

"All you need to know is that I'm handling it. There may be a few men in the Court of Honor who are not pleased with me as vizier, but that doesn't mean everyone is upset."

"Like Jafar."

"Right. Jafar and some of the others seem glad I'm vizier. I think they're just relieved to have someone they already know. Someone who thinks for himself."

"Do you?" I asked. "Earlier, it sounded like you were more worried about what the people all think, more worried about keeping up Hashim's illusion, than you were about doing what is right." He pulled back slightly, and his eyes reopened. Even I was surprised at my words. They had come pouring out of my mouth, knotted into little bows of frustration.

I was starting to sound more like my sister.

"I was caught off guard," he explained. "I didn't expect Ibrahim to show up right then."

"But isn't that when our true selves are most visible? When we're caught 'off guard'?"

He pinched the bridge of his nose and nodded. "I'm not sure I want to know what you think of me now."

"I think you're going to be the best vizier yet."

I was about to say more, but he threaded his fingers in my hair and pulled my face closer. Then he leaned down and brought his lips to hover right above mine. But he did not bring them any lower. I could feel the warmth of them, but that was all he would give me.

He sighed and shook his head. "You're going to bring me to ruin right here, in my garden," he said. "Every breeze that blows brings your scent to me. Every bird that sings calls out your name to me. Every dream that appears brings your face to me."

"What is that from?" He could not have come up with those words so quickly on his own.

"*Layla and Majnun.* The story of two lovers who were torn apart by their families."

"Let's hope we don't have the same fate," I said. And just then, Kamal's door opened and hit the wall. I pulled away from Kamal and retreated into the garden while Ibrahim marched into the room.

Kamal whirled around. "What are you doing here?"

Ibrahim held out his fist and uncurled his fingers. There in the center of his callused hand was a diamond that had been in my hair. "Your jinni was here. Spying on us."

"That's just a diamond," Kamal said. "It could have come from anywhere. And besides, I didn't see her. Did you?"

Ibrahim shook his head. "No one saw her, but we don't need to. They can go anywhere they please now that the wards are down." The truth was that the wards had been reinstated, but they were not at the same strength as they had been before Zayele destroyed them. Jinn could not transfer directly into the palace, but they could enter through the Lamp. No one seemed to notice that I could still transfer in without using the Lamp, though.

"I think you're imagining things," Kamal said. "They're not malicious. And, as I said, that stone could have come from anywhere."

"It's a *diamond,* Kamal. They don't fall off trees. And if I remember correctly, she had dozens of them strung into her hair. She's a temptress, and she's using you and your 'gift' from Father to undermine all we've worked for."

Kamal crossed his arms. "First, she's not a temptress. Second, what are we working for, exactly? Where has all this fighting gotten us? Is there something we need from them that they won't give us if we just ask for it?"

Ibrahim tossed the diamond onto the floor. It skidded across the stone and stopped at my toe. My invisible but solid toe. "I can see I'll get nowhere with you tonight. But tomorrow, after prayers, meet me at the stables. We'll discuss this 'peace treaty' while we go for a ride. If we're outside in the open, there will be no shadows for anyone to lurk in." Then he turned on his heels and stormed out of the room, not bothering to shut the door behind him.

I bent down and retrieved my diamond. It was the size of a lemon seed, and just as smooth. "I'm sorry, Kamal," I whispered.

"It doesn't matter. He can't prove it's yours. But I suggest you go home, and stay there until I call for you. Tell your master that I will send for you. In fact, if you return before I call, I will . . . I will consider it a breach of our negotiations."

He had to say that. At least, that's what I told myself. His request hadn't been listened to before, and now he had to be firm. Either way, the harshness stung a little, even when I was just smoke and flame, falling down, down through the layers of sand and oil and rock.

✦ 23 ✦

ZAYELE

ATISH AND I turned around to find Melchior sitting on the Diwan's dais. He was leaning to the side, resting his head on one hand as though he was disappointed.

"As I said, I knew you'd come for Yashar. He didn't want to leave with you, though, did he?"

I forced down every angry word that flashed in my mind. "Actually, I didn't come to free him. I only wanted to see how he was doing. This could have been arranged if you'd—"

"Silence! You were told to leave him alone. He needs total isolation in this weakened state. He cannot be with anyone who cannot control her emotions, her fears, or her impulsive nature. And that means you above all, Zayele."

"He is not your newest project!"

"He is not yours either," he spat. Then he seemed to shimmer with anger and fire, and pointed at the doors. "Now get out of here, both of you, before you cause more harm."

The doors blew open and we were thrown through them

and onto the crushed rock outside. I picked myself up and brushed off all the bits and shards. I was going home.

I knew it was a bad idea, but the second it crossed my mind, I could not give it up. My mother, my *adoptive* mother, didn't know where her son had gone.

Would she think he'd fallen into the river? Would she wonder if he had had enough of the way they'd treated him—they had made him wash the women's rags!—or would she have that knot in her stomach like the one I had been carrying with me ever since I'd taken him with me to the desert?

Would she wonder if I had come back?

That was what had given me the idea: I could go back at any moment. I could go to Zab and tell her where he was. I could tell her all that had happened.

Atish walked me to my door, but we did not speak much along the way. I was grateful, because my mind was whirring with plans and worries, and it wouldn't take much for him to figure out what they were. I couldn't take him back to Zab. This was something I needed to do alone. I said goodbye before opening the door, and the moment he was out of sight, I stepped away from it.

There was no one out in the open this time of night, thankfully. I closed my eyes and wished myself home.

I delivered myself to the same place I'd brought Shirin and Atish, when we'd come to find Yashar. From there, I climbed carefully down the narrow goat trail to the bank of the river. It was dark, but the moon was full and helped me find my way.

With each step, an anxiety I hadn't expected built up within me until, by the time I could see the village fires, my breathing was shallow and quick. A rush of thoughts flooded me. I should be there with my mother. I should be in the Cavern, pressuring Melchior to let Yashar go.

I waited at the edge of the village, watching a beetle scurry over the broken rocks. It wasn't until the beetle had disappeared from view that I realized I'd been sitting out in the open moonlight the whole time, easy for anyone to see.

I started for the village then, hesitating between making myself invisible and walking in as though nothing had happened. What would be less frightening to my mother?

But someone else made the first move. I was grabbed from behind. A man gripped my shoulder, tightly, and thrust me against the cliff wall. My face crashed into the rock, and I felt tiny bits of crystal bite into my cheek. I tried to turn around, but my head was held tight.

"Who are you?" a gruff voice demanded. "Are you a jinni?"

My stomach dropped. I had not dressed for Zab. I was still wearing the clothing I'd borrowed from Najwa, and in an effort to look more like a jinni and yet still feel like me, I'd worn a hijab littered with jewels. In all the stories we'd been told by the fire, the one that popped into my head now was of the jinni temptresses, and how they lured men into the shadows of the night.

"It's me." It was hard to talk, because my mouth was pressed against the rock. "Zayele."

"Zayele is in Baghdad," the voice said. It was strained, but I recognized him now: Afran, one of my father's favorites.

"No, I'm not. Afran, it's me. I'm here to see my mother."

He pulled me away from the wall and took in my face. His eyes narrowed and he frowned before shaking his head. "You look the same, but you cannot be her. You're a jinni."

I wrenched myself out of his arms and shook my head. A second later, he came at me again, grabbed me by the wrist, and dragged me away from the village.

"Where are you taking me?" Afran was the most hot-tempered man in the village. Why could it not have been one of the many others, the men who were understanding and gentle? Why did it have to be Afran who had found me? I tried to pull my hand out of his, but the many years of working the herd had made him strong.

"Away from my family," he said. "You come here and change your shape, like a monster, to look like my cousin. But you are not my cousin."

He was going to kill me. I knew it like I knew that with the night came fear. It did not matter if I acted as humanly as possible—he did not believe I *could* be Zayele. And anyone who looked so much like her could only be a shape-changing jinni.

He dragged me to the edge of the river.

"What are you doing?" I asked, panic rising in my voice.

"Jinn cannot swim," he said. And without blinking, he pushed me into the water.

I always think of useless things when I'm in trouble, and this time, I thought of the undergarments Yashar had dropped into the river and how I'd be joining them soon.

I clawed at the water, but it was like climbing the air. It caught me, a storm of current and rocks, hitting and crashing and pulling me down.

When my head bobbed at the surface, I gulped in some air and whispered, *"Mashila."*

It was supposed to transport me back to the Cavern, but it didn't work. I was in the water and I could not turn to flame.

Afran was running alongside me, carrying his bow. He notched an arrow and pointed it straight at me.

The current poured into my mouth and I tried to spit it out. Then something hit my upper arm, and when I screamed, more water rushed in, cold and forceful. Tumbling, I rolled along the rocks, turning my body so that my feet faced downstream and then curling into a ball. *Afran had shot me.*

I knew this portion of the river. The rapids did not last for long before the river split at a rise in the riverbed that formed an island just large enough for a few ducks to nest on.

It was racing toward me, the slice of dirt and rocks that cleaved the river. If I could make the little island, I would have a chance. If I missed it, I would continue to tumble down the river, past the village, and to the next set of boulders.

Tucking my knees beneath me, I swam, chopping at the water as hard and as quickly as I could, until I was directly in front of the island. It loomed, a dark slice in the even darker river.

Twenty feet. Ten feet. Five feet. *Now.*

I pressed my feet into the riverbed and pushed, launching myself toward the sandy point. Only my shoulders made it out of the water, but it was enough. I caught the earth and clawed my way onto it, into it, my fingers sinking in the wet sand and grabbing hold.

For a moment, I feared the current was too strong and would pull me away again. But I held on, and one foot found the ground and pushed back. I climbed up out of the water and lay heaving on the island that was barely long enough to hold me.

I was out of the water. My upper arm throbbed, and I found a broken arrow lodged inside. I was bleeding, but the cut was clean. I knew I should pull the arrowhead out, but I couldn't bear to do it. Instead, I pushed myself onto my side and sucked in more of the cold air. When my eyes found a focus, I saw I was right in front of the village, and I was being watched.

Afran had run along the river road, shouting at the village. Many people had come to the riverbank, carrying torches and oil lamps. Most were standing there, shock spreading like a fever across their faces, but some were screaming for rope or tree branches. Afran was screaming out that I was a jinni, an impostor who had taken Zayele's form.

"Stop," a deep voice commanded. The crowd peeled apart, revealing the man I'd always thought of as my father. He took one look at me and cursed. Then he shouted over the river, "Why have you returned?"

I pushed myself up onto my knees. Instinct told me to look down, to show him I was meek, but I was never one to live by instinct alone. I looked him straight in the eyes and said, "I learned the truth about who I really am."

His face darkened, and my stomach twisted. He stood still, a solid form in the soft light of his lamp, while the villagers moved and flowed around him like water. Then he said, "Afran is right. This is not Zayele. This is a jinni who has taken her form, and we will leave her there to bleed out."

Then my—Yashar's—mother came to the edge of the river. She was wearing the same clothes I'd last seen her in, but now her eyes were dark with worry. "Zayele," she said, and I knew that although she wasn't my real mother, she had loved me. She loved me still, even though I was only half-human. She held the hem of her hijab against her mouth and sobbed. She knew, without doubt, that I was truly Zayele. Her Zayele.

I was not going to die on the island.

Pushing into the gravel with my good arm, I stood up. My clothes clung to me, ripped and revealing too much. My hair was matted, plastered against my uncovered head. But it didn't matter that they could see my body. All the villagers could see was a jinni. An impostor. The enemy.

I pulled my shoulders back, wincing at the pain, and then looked at my father. "Hashim is dead." Then I looked at my mother. "I found my sister," I said, smiling. This seemed to surprise her, and her eyes cleared for a moment.

Then I turned to the villagers. These were the people I had grown up loving and living for. These were the people who had raised me. My cousins, my aunts and uncles. My family. To them, I said, "I'm half-jinni, but I always have been. And I am the same Zayele you've always known. Hashim was using me, using our tribe, to deepen the hatred between jinn and humans, but he was stopped. My sister, Najwa, saved the caliph's life and is now a consul to the palace. I came back to tell you that I've saved Yashar." A lump formed in my throat, and I began to cry, coughing out the words. "You won't have to be troubled by him anymore. I will take care of him." My mother gasped and turned away. When no one said anything in return and my body had begun to shake uncontrollably, I whispered, *"Mashila."*

The water, the chill, and the pain all slipped into the air when my body twisted into flame and poured into the island, pushed through what little water lay beneath, and raced to the Cavern. To my home.

✦ 24 ✦

NAJWA

A MEMBER OF the Corps, a man a few years older than me, happened to be standing beside Delia when I transferred into the Eyes of Iblis Command. He jumped in surprise and shrieked.

A corner of Delia's mouth twitched. "Najwa, come with me."

I nodded to Delia, gave the man a sidelong glance, and went with her to the room with the Eye of Iblis. The images I'd recorded shone on the flat crystal tiles, lined up in order. First there were the tables set for a feast, surrounded by many of Ibrahim's higher-ranking soldiers. Then there were several of Ibrahim, one of the mysterious man with the braid, and more of Kamal than was necessary.

"Those came in fairly soon after you left, but then there was nothing," Delia said. "I was starting to worry."

"I'm sorry. I was in Kamal's garden."

"Did they discover you?" she asked.

I shifted on my feet. "Not exactly." I wanted to look away. At the floor, at the smooth, bare walls, even at the Eye with its record of the evening. But she held my gaze. "Kamal and I spoke, after. I made sure he didn't break his vow to his father, so he didn't see me. But then . . . Ibrahim came in." I ran a hand through my hair as I told her about the diamond, feeling where the gems studded the strands. Nearly every jinni had gems in her hair, but I was the first to leave one behind as evidence.

"Before you return to the palace, I want you to strip off all those gemstones, and anything else that would mark you as a jinni," Delia said.

I pulled off one, a small chip of turquoise, and squeezed it in my palm. She was right, except that I wasn't supposed to return.

"Kamal said that if I came again before he was ready, he'd consider it a 'breach of negotiations.'" The words tasted slimy, even though they weren't my own.

"Well then," Delia said. Her face drew tight, until her mouth was pursed and her eyes were narrow. "You'll have to not get caught next time. I don't think Melchior will care much about these negotiations, and he is the master now."

"Yes, ma'am," I said.

"You look like you're going to collapse at any minute, Najwa. Tell me everything you saw and heard, and then you can go home."

I left the Eyes of Iblis Command feeling like one of the caliph's performing monkeys. Mindlessly, I watched the woman take the copper disk with my name on it off the wall of tiny pegs and set it in the tray on the desk. She said something about it being "nice out tonight," but I was too tired to respond.

Of course it was nice out. The weather never changes in the Cavern. The sun never bakes the cobblestones so that they burn your feet. The stars never shine down on the Lake of Fire; they never lead us north or outline pictures on our ceiling. There isn't a need to know which way is north when you can see everything all at once if you only climb up a gypsum shard or two.

I trotted over the dependable cobblestones, passed the fountain where Zayele first arrived in the Cavern, and went to the canal bridge closest to the school. It was halfway between the waterfall and the lake and made of cream-colored bricks, each printed with a phase of the moon. I leaned against the railing and traced my fingers along the curve of a crescent. It was both smooth and rough, like pumice, except for the edges where, across the centuries, hundreds of jinn had set their hands so they too could lean out over the canal and watch the water flowing by. Most of them would have only stopped on the bridge during the Breaking, to throw in their pain, their memories. But others, like me, paused to hold on to something made by jinn long forgotten.

Before I met Zayele, I'd never seen the moon. I knew of its phases only from these bricks. I knew only of its light and its absence of color from the books Faisal had given me to study. But someone, long ago, knew the moon and wanted us never to forget it.

Of all the people who first came to the Cavern, I only knew one name, Iblis. All the others had been lost to time, their bodies gone back to the flames, and their memories caught in their

Memory Crystals, ricocheting against the cold, glassy walls. Those, if they hadn't cracked or been lost, would be set somewhere in the funeral plain, below the Cavern's floor. Where Faisal had gone. Where my mother's memories waited for me to watch.

What did it mean to be a jinni? Or a human? What sort of being was I? And did I have to choose?

The moon bridge would not answer my questions, so I left it and wandered aimlessly.

I was drawn to Faisal's and Mariam's crystals like a fly to honey. I was there before I even realized where I'd headed. This time, I nestled myself between the two of them, green on my left and yellow on my right, and told them what had happened that night in Baghdad. Then, without meaning to, I slipped into Mariam's memories.

I was lost in them. Although Faisal had only been able to recover a small number of her memories, they were intense. Her spirit was constant. She was strong, brave, and impulsive like my sister, but she was observant and quiet too, like me. She loved Faisal deeply, but he was like a brother to her and it pained her to know he wanted more and she could not give it to him.

But nothing hurt her more than being cast off by her own father.

I lived her memories, looping through them over and over again until I started to forget which were hers and which were mine.

I awoke with a cream-colored blanket wrapped around me and a satin pillow tucked beneath my cheek. Confused, I stretched and sat up, then found a tiny scroll tucked into my fist.

I was still in the burial chamber. How long had I been here?

Trying not to panic, I opened the scroll and read the handwriting.

> Najwa,
> Grief is a powerful force, but it will get easier if you let your loved ones go. You have a vibrant life of your own to live.
>> Your friend from the lake,
>> Firuz

He didn't have to say it, but it was clear enough that he thought I was one of the Haunted.

Maybe I was.

✦ 25 ✦

ZAYELE

I STUMBLED INTO the house and was relieved to find Shirin there with Rahela. I sank to my knees, reached out for Rahela, and saw her mouth open into an O before I fell to the side. They rushed to me, and their voices were too loud. I tried to reach up to cover my ears, but my left arm wasn't working.

"What happened?" Rahela asked, filling my entire field of vision.

"I went home. Zab," I said. The words slipped out with a weak breath.

Shirin was pressing into my arm, mumbling a wish. I sucked in another breath while Rahela cursed. A moment later, I was flooded with warmth and comfort, and I sank deeply into the floor. The marble was wrapping itself around me, like a cloud, and I let it. I welcomed it.

I woke up in the hospital to find Taja sitting beside me. Alarmed, I felt for the place the arrow had entered, and found it was nearly healed.

Taja huffed. "You missed your lesson. Melchior isn't too pleased."

"Well, he can go to—"

"I can go where?" Melchior was on the other side of me, standing next to Razeena. They looked like a pair of chess pieces, calculating and deadly.

"To Zab," I finished. "To tell Yashar's mother why he hasn't come home." I knew it was daring to talk that way to Melchior, but at the moment, I was too upset to care.

Melchior blinked, like a snake. "It is my understanding that Yashar was not well treated in the village and that his parents would be relieved for him to find a place elsewhere."

I turned away from him and sought help from Taja, but she was purposefully looking at the tray of medicines on the table beside me.

Anger, frustration, and desperation burned inside me. They twisted in my veins like a poison, consuming any care I might have had for my own safety. At last, the feelings bubbled up and I spit the words at Melchior.

"Why haven't you told me you're my *grandfather*?"

He smiled, but his eyes narrowed in suspicion. "It seems I didn't have to tell you."

I pushed myself up into a seated position. I couldn't face him looking like a victim. "How can you stand there smiling when you know you're the reason *all* of this happened!" Razeena reached forward, and I knew she was going to use a calming wish on me, so I swiped her hand away. "Don't do that," I snapped.

Melchior crossed his arms and raised an eyebrow. "I'm the reason all of what happened?"

I groaned in frustration. "You made Hashim think all jinn were bad, so when he met my mother—who had been banished *by you*—he killed her and blamed it on a jinni! The war started because of that. Because of you. And you sit on your jinni throne and act like none of it's your fault."

"That's because it is *not* my fault. Angering a person does not make you responsible for their actions, granddaughter. I forced your mother to make a choice, yes, but *she* chose that life. Her fate was a darkness on us all." He was tapping a finger against his arm, slowly.

I could not believe he could cast it all off so easily, and the fire in my veins flashed bright. My skin began to pulse with an orange glow, and they all looked down at my arms.

"Hold her down," Razeena told Taja. Her eyes were wide in alarm, and that frightened me. She didn't seem like the sort of jinni who was easily disturbed.

I fought them at first, but my skin started to glow brighter, and I let it go. Razeena's hand was on my forehead—she was whispering something—and my head rolled back.

This time I woke up in my house, with Shirin by my side. I shook off my blankets and she picked up my wrist and began to examine it.

"What happened?" I asked. My throat was sore. Had I been screaming?

"You got so angry, the fire in your blood started to boil

everything. But I think you're fine now." Shirin was everything Razeena was not. Her touch was soft, and her eyes were luminous and caring. This was what a physician should be like, I thought.

"Is that normal?"

"Not for jinn, but you're a little different. I think you were burning up the human part of you."

"Would that have killed me?"

"I don't know. No one knows. It's not something anyone expected. It's never happened to Najwa."

I sighed. "That's because she never gets angry."

"Oh, she does. One time—"

"I mean she doesn't get as angry as I do. But even I have never gotten that angry before. Especially that quickly."

She squeezed my hand and set it on my stomach. "Rest for now. I'll make you a tea that will calm you. You need to be ready for something big tomorrow."

"What?"

"When Taja brought you, she told me to get you ready. You're training with the Shaitan tomorrow, so you need to be healthy."

While she left to make me tea, I lay back and thought about all that had happened that day. My adoptive father had sent me away because he didn't want a half-jinni girl in the village anymore. And when I returned, he told them to let me bleed out in the river. Would Melchior have done the same if Mariam had managed to return home, bleeding from a wound made by Hashim?

Melchior didn't seem to have any regrets. This was the

most dangerous sort of man, and I could not afford to appear so angry before him ever again. Like him, I needed to be calm and calculating.

I drew in a deep, slow breath and watched my new friend pour boiling water over a cup of herbs. While the steam rose, I tried to think of a way I could direct my anger the next time fire flushed in my veins.

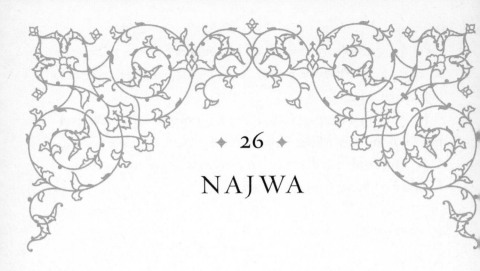

26

NAJWA

I RETURNED HOME without looking at another person, slipping in through the door without making any sounds. I was too tired to speak, too tired to say that yes, I spent the night in the burial chamber. Too tired to even lift my eyes, or my chin, or my hands.

I was not prepared for what I found inside the house. Rahela was at her loom, working on a rug that looked nothing like all the others. It was full of color, as if a collection of precious stones had turned into something fluid and been poured onto the threads. She had finished two feet of the rug, but it was already glistening in the weak light of three oil lamps. This, however, was not what surprised me the most.

A man sat beside Rahela, handing her whatever tool she needed next and sorting the jewel-toned skeins on his lap. I watched them for a moment, thankful that their laughter and the plucking of the warp had covered the sound of my entrance.

I knew him. He had trained with my adoptive mother, Laira. He was one of the weavers, one of the spider-marked:

Abdas. He had always been kind, laughing more often than not and bringing everyone into the conversation of the moment, but this was true of most of the weavers. But how had he ended up here, with a human girl who, up until a few weeks ago, had been afraid of jinn and was still not the sort of person to leap into conversation with one? Especially a man, alone.

Her back was straight but relaxed, and her fingers moved assuredly across the loom. She was comfortable with Abdas, and although I was happy she had made a friend and had moved on from her darker rug colors, I hadn't expected him here. He was all energy and smiles, and at the moment, I wanted none of that.

"Rahela?" I asked. They both stopped and turned around, neither of them showing any embarrassment at their being caught alone.

"Welcome back," she said. She smiled with her lips together, sweet and warm. "This is Abdas."

Abdas bowed his head at me. "Najwa, it's nice to see you again."

"You know each other?" Rahela asked.

"Of course! Her mother was my teacher, before I got my mark." He nodded at the spider marked onto his skin. "I've known her since she was seven years old. She used to watch us weave, never saying a word. I always wondered why you were so different from your mother, Najwa. And now we know." He said the last part as though he had found something long lost. His cheeks and eyes were shining, and I felt myself pulled into this happiness, this freshness.

Rahela scooted back her bench and came over to me. "You

look so tired, Najwa. When Zayele's eyes start getting red around the lids, I know it's time to get her to lie down." She half carried, half dragged me out of the room, calling out at Abdas, "I'll be back in a minute."

"Why is he here?" I asked, sounding surlier than I had meant to.

"I was out of yarn yesterday and went to the market to find some more, and he started talking to me." She shrugged. "I know it's unusual for me to befriend a strange man, but he is so kind. Is he truly this way?"

I nodded. "I don't think he could be deceitful if he tried."

She helped me through my door and to my bed, then lifted my legs up onto the mattress. "I'm relieved to know this. He suggested I try these other colors, which were in a bin hidden behind the table. He works at that store, and he made those yarns. When I first felt them under my fingers, they reminded me of the poppies that grew in the fields by my village, vibrant and strong."

I laid my head on the pillow and let her lay one of Laira's blankets on me. "I'm glad you've found something that reminded you of home."

"Please don't think I am trying to attract Abdas," she said quickly. "Because I am not."

"I don't." I didn't think Abdas was the kind of man who noticed a woman. His passion was for weaving, through and through.

"I've sworn off marriage and men. I'm going to throw myself into this new rug, and then maybe another. Abdas said he might talk to Laira and see about getting some help from her."

I almost sat up at that. "No, don't let him do that. Laira is still . . . wary of humans. Even ones like you."

"All right then." She smiled, contented. "Before I switched to these yarns, I felt so heavy and dark. My fingers stumbled along on the loom. But now they're flying, finding their way through the warp like a sparrow in the orchard. We've been up weaving all night, and neither one of us is tired. We keep saying we're going to keep going until it's done. It feels like . . . magic."

I tried to tell her I was happy for her, but I felt heavy myself, and it didn't take long before I was gone, dreaming of birds trapped in the Cavern, wings tired and drooping from too much flying up against the crystal ceiling.

27

ZAYELE

THE SHAITAN COMMAND was a fortress. Jagged, knee-high points of granite topped a surrounding wall drenched in silver. At each end of the wall loomed an observation tower made of polished bronze. Two golden lions flanked an iron gate, and I half expected them to roar as I approached. If there had been any sunlight in the Cavern, the Shaitan Command would have been blinding.

A tall, muscular guard stopped me at the entrance by stepping in front of me and putting his hand on the hilt of his dagger. "Are you expected?"

I tried to stand a little taller. "I'm here to see Taja."

He nodded and let me pass through, but I was stopped again at a desk with another guard sitting behind it. Behind him was a wall of copper disks, just like at the Eyes of Iblis Command. "Will you be coming here again, or is this a one-time visit?"

Taja walked up to the desk, appearing from within the

fortress, and smiled at me. "She'll be here often, Tamil. Go ahead and make her a disk."

I held out my finger so he could prick it for a drop of blood. He put the blood on a new disk he took from a box, blew on it till it was dry, and then hung it on the board behind him.

"They're ready for you," Taja said while I shook the pain from my finger. Tamil waved me on, and I caught up to Taja, who had already passed through the entrance.

The interior of the Shaitan Command was a huge rectangular training yard. Pillars held up a second floor along the inside of the wall, but there were no structures in the center. It was clear that the primary activities in the Shaitan took place in this dirt yard.

A group of soldiers stood in two lines, not far from the entrance. At their front stood Aga, Melchior's dyad, and Captain Rashid. Aga saw me and raised a brow, but Captain Rashid smiled and advanced toward us.

"Good morning, Taja. Zayele, I'm relieved to see you're ready to begin training with us. Are you able to run?"

"I think so."

"I need you to be certain," he said. His face scrunched into concern.

"Yes. I can run." Maybe.

"Good. We will do our exercise first, and then I will introduce you to the top candidates for your dyad." He smiled, as though I should be excited to meet the man who'd be my lifetime partner. The partner I wasn't able to choose for myself. Then he added, "Don't worry. Atish is still a candidate."

Taja took my arm and pulled me aside after a nod at Captain Rashid. "They're going to run in the tunnels today. Do you think you can manage it? I'll be there too."

My stomach turned, but I shrugged it off. "Of course."

"Good. Let's get in line."

We walked down the line, and I looked at the collection of Shaitan, wondering who were the others at the top of the list. I saw Atish, but he was at attention and could not turn to acknowledge me. He was wearing the same thing as the others: a pair of soft trousers, leather boots, and a vest. The women wore a tunic in place of a vest. They were dressed for physical activity. I, however, was wearing a dress that came to my ankles and had only managed to tie back my hair.

Taja saw me eyeing my clothes and chuckled. Then she made a wish and pointed at me. My dress peeled apart to reveal the same attire the Shaitan were outfitted in. My tunic was soft and loose, like Taja's, and my hair was tied back with a leather cord.

"Thank you. I should learn that wish right away."

"I do what I can," Taja said with a grin.

The tunnel entrance was directly behind the Command, which was a relief because we jogged to it. It was wide enough for three columns to run side by side, and it was lit by the occasional wishlight along the way. There were two deep grooves in the floor, like something large had been dragged through the tunnel. The fluttering began in my stomach now, more intense than when I had gone to my first magus training.

"This is one of the Shaitan's tunnels to the surface," Taja

said. She spoke easily, as though we weren't running. "More specifically, this is the tunnel to Samarra. The Shaitan army runs the length of this tunnel. They don't transport to the entrances, because it's a waste of wishpower. It's also not a good idea to transport en masse."

The Cavern reached out to so many places, it was like a central connection to anywhere in the world. "How far do they have to run?"

"This one is roughly fifteen miles in length."

"Oh."

"And it's slightly uphill."

"Slightly," I repeated with a groan.

She smiled. "You'll get used to it. At least you'll never have to pull the carts of supplies too. They're full of weapons and replenishments, and they're heavy."

"So that's what those grooves are from?" I asked, pointing at the floor.

"Yes."

"But why are *we* running? Can't magi just transport everywhere?"

"When you are bonded to a Shaitan, you'll be running right alongside him. If he has to run, you run. If he has to jump, you jump."

"We're running to Samarra *now*?" I was breathing heavily already.

"I never know how long Rashid will have us run. We go until he gets tired."

That didn't make me feel any better. Rashid didn't look like the sort of man who tired quickly.

We didn't talk for a while after that. I focused on keeping one foot in front of the other, trying not to trip over anything that might be lying on the tunnel floor. I had never run this distance in my life, but I used to race the others up and down the gorge, back in Zab. We'd never gone far, but the terrain was tough and there were animals, weather, and strangers that we had to be wary of. At least this time, I could shuffle along and not worry about falling into a river.

This training session had nothing to do with magic. It was all about pushing oneself past the pain. This I could do, so I tried to keep my breathing even and watch the Shaitan jogging in front of me.

As I ran, I thought about what had happened the day before. I thought about how it felt to arrive back in Zab and hear the soft swooshing of the river flowing past. But then I thought of being thrust against the cliff face and being tossed into the cold current. An arrow had pierced my shoulder. I had nearly drowned, but I had managed to drag myself onto the spit of land and stand up—not just onto my feet, but also against my entire village.

I picked up my pace and kept going, trying to ignore the burning in my shins. Running uphill, I found, was not painless. But the Shaitan could do it, and human or not, I was going to make myself run as well as they did. Finally, someone blew a whistle and the columns turned around.

"Now we're at the front," Taja said. "We get to keep the pace."

I nodded, but I couldn't speak.

When we finally emerged from the tunnel, I was stumbling more than running.

Melchior was standing in the center of the training yard beside Aga, with his arms crossed. We eyed each other while a half dozen young jinn ran to us and handed out bowls of water.

I grabbed one of the bowls and dunked my face into the water. When I had drained the bowl, I found Melchior standing in front of me.

"You made it back," he said simply.

"She did very well," Taja said.

I wiped the water off my face with the back of my sleeve, which was a waste because my clothes were dripping in sweat.

"Hmm" was all he said. Then he went back to stand beside Aga, who clapped her hands together and called the exhausted Shaitan to attention.

"Everyone is released for the rest of the hour, except for the remaining candidates."

Five Shaitan separated from the others and made their way to Aga. Atish caught my eye and smiled, but it was a tired smile. Was he worried he wouldn't be chosen?

Aga brought them over to me and told me their names. "Zayele, these are the last five, or top five, if you prefer. We will continue to test them until it's time for you to make the final choice."

They were letting me have a say in this after all! I studied them. Atish was warm and friendly. Samir was just as serious as he had seemed during his fight with Atish. And Arzada was smaller and wirier than the others. He smiled and bowed his head at me. His eyes were bright and kind, which was a change from Samir's. The other two, Akbar and Kian, who looked like they could be twins, were both sturdy and quick.

"Thank you, Aga," Taja said. She clasped my shoulder. "We all need to get some rest now. Tomorrow's training will be both mentally and physically challenging."

Melchior nodded in agreement. "And Zayele seems to need more rest than the average jinni."

Because I was human. He didn't say it, but he didn't have to. He nodded at the other women, then at me, and headed straight for the gate. After he was gone and Aga and the Shaitan had left us alone, Taja toed the dirt at our feet.

"Melchior is going to be there. Tomorrow is important."

28

NAJWA

"NAJWA, COME," DELIA said when I entered the room with the Eye. My images from the day before were still spread across the entire wall, as if they'd been etched onto the crystal. Kamal, smiling as he took a sip from his cup. Ibrahim, looking sidelong at the man beside him. The peacock, tail flushed out like so many eyes, so many jewels, and a hard, yellow beak. "I have a message for you."

She picked up a scroll off the table and handed it over to me. It had to have come from Kamal. My fingers shook while I uncurled it.

> To Jinni Consul Najwa al-Rahman:
>
> You are invited to meet with several members of the Court of Honor. We will be convening in the House of Wisdom's great hall following tomorrow's Dhuhr prayers. You may bring an escort for your personal protection if you wish, but we will be unarmed.
>
> Cordially,
>
> Kamal ibn Mansur al-Abbas, Grand Vizier of Baghdad

I brushed my finger over the ink, grateful the Lamp had transported it without changing the way the letters slanted just a little too far to the left. This was Kamal's handwriting, without a doubt.

"Dhuhr prayers are in the afternoon," I said. "I don't have much time to prepare."

"We need to select an escort for you too." Delia took the scroll from me and set it back on the table, where I could no longer touch what had been in his hands.

"I need an escort?" I asked.

She nodded and turned to look at the wall of images. "I'm sure Kamal would not invite you if he felt there would be any threat to you, but I do not trust Prince Ibrahim, or that man there," she said, pointing to the man at Ibrahim's right side. "Badr al-Din. His influence stretches from the Court of Honor deep into the army. He is Ibrahim's trusted friend, and he will be there to greet you, without a doubt. Another man, Zakariyya Hadrami, will be there too. Both of these men are supporters of Ibrahim and have already started spreading the word that Kamal is not the best choice for vizier."

Badr al-Din looked like he had gone to the army when he was young and had never left. He wore half of his armor at the feast. It seemed stuck to him, like a second skin, or scales. Zakariyya Hadrami, on the other hand, wore no armor, but his beard was long and gray, and his robes were spotless and black. In the image, he was frowning at a plate of grapes, as if they had said something heretical.

"You know *everything*," I said.

Delia almost smiled. "There is much to be learned in the

corners of teahouses. A little experience helps too. I want you to memorize these men's names and faces, as well as decide how you will dress for the meeting. Come back in an hour in those clothes. I am going to go choose your escort."

"But I thought . . ." I let the words trail after one look from Delia.

"You may be the appointed consul, but you're not going to be in charge of this mission. There are some in the Corps who have asked to take a more involved approach." She sighed and clapped a hand on my shoulder. "I know it's frustrating, but you are so young. Imagine if you had been in the Corps for years and years, and suddenly the newest member is the most crucial piece in the puzzle. You'd have trouble believing she could do all that is required too."

Her words stung but I nodded.

"I will see you at the Lamp," Delia said. Then she guided me to the door, patted my back, and sent me on my way.

I left the Command feeling as though I'd been pricked by a thorn and everything was spilling out.

I returned an hour later wearing a hijab in the Baghdad style, with my hair unadorned and peeping out beneath. I wore a simple gray gown embroidered on the sleeves with green thread that curled in on itself over and over again in small, soft waves.

A man stood facing the Lamp, with his back turned toward me. He had short black hair, a charcoal tunic that fell to the back of his knees, and matching trousers. I didn't recognize him, but I knew in a flash what sort of man he was, because of the emblem embroidered with red thread onto his sleeve. It was a bat, which meant he was from the Mark of the Law.

Why would someone whose job it was to uphold our laws be here, by the Lamp? Certainly he wasn't going to be my escort.

I looked over to Delia, who stood beside him but was facing me. She took in my clothing choices, nodded, and tapped his shoulder. The man turned and my face flushed. It was Firuz.

"Hello again, Najwa."

Delia looked at him. "You've met before?"

"Only . . . once," he said.

He had a dagger tucked into his belt, and since Kamal had mentioned everyone would be unarmed, I'd expected my escort would be also. This dagger looked ornamental, but I knew what it was. It was *Shabawez,* the Knife of the Law.

"I did not fully introduce myself before." He bowed and clutched the hilt of his dagger. "I'm Firuz, from the Mark of the Law."

I bowed in return, and waited for Delia to tell me what I already knew. She inhaled for a moment, as if she needed to think carefully before she said anything, and then came to join us. "We've chosen him to accompany you to Baghdad. He will have seniority over you, but of course they will not know that. To the humans, he will appear to be nothing more than your guard."

"Won't they know what he is by the symbol of the bat?"

They exchanged a tight, knowing smile before Firuz answered me. "The humans do not know all of our symbols, but this is a good question. I will hide it while we're there.

They may, perhaps, confuse me with one of the Shaitan. This will afford you greater protection."

"Firuz is the wisest choice," Delia said. "He is trained to notice dishonesty, which will be helpful when you're speaking with the ministers in the court."

They were risking my safety in exchange for someone who could gather more information. They did not trust me to do my job.

"Before we go, there is a wish I must perform so that I can send my thoughts into your mind," Firuz said.

I backed up, careful not to knock over the heavy Lamp. He was not smiling, and his eyebrows had gone very straight. "You're going to open up the channel between our minds," I said dryly. "Can you also listen to our thoughts without such a wish?" Had he read my mind before, when we first met? And what had he seen when he'd found me at my mother's Funeral Crystal?

He flicked his hand in the air. "Not until you've given me permission. Once we're back in the Cavern, I will release you and your mind will be your own."

Delia cleared her throat. "Najwa, we trust that you will glean any information you find useful, as well as represent us. And our goal is peace, Firuz. Please do not forget that while you're up there, sending your thoughts into this girl's head."

Firuz nodded and then, without any warning, placed his palm on my forehead. It was warm, and I relaxed beneath it, my eyes softening, my jaw loosening. He whispered, quiet as a beetle in the dark, and lifted his hand.

Can you hear me?

It was less a sound than a feeling of words forming into things and spreading through the roots of my hair. I placed both hands on my veil, pulling on it, and I nodded.

"That is the strangest feeling," I said.

"You'll be used to it soon enough. Now try to speak to me. All you have to do is say the words in your mind. They will find me on their own."

I was starting to wish I had never met this man. As powerful as he was, he was making me more uncomfortable than I'd been in a long time. But I had to do this. Not only because it was my job, but because this meeting needed to happen. I needed to show the rest of the Corps that I was fully capable, no matter my age.

You'll have to do better at controlling your emotions if you want them to be impressed with you, he said.

I miss Faisal. The words slipped out, and I could not retrieve them.

I know you do, he said. *I'm glad this is coming easily to you. Most jinn cannot tolerate the sensation.*

"Are you satisfied?" Delia asked, staring him down. He nodded, and reached out to rub his hand over the back of the Lamp.

"She learns quickly."

"She does. And just so you know," she said, turning to me, "*I* was not the one who felt an escort was necessary. You're released for the night. Come back tomorrow, in the same attire. Firuz and I will be waiting for you here."

29

ZAYELE

THE NEXT DAY, Iblis's Palace looked different to me. Instead of seeing a spiky, lizard-looking building scraping up the far side of the Cavern wall, I saw the spire where Yashar had chosen—*chosen!*—to stay. But they'd forced him to live there, at first. He should have hated it on principle. Like I did.

I took the steps leading down to the palace's iron gate. I made my way inside, dreading every step that brought me nearer to the training garden, and this time I paused to take a closer look at the main hall.

There, in an alcove to my right, was the imprint of a long, wide feather. It was too intricate to be anything but an impression, a stamp in muddy stone left to dry. And although I had not been all over the world, I knew enough about the birds in the area to know that the feather that made that mark had not come from any bird. Birds didn't have feathers that long, and they didn't curl inward at the tip.

It was the angel's feather. Seeing it, or the impression it left in the stone, proved to me the story of Iblis and the angel was true. It was more real than any innate power, any magic, and any bit of the fire in my veins.

"Sometimes I forget how it made me feel when I first set eyes on the feather." It took me a jolting second to realize Melchior was standing beside me, his hands together at his waist. He glanced sidelong at me. "You've just reminded me of that. Thank you."

I didn't know what to say. Melchior was not the sort of man to ever say thank you to anyone, much less to me.

"Where is the feather? Did it fall apart?" I asked.

"Iblis never touched the feather. But one had fallen off the angel's wings and lay on the ground. When he left, it burned an impression into the earth and turned it to stone. Years later, when the palace was near completion, Iblis went back to the site and dug up the stone."

"So the legend is true."

He nodded. "It is all true. Even, I am sad to say, that the angel had been thrust out of the heavens." This shift in tone, from critical to understanding, left me wary. And what he meant was that jinn were created by a fallen angel. There was only one I knew of, and his name was the scariest of all. "But all of this is not our doing, and it happened long ago." How could he be so dismissive?

"So we come from an evil source," I said. "Just like I've always been told. How can any jinni claim to be good if she comes from the spite of a malevolent angel?"

Melchior pressed his lips together thoughtfully. "In your faith, everything comes from Allah, yes?" I nodded. "Then how can anyone or anything be evil? At our beginning, we are potential, and it is our choices that divide us between darkness and light." He waited a moment. "To the magi's garden, then." He turned around quickly, and his mouth settled back into its usual stiff frown. It was like a mask, but I wasn't sure which face was the real one. Was Melchior the critical, unapologetic magus, or was he the thoughtful, understanding grandfather?

It didn't matter what he truly was, because for now, he was the magus, and I followed his sure steps out of the hall, through the gate, and into the garden.

Taja was there, holding a small wooden bowl. "Ready?"

"I think so." I didn't see any hornets in the cup. She saw me eyeing it and held it out to me.

"This is for you." I took the cup. It was made of a soft brown wood with yellowy marbling. "How much do you know about the origin of the jinn?"

I shifted uncomfortably on my feet and told her all Melchior had just told me.

"Do you know why the angel fell from the sky?" Melchior asked. "Some say it was because he fell in love. Not with a woman, but with her voice. He would lean down from the treetops and listen to her sing while she worked in the fields. He would follow her while she led the animals out to pasture. But his favorite was her song for drawing up the water.

"One day, the angel was so taken by her voice that he ached to hear it from within the well. He climbed down into it, and with each note she poured down to him, the deeper he sank. Before long, his wings were wet and he could not fly out. He had to beg an old man to pull him from the well."

"Iblis," I said, finally catching on. "The man who saved the angel."

Melchior nodded. "When the angel's wings were dry, he grew more daring and gave Iblis a choice: bring him the woman or suffer. Iblis was a good leader, and he chose to suffer rather than hand over the woman. The angered angel made a spiteful wish on Iblis, turning him into a being of flame instead of clay, and then he spread the wish upon the whole tribe. The singing woman, however, had disappeared."

I frowned. "Didn't Iblis know where she'd gone?"

"Iblis had never seen her before. He was protecting a stranger, a woman who did not belong to his tribe. She had only been seen by the angel."

I gasped. "Is that who's inscribed in the—"

"Shh," Taja said. "Don't say her name, or she might tease you away."

I rolled the cup in my hands. "What am I supposed to do with this cup?"

"You need to bring it back full of water from Iblis's well," Taja said.

"But I don't know where that is!"

Melchior frowned and crossed his arms. "I expect you to use your wits and figure it out. Taja and all the other magi before her did this on their own. Even you, with only half the blood of a jinni, should be able to think this through. I will give you the same information I gave everyone else: find the source." With that, he swept around and reentered the palace, leaving me alone with Taja, who raised her brows.

"Good luck. The well is far, and you need to return before

the wishlights dim." She hesitated, then whispered in my ear, "This is the final test."

This was the last one. A thrill snuck down my shoulder blades, as if I had feathery wings brushing my skin there. I swallowed her words and watched her step back into the shadows, leaving me alone to think this problem through.

The well's source could be anywhere. I mentally listed all the strange things in the Cavern, like the blue, harmless flames that erupted from the lake, the gushing waterfall that stirred air and water, and the side tunnels full of gemstones and glowing worms.

Najwa had told me the Cavern had been here before Iblis, although he had built the palace and the surrounding city. He and his tribe discovered it when they fled underground following their transformation into jinn.

I needed to find Iblis's entrance. The well would have to be nearby, on the other end. Shuddering, I remembered the last time I ran into a tunnel. It had been behind the waterfall, and I'd gotten lost in the dark. Atish came in and found me, but that was when he discovered I wasn't Najwa. It was obvious, apparently, because I hadn't used any of my wishpower to help myself. I'd been too weak, and that tunnel had been too long for my lamp to keep lit.

It wasn't through a tunnel, I realized. Iblis must have come through another way. A shorter way. I tucked the cup into a small bag on my waist, jumped up, and studied the walls of the Cavern, but I was behind the palace and couldn't see much. My hands shook when I put them on the black square and opened the door. I ran into the palace, kicking the fallen petals out of my way, and spotted the beam of sunlight. Then I raced to the apricot tree.

I had almost forgotten about it, and it seemed as though every time I left its presence, it slipped from my mind. It must have been a strange sort of wish, making us all forget about it. It was the perfect way to protect itself.

The branches, the leaves, and the fruit were all perfectly normal. There wasn't a hint of magic stirring in the roots, which meant the tree got what it needed through a natural source. Its light—and whatever pollinated the flowers—came from above. I peered up at the hole in the wall from where the sunbeam poured down.

It seemed impossible that light would make its way into the Cavern. It was thousands of feet below the surface of the earth. But somehow, the light was here, and it had to come from outside.

I swallowed and took a deep breath. This time, they hadn't said I couldn't fly. With a last look at the tree, I closed my eyes and wished myself back into a wallcreeper.

My wings weren't long, but they were a rich crimson beneath the black. The little cup had been in the bag at my waist, but that had disappeared with my clothing and I could only hope it would reappear when I turned back into my normal form. I stretched out my wings, hopped up, and flew into the beam of light. It was blinding. I blinked, feeling more than seeing my way up to the hole in the wall.

My feet clung to the gray stone edge, and I blinked again. I was at an entrance to a narrow tunnel just wide enough for a person, and the light came from a bright circle a foot or two inside the tunnel. I hopped to the circle and the light vanished. Farther up the tunnel, at an angle, was another circle of light. I hopped to that circle, and discovered an array of polished silver mirrors that brought the light down from above.

Najwa would like this.

I shook off my wallcreeper form and was relieved to find the cup was still in my bag. Then I walked the rest of the way along the mirrors, following the light. At one point, I came to an old ladder that went straight up the side of a cliff for several hundred feet. The tunnel was wider here, and shared the space with swirling dust and moths. Although I could fly, I had a feeling I needed to stay in my normal shape. I draped the hem of my hijab over my face, tied up my skirt, and began my ascent.

My arms were tired within twenty feet. My muscles were sore from climbing and running, but I pressed on, knowing the sun and fresh air were at the end. When my hands grew slick with sweat, I wiped them on the opposite arm and kept climbing. I didn't glance down.

As I climbed, I thought of what Melchior said. The angel had chased a strange singer and had gotten himself stuck in a well because of her. When his rescuer would not help him find her, he retaliated.

Everything, it seemed, was related to the woman whose name was inscribed on the Cavern's ceiling: *Allat,* one of the three daughters of Allah.

I didn't know much about Allat, but I'd heard her name many times. She was one of the threads woven into our lives, my aunt had told me. That was all I knew.

❖ ❖ ❖

The jagged cliff top dug into my palms. I pulled myself up and squinted in the brightness of midday. The sky was an eternal, rich blue and it made me homesick. For all the Cavern's wonders, it lacked the purity of the open sky.

Once my eyes adjusted to the light, I checked my surroundings. I was up against a reddish mountain, and the valley swept out before me, craggy and dotted with trees until it met a wide, glistening river in the distance. I did not know if it was the Tigris or some other river.

A few feet away stood a pile of rocks stacked one on top of the other. Someone had been here. I scrambled over the earth to take a closer look, and saw a string of pebbles, each no bigger than a bean, set into the shape of a crescent. Whoever had set these stones had done so since the last windstorm.

Had it been Allat? Was the story true?

I shook the thought away and scanned the area for any sign of a well or anything else that showed people were nearby. *There!* I saw it—a short walk down the slope was a grove of three acacia trees. I crept over, hoping no one would be present.

In the shade of the trees, just as I'd hoped, stood a well. It was enshrined in wild jasmine. Thin strips of faded green ribbon were braided onto the cover's wooden handle. Goose bumps spread down my shoulders, and I knew without a doubt that this was the place where Iblis had encountered the nameless angel.

It was quiet there, and smelled of sky and jasmine. I took in a deep fragrant breath, and as I let it out, the weight of all I'd gone through rushed out of me. I wept as I bent over the top of the well. Hot, heavy tears splattered the green ribbon, making wide dots of darker green. I let the tears fall for a minute, then wiped my eyes and stood straight.

"Let's pass this test," I said to myself and any goddesses that might be lurking nearby. I pulled the jasmine and ribbon off the wooden lid, then, using both hands because it looked heavy, tried to lift the lid off the well. It wouldn't budge. I struggled, tugging and twisting the top until my arms and back ached. Frustrated, I muttered a curse and the lid creaked. Quickly, I twisted it off and set it on the ground.

A long rope had been tied to the side and dropped down into the well, which looked as deep as the earth itself. I pulled the rope up and found a small brass bucket on the other end filled with clear, quiet water. My climb had exhausted me, and without thinking, I drank from the bucket. The water tasted as fresh as snowmelt, and before long, I had drunk every drop. The water chilled my stomach and I worried, *Was it forbidden to drink from the well?* I shook my head at myself and dropped the bucket into the well again, pulled it back up, and filled my tiny cup. With a wish, I sealed the water inside, shaking it upside down to check the seal.

When I had replaced the well cover, rethreaded the jasmine and ribbon, and paused to appreciate my work, I heard a few notes of a song. They lilted, climbing like a bird's, and stopped. The echoing silence that followed was chilling.

Her voice was, indeed, the most beautiful I'd ever heard.

"Hello?" I turned around, but saw no one. I was alone in the acacia grove with my sealed cup of well water.

"Thank you for the water," I said. "And the song."

Then I ran, afraid she'd step out from behind a tree trunk.

When I got to the tunnel, I turned into the bird again, hoping against hope that the cup was all right, and flew straight down like a rock tumbling off the edge of a mountain.

When I returned, Taja and Melchior brought me to the end of the pier. Taja was having a difficult time holding back praise, it seemed. Melchior's face was stern, but not unkind.

"Take out your cup," he instructed. I pulled the cup out of my bag and wished away the seal. "Now bring it to your lips and blow across the surface."

I cocked an eyebrow at him, but I did what he said. As my breath slipped over the top of the water, it turned blue, like the flames on the lake. I gasped in surprise, and the flame was pulled into my mouth. "What was that?" I coughed.

"The flame is now a part of you. Next, you must pour the water into the lake," Melchior said.

I upended the cup and watched the water fall and splash.

"You have now done your duty as a member of the magi, in bringing the magic of the well into the Cavern."

I gaped. "You mean the water isn't naturally like this?"

Taja shook her head and smiled. "The water in the well was transformed after the angel made his wish. The lady who guards the grove only allows those of us with the blue flame to take from her well, so only a magus can bring a fresh cup to the Cavern. We come from the well, and by bringing it here, we replenish the source of our magic."

I dropped the cup.

✦ 30 ✦

NAJWA

THE NEXT DAY, I met Firuz and Delia in the Command of Iblis. I didn't have to wait long before Delia reminded me who to watch at the meeting, as well as the fact that Firuz was actually the person in charge of the mission. Once Firuz connected our minds again, we slipped into the flame that flickered out of the Lamp. A moment later, we appeared in the hall beside the Baghdad Lamp, stepping away from each other quickly. Transferring beside Firuz had been too intimate, and I felt a sudden lightness when our forms separated.

Kamal stood close to the wall and was leaning forward on the balls of his feet. His eyes shone from beneath a clean indigo turban. On Hashim, the turban of the vizier had been menacing, with all the ferocity of an asp, but on Kamal it was just a long strip of dyed cloth.

He took in Firuz's tall and thin frame and then bowed to us. "Welcome back, Consul al-Rahman," he said to me, and my face flushed with embarrassment. I had never had a surname until I'd discovered I had a human father. Kamal's mouth twitched at the corners, as though he knew the name had startled me, and his eyes lingered on my pink cheeks.

I bowed in return, bending at the waist to hide my blush, and sensed Firuz standing behind me, straight and watchful.

So this is the great Prince Kamal, he said to me. I did not give a reply.

"This is Firuz, my escort," I said. Kamal's eyes narrowed a tiny amount. He glanced at the distance between Firuz and me.

Kamal bowed his head at Firuz. "Welcome to Baghdad. I am grateful you've come to watch over Najwa, although she will not need it. She has the caliph's protection."

Firuz smiled, but it was thin and forced. "I am honored, Prince Kamal." Thankfully, he had no reason to say more.

"Where are the others?" I asked. "In the House of Wisdom?"

Kamal nodded. "Yes. They have been waiting."

"Am I late?" I asked while Kamal came to my side. We began walking toward the House of Wisdom, traveling along a hall with walls of enameled plaster arabesques in alternating blue and green.

"Not at all," he said.

While we walked, Kamal explained why we were meeting. Not everyone from the Court of Honor would be present, he said; there would only be five. Zakariyya Hadrami and Badr al-Din were there to present the concerns of the palace, mainly those of Ibrahim, but Jafar al-Jabr and Ya'Qub Ghamdi were eager to speak with me. The fifth man, Muntasir Arafat, was the palace's legal expert and did not seem to care if the war continued or not. He, Kamal explained, was the one we needed to speak with the most.

"What about Hadrami and al-Din?" I asked. I kept my voice low and my lips covered with the edge of my veil. "Are they dangerous?"

Kamal shook his head. "Not to you, specifically. But they are not convinced."

"What is there to convince? We jinn are innocent of the attacks Hashim blamed on us. The war has continued without a need for retaliation. People—on both sides—are dying. For *nothing.*"

Kamal paused, and I stopped to match him. "You will see what I mean soon enough." Then, with a quick glance at me, he smiled. "Dressed as you are, you may need to convince them you're a jinni again."

Then he pushed open the doors, and the air rushed out at us, cool and soft.

This is the library, I said to Firuz. The House of Wisdom was the largest library in the world. The center was open to the domed ceiling, from which hung all manner of brass celestial models. The two stories of walls were lined with books, scrolls, and maps. I had been here before, when I'd found a Memory Crystal of Melchior's time in the caliph's prison, as well as a diary written by Faisal's brother, who had been the last jinni scholar to study with the humans. The House of Wisdom smelled of paper, stale air, and ink, and fine particles of dust drifted through the golden beams of sunlight that streamed down from the high windows.

I've seen libraries before, Firuz said.

Of course you have. I had to stop myself from thinking any more words. Firuz was, after all, in command. He didn't need to hear me rushing on about how these were all *human* books, filled with lines and poems and numbers he had never even thought of. He wouldn't care about the models of the planets and sun, or about the table covered with astrolabes and charts, pointing to all the stars, all the balls of light that put our gems to shame.

But in front of the arches of brass and the enameled globes stood five men in black robes edged with silver. They all had beards ranging from short to long, dark to light gray, but they were not all frowning. Jafar al-Jabr, mathematician and head of the House of Wisdom, smiled and came toward me.

"Welcome, Najwa. I do not believe you've seen our library," he said. I had never told him of the time I'd snuck inside, invisible. "Is it not beautiful? It is twice the size of the one in Rome, they say." He held up two of his fingers and shook them at me.

"It is much, much larger than the one we have in the Cavern," I said. It didn't seem wise to admit I'd taken the diary from the House of Wisdom and given it to the librarian in the Cavern.

"Oh," he said, eyes shining, "I would love to hear what sort of sciences they are studying in the Cavern."

"Maybe one day you can come visit, and see it all for yourself," I said.

His pupils widened. "I hope that soon there will be peace and trust between our races, so that I may do just that. I have always regretted not having gone to see the Cavern before."

Kamal laughed. "Jafar, you will lose your mind in the Cavern."

Someone shut the doors behind us, ending our conversation, and I turned to the other men. "Thank you for inviting me to this meeting," I said, bowing low.

Badr al-Din, whom I recognized from the images I'd collected at the banquet, nodded. "There is much to discuss. We should begin. Come," he said, and he pointed to a low table nestled in a spray of green and red cushions, set beneath a large screen made of short, angled pieces of wood fastened together in a replicating diamond pattern. The result was a wall of chrysanthemum cutouts through which sunlight and breezes could pass. The light scattered across the tabletop, the cushions, and the floor, outlining the area in color and shadow.

I was taken to my seat, where I placed my hand onto one of the perpendicular shapes of light and let the warmth fade into my skin. The dappled light made the table, and all those sitting around it, half unseen. We were there to speak openly, but none of us were fully there, in the light.

Kamal raised an arm, and a servant appeared from behind a stack of books, carrying a silver tray of tea and cups. After the men each retrieved their cup of tea, I took mine. Years of training to avoid human touch had left me wary of brushing against their fingers. Although I knew no one would dare demand a wish from me at this time and place, I was very aware of their hands. We were close, knees nearly touching, and I was grateful to be farthest from the window. If I needed to get away from the table quickly, nothing was penning me in.

There is no one else here, Firuz said. He had remained standing, settling himself beside a column several feet away. *Is this library always this deserted?*

I did not like how he could speak so freely into my mind. His words left traces, like fine powder, all over my thoughts.

I don't know, I answered. *Please, let me focus.*

Kamal took a sip and held the tiny cup between his fingers, then nodded at the men. "I would like to begin now, Consul al-Rahman," he said. "While you were away, we held many discussions on the best way to proceed from here, such as how to end the conflict, how to help others see jinn in a more favorable light."

"Prince Kamal, we believe that the best way is to proclaim to the entire caliphate, through a series of proclamations and notices, that the former vizier Hashim forced the war by murdering both humans and jinn in the attack in Zab. We understand it will take great courage for the caliph to declare the truth, but we believe he is a strong enough leader to do so." In the back of my mind, I was astounded that I had not only been able to speak in front of these men, but that my words had been so clear.

Zakariyya Hadrami sucked in air through his crooked teeth, and everyone turned to him. He smiled. "Consul al-Rahman, you must also understand that war, especially one that has continued for so long, cannot be stopped cold. It will require tempering many fears."

"What sorts of fears, other than your worry that the caliphate will revolt?" I asked.

Hadrami frowned. "Well, the people have many. What

would be the guarantee that the jinn would not slaughter us in our beds, for instance?"

Firuz snorted behind me, and I knew I had to think quickly. "Councillor Hadrami," I said, "jinn have never once slaughtered humans in their beds. There is nothing to base this fear on. It is a rumor based on prejudice."

Badr al-Din leaned forward and set his elbows on the table. "What he means is that we have no proof of your goodwill. What good is the word of a jinni?"

What good is the word of a man? muttered Firuz, and for once, I agreed.

"There won't ever *be* proof," Kamal interjected. "Only trust. And trust is a choice."

I nodded, forcing myself to keep my eyes on Councillor Hadrami. "Yes. And this is true for us as well. We would be placing ourselves in harm's way, should we choose to walk amongst humans. Every human in the city knows that if they can touch a jinni, they can command a wish."

Good. Get them to think we are the weaker race. This will—

Please, Firuz. Every time you do that, I nearly jump.

My apologies. I will tread more softly.

"Should an agreement be reached, there will be a law against jinni enslavement," Muntasir Arafat said. His voice came suddenly, like a cold wind under the door. Everyone turned to look at him. "I trust there are lawmakers in the Cavern, and there are those that enforce such laws?"

"Yes." I had to resist the urge to look at Firuz.

"Then what we need are papers for us all to sign, and it will be done. That is, if we choose to find any trust between us," he said. Instead of leaning forward, as Badr al-Din had done, Muntasir leaned against the wooden window and crossed his arms over his rounded stomach and surveyed us all.

"Is it that easy?" Kamal asked. It had not been a question, and he showed it clearly by setting his cup onto the table a little louder than necessary. "I had been informed earlier that our army could not stand down. Ending the war would, apparently, 'cause those in command to no longer be necessary,' and this would cause the city to collapse in on itself."

Badr al-Din glowered. "That was not what Prince Ibrahim meant. What he *said* was that there must be reparations. Our army has suffered heavy losses over the years, and if those who lost everything were told that it has all been for nothing, they would riot. The army would dissolve, leaving us open to attack. And not just from the jinn, but from our enemies in the east as well. The Mongols have been waiting for years for their opportunity to advance on us. With the exception of Toqto'a, of course."

Najwa, the mention of the Mongols has set off a series of thoughts from someone here. I cannot pinpoint whose they are, but he is not afraid. And more, he is thinking of a partnership between jinn and the Mongols.

Do we have anyone working with them?

I do not believe so.

The men were silent now, watching me. "What sort of reparations?" I asked weakly.

Badr al-Din blinked, looking more feline than human. "Coming from the jinn, I would assume they'd be items from the Cavern, such as gold and precious stones. Items of wealth. These would be used to calm the sores."

I could feel Firuz's agitation shooting off him like bolts of lightning from a cloud. *Why should* they *receive reparations? We are the ones who have suffered most.*

"What of our army?" I asked. "What would the Shaitan receive from the caliphate, to ease *their* wounds?"

Badr al-Din spat at the floor, then flared his nostrils. "They could have my condolences," he said. "Because if this war is to end, it will be because we have ground the Shaitan into dust."

Everything erupted at once. Jafar al-Jabr knocked over his cup of tea, Kamal stood up from the table, two of the other men began shouting at each other, and Badr al-Din sipped his tea, cleared his throat, and stood to face Kamal.

"I understand why you did not want your brother here," he said, pulling his shoulders back. He stood several inches shorter than Kamal, but he appeared bigger somehow. "If he had heard that, he would have slain your 'pretty princess' right there on her cushion."

I could not move from the table, because the fire in my veins was heating up and I did not want to harm anyone in the room. I heard them arguing, with Kamal's voice piercing through the angry fog in words like "compromise" and "bias," but I did not join them. Finally, I looked up and saw that one other person was not joining the fray: Muntasir Arafat. Instead, he sat motionless, watching, and I could not tell whether he was pleased at the words around him or not. I pressed the eye mark between my thumb and forefinger, and captured the image of his face.

Eventually, Badr al-Din marched off, slapping his heels against the marble floor. Zakariyya Hadrami scooped himself off his cushion and followed without giving us a glance. Kamal turned around, nearly bumping into Firuz.

"My apologies," Kamal said. "To all of you. I had thought they were ready."

I cleared my throat, but it was too sticky, so I took a sip from my now-cold cup of tea. "Prince Kamal, it seems the army despises the Shaitan. This may be the crux of our problem."

"Yes. It would seem so."

"Why?"

Kamal wiped at his forehead. "My brother's soldiers are the strongest army in the world, but every time they've attacked the jinn, they have lost more than they've gained. For those that have made fighting their way of life, it stings. And after many years, the sting is difficult to ignore. Ibrahim is not the type to forget."

"Then what can we do?" I asked.

At last, Muntasir Arafat spoke. "You must get the caliph to agree to the end of fighting. But he too will want something from the jinn. Be it jewels or promises, he will not give peace away for free."

I looked over to Kamal. "Can we convince him?"

"I don't know. He is not fully recovered, and Ibrahim has been with him more than I have."

"Please, Kamal, speak with your father. It's the only chance we have. Otherwise, Ibrahim will run us all into the ground."

Arafat is watching you.

Why?

He was lying when he said an agreement from the caliph was all we needed. He's pleased all of you believed him.

"Councillor Arafat," I said, turning to the wizened man, "if you provide us with the papers needed, I will get them approved by the Cavern. Please send them through the Lamp." I stood up slowly, careful to keep myself steady. "Kamal, I think it's best if I return now."

The rest of the time in the palace passed quickly. Kamal took us back to the Lamp, and although I wanted desperately to take his hand, I could not look at him. I had not said the right words, and the result was that the meeting had burst open, revealing the hate, the wounds, and the disease of so many years of fighting. I was not sure I could seal the seam. Not with words. Not with *my* words.

+ 31 +

ZAYELE

SOMETHING HAD HAPPENED at the last training exercise. I saw it in Melchior's eyes when he told me to go home and rest. The annoyance, the self-righteousness, and the comments about my human father were gone, and in their place, he had bowed his head. The bow hadn't been a very deep one, and if you didn't know Melchior, you might have thought he was only taking a deep breath. But it had been a bow. A nod. At last, I had done something *right*.

Because of this, I was only mildly surprised when I received a message from Melchior instructing me to meet him and Taja at the Shaitan Command again. He and Taja were waiting for me at the entrance, beside the guard's table.

"You've arrived," Melchior said. It was less a statement of my presence and more of a greeting. I glanced at the guard, who picked up the disk with my name etched on it and hung it on the wall.

Taja smiled. "From now on, you're part of the Shaitan. Not a full member, but as a magus, you can go nearly anywhere."

I glanced at Melchior. "I can come see Yashar whenever I want to?"

"If you can control your mind," he said dryly.

Melchior and Taja had their disks placed on the wall with the others, and then we all went through the arch and stepped out onto the training grounds of the Shaitan. Before, I had only been looking for Atish and hadn't had time to look closer, but now I noticed a line of blackened columns at the far end, at which the Shaitan were lining up and throwing fireballs. Loud, explosive sounds reverberated across the open space, and I blinked involuntarily each time one of the balls of fire hit the target.

"You'll get used to that," Taja said. She walked between Melchior and me, slow and steady, until a jinni I didn't recognize stopped throwing fireballs and turned around. He saw us approaching and grinned widely. Taja's pace quickened, and with a sideways glance at me, she said, "That's my dyad, Saam."

I had only seen one Dyad together before: Melchior and Aga. They were older, wiser, and stiff as reeds. Taja and Saam, however, were a force of nature. Saam wrapped his arm around Taja's shoulders and spun her to face me.

"This is your newest magus, I see," he said. He wasn't much taller than Taja, but he was powerfully built, like a stallion that hadn't yet grown out his legs. "Welcome, Melchior," he said, bowing his head at the Master of the Corps. "And Zayele."

"Where is Rashid?" asked Melchior.

"Over there," he said, pointing to Rashid, who was entering

the training grounds from the opposite side with Atish, Samir, and Arzada beside him.

A Dyad wasn't a romantic arrangement. It wasn't a marriage. But it could be, and often was. From what I'd heard, sometimes that invisible bond twisted around the pair, like it had with Taja and Saam. A blush spread like a rash over my face, and I couldn't do anything to hide it.

"Zayele," Rashid said. His voice was deep and rumbled. "Are you ready to see what we can do?"

Melchior almost sputtered. "Is this what you intended when you said 'formal introduction to the Dyads'?"

"I don't have time for anything more than this, unfortunately. I've just gotten word from Delia that Ibrahim's army didn't stop at Baghdad to join their leader," Rashid said. "You probably already knew that. Anyway, I have to speak with my lieutenants and see about sending out a patrol. I'd like to know where they're headed."

Melchior's face was poppy red. "It seems I need to speak with Delia. And this young woman's sister," he said, gesturing at me. "Zayele, Taja and these Shaitan jackals will tell you what you need to know." Then he was gone, strutting beside Rashid, who had frowned at us all before leaving.

The moment they were out of earshot, I turned to Atish. "What's going on?"

"Well, hello, nice to see you here," he said. When I didn't smile, he sighed. "I think Melchior's upset because Rashid knew about something before he did. Don't worry about it. Anyway, we're going to watch a Dyad work together."

"We have to get you ready for the Bonding," Saam said. He exchanged a knowing look with Taja.

I set my hands on my waist. "Is there a secret ritual? Or do we just clasp hands?"

"There's a little more to it than clasping hands," Taja said. She tugged on my arm. "Come. First you need to see what a Dyad can do, compared to all those other soldiers out there," she said, nodding at the line of Shaitan throwing fireballs at the columns. They continued to pop louder than I liked, but I wasn't blinking anymore.

Saam and Taja took us to the line of Shaitan and asked one of the soldiers, a woman in her thirties, if they could take her place. She stepped back and shrugged. Then Saam pointed at the ground. "Arzada, show Zayele what a single Shaitan can do."

Arzada widened his stance, narrowed his eyes on the column, and took in a sharp breath with his nose. Then he threw his hands forward and hissed, *"Narush."*

A blood-red ball of flame erupted from his palms and shot forward, slamming into the column. I winced and covered my ears while the fire wrapped around the column, leaving behind a charcoal-colored mark in the marble.

"Impressive," I said. I might have been more interested if I hadn't just seen every other jinni on the line do the same thing.

Arzada raised his brows at Saam. "Let's see what you can do, oh mighty *Dyad.*"

When Taja and Saam had lined up, Atish leaned close to my ear. "We'll do better, when our time comes." I hoped he was right.

They stood shoulder to shoulder and nodded once at each other. Saam let loose a chain of fireballs that spiraled around the column like a thorny weed of fire. Then Taja shouted a word that sounded like a rock cracking open.

And the column *did* crack. A line crawled up through the column like a bolt of lightning, and then the marble crumbled into a pile of dust and newborn gravel.

I was about to clap when Taja smirked at me and pointed one finger at the column. With her eyes on me, she whispered something, and the air stilled around the fallen rock. Then it wound around in the opposite direction from which it had come, swirling and spinning until every last grain of dust settled back into the column, leaving it pristine and unscarred.

They turned as one. "I dare you to try *that*," Saam said.

I was gaping. "I . . . don't even know how to make the *sound* you just made, much less do something with it."

"That's what we're here for," Taja said. She was smiling at me in a way that spoke of friendship. I wasn't sure what to do about it.

32

NAJWA

FIRUZ SPUN AWAY from me the moment we returned to the Cavern, but before he turned, I noticed his brows were drawn together in confusion. I shook the strange sensation of transporting out of my head and thought, *What's wrong?*

I will let go of your mind now, Najwa. You did well.

"Firuz, what did you see?"

He stopped and rubbed his chin with one hand, lost in thought. Until then, the round hall that housed the Lamp had been empty, but Delia and several other members of the Corps came trotting into the room.

"What happened?" she asked me.

"There's something going on in the palace," Firuz said, suddenly alert. "More than the prince and his friends are aware of."

Delia's eyes narrowed. "What do you mean?"

"I think it has something to do with the Mongols," I said. "Did we ever find out more about that man Ibrahim hired, Toqto'a?"

Delia nodded and we followed her back down the hall to the room with the Eye. One of the panels held the image I'd captured of Muntasir Arafat.

"Tell us what you heard, Mind Reader," one of the officers said.

"There are jinn working with the Mongols, and they are in communication with someone who was in our meeting."

The officer whistled and looked at the other members of the Corps. "Mysterious jinn working with the unstoppable Mongols?"

Firuz bristled. "So it seems. And, unfortunately, the humans are more inclined to continue the war *now* than they were a few hours ago."

My face flushed in shame. "It is true. I offended them somehow. They were speaking of reparations, and I mentioned the losses the Shaitan have faced, and the meeting erupted."

Delia shook her head. "I do not think you could have changed their minds in either direction, Najwa. The caliph's army is set on the war. They were looking to find fault with you. What concerns me is what Firuz has discovered." She leaned forward on the table and sighed, dropping her head between her shoulders. "Firuz, the thoughts you were able to glean—was there anything identifiable about the jinni and his relationship with the Mongols?"

"Jinn. There is more than one. But I did not get anything more than I've told you. Just a whispering of a thought."

"But who would betray the caliph? Who would harbor positive thoughts regarding another group of jinn?" Delia asked. She rapped her fingertips against the table.

I scanned through my recent memory of the House of Wisdom. Someone there had not been completely honest. Badr al-Din had not wanted any peace between us, but his whole life had been wrapped up in the caliph's army, and any conflict between them and the Mongols would be devastating. It didn't make sense for him to be the traitor. The same could be said for Zakariyya Hadrami. They were Ibrahim's men.

Jafar al-Jabr didn't have a dishonest hair in his beard. Kamal would certainly not betray his father or the caliphate. That left Ya'Qub Ghamdi and Muntasir Arafat. I could not imagine Ya'Qub offending a flea, much less daring to communicate with the infamous Mongol army.

I pointed at the image of Arafat. "It's him," I said, watching everyone turn to look up at the Eye. They squinted in the brightness coming off the wall. "He is the only one who would even think of working with another army. He didn't seem to be afraid of us."

"Najwa is right," Firuz said, surprising me. "Arafat's thoughts regarding us were uncommonly comfortable. I thought it meant he was keeping an open mind about the negotiations, but perhaps he is used to speaking with jinn."

Delia stepped closer to the Eye and studied the image of Arafat. "I need you both to go back. But do not let yourselves be discovered. Find out more about this man, and his dealings with the Mongols. If they are nearby, this does not bode well for us—humans *or* jinn."

"Delia?" I asked. "Who would these jinn be?"

She was about to speak, but Firuz answered first. "They must be descendants of the Forgotten."

No one had run across them in hundreds of years. Why would we meet up with them *now*?

"Could it really be the Forgotten?" I asked Firuz.

"Unless the dark angel turned *another* tribe of humans into jinn on some other corner of the earth, then it must be."

The mutterings within the Corps stilled, and we all avoided each other's gaze, not ready yet to acknowledge the weight of Firuz's words. If the Mongols were working with the lost jinn, and if they were preying on the caliph's army, the result would be catastrophic.

✦ 33 ✦

ZAYELE

I TOLD TAJA that I wanted to see Yashar again, and she surprised me by pointing me across the training field. He was sitting straight-backed against a statue, with his face turned toward the Shaitan, as though he were watching their exercises. As though he planned on learning from their technique.

"He's here?" I asked her. How had I not noticed him earlier? He stood out in the midst of the soldiers, the lone, thin boy dressed in black.

"Melchior has been teaching him to control his response to what he sees, so this must be a test." She shrugged. "I think he just got here, though."

"I can't believe Melchior is testing him already. He's a *child.*" Gritting my teeth, I marched over to where he sat. When I was close enough that I could hear him sigh, he turned his head toward me.

"Zayele," he said, and the sigh was gone. "How are you?"

He sounded *normal,* and I looked closer to make sure it was really him. How could he act as though nothing had happened? "Good. And . . . you?"

He was still smiling. "They're training me."

"To be a Shaitan?"

"No," he said, laughing. "They're teaching me how to use my sight."

"What do you mean, 'use' your sight? What can you do with it?"

I took a few more steps, stopping when I was just out of arm's reach. He blinked and rubbed his mouth.

"The shadows I see? When I really focus on one of the swirls of smoke, I can get a feeling. It's like . . . it's like a dream. I can see it, but not clearly, and after I look away, I know what it is. Each one is a fear."

"You see fears?" I couldn't have given him the ability to see *fear.* It was impossible. It was horrifying.

"There's one twisting around you now, around your throat," he said. He was watching me out of the corner of his milky-white eye, and I stared back, watching his useless lashes move up and down while he blinked. "What are you afraid of?"

"The same things as anyone," I muttered, and I sank to the low wall he was sitting on. It dug into the back of my thighs, but at the moment, I didn't care.

"Melchior said most people are afraid of not being wanted. Or they're afraid of getting hurt by something, like a spider or a snake."

"Do you know what my fears are just by looking at them?"

"No, but I think I will be able to do that soon." He said it so simply, so earnestly. "I am trying to make a chart in my mind so that when I see a shadow, and I ask the jinni what they're afraid of, I can learn what that shadow means. Like another language or a code."

"What good is it to know someone's fears? What is Melchior planning to use you for?" I wasn't expecting him to answer, and he shrugged.

"Melchior said that in a fight like that," he said, pointing at two women sparring, "I could change what happens. I just have to tell him what one person is afraid of, and he'll make that fear happen, somehow."

Why would Yashar want to help Melchior that way? "So if that woman is afraid of, say, snakes, and I make one appear in front of her, she'll get distracted and lose the fight?" I asked.

"We haven't tried it yet. Melchior said he's coming back this afternoon to work with me on it."

I had never seen him so *full* before. His cheeks were stretched from smiling, and his forehead was easy and smooth. He tapped his fingers gently against his thigh while he looked over the field, and then back to me. "You seem happy," I said.

"I've never been useful before. They like having me around. And no one is afraid of my eyes. I can tell."

My eyes were starting to water, and I needed to get away before they overflowed. I stood up quickly and brushed the dirt off the back of my legs. "I'm glad they're taking care of you. But promise me something."

"What?"

"If you *ever* want to leave, tell me. I can get you out of here. All you have to do is let me know."

He chuckled. "Stop worrying so much." Then his laughter stopped and he grew serious. "I don't want to go home."

"If you want this to be your home, then that's fine. But remember, you're not a jinni. You're human, and they'll never forget it."

"Being human doesn't mean I'm weak. Just like being blind didn't mean I couldn't do anything."

"What do you mean?"

He shifted on the wall. "Zayele, you always wanted to fix me, but I was fine. I wasn't excited to lose my eyesight, but I was managing. Sometimes, being in the dark lets us notice other things. It makes us listen. You should try it sometime."

This was making my stomach turn over on itself. I thought I'd been listening to him, but my worries might have been louder than him. "I'm sorry I wasn't paying attention, Yashar." Tentatively, I reached over and squeezed the back of his hand. "And I'm sorry I've forced you to see fear all around you, instead of light."

"I think I'd always sensed other people's fear before. But it's clearer now."

He was probably lying for my benefit, but I allowed it, and told him I'd see him soon. I left him there on the low wall, sitting as still as a lizard in full sun. My chest was twisting and burning, and I ran from the Shaitan headquarters, flashing a frown at the soldier at the entrance. I scrambled along the crystals poking out along the wall, and found the shard Atish had shown me. When I climbed up, I found him already there, leaning back against a roll of blankets, clear eyes blinking with no surprise.

Without a word, he drew me into his arms and held me tight. I burrowed into his neck and breathed in the smell of his skin, the fire in his blood, and the metallic tang of the wide necklace he wore.

For a moment, before I could thrust the thought away, I wondered what fears Yashar would see circling Atish. Was he afraid of failure too, or was he afraid of not being wanted? He never said a word about Yashar, and for that, I kissed him.

34

NAJWA

THIS TIME, I was wary of loose diamonds and anything else that could betray me. I had stripped away all jewels, I was barefoot, and I made sure not a strand of hair could fall onto the palace floor. Firuz was accompanying me and was dressed as plainly as a jinni could be. For him, this meant he only had to take off his sandals. Our mission: monitor Badr al-Din and Prince Ibrahim, as well as report any possible threats to the Cavern.

Because Firuz was coming with me and could not transport directly into the palace, we transported through the Lamp. We were lucky no one was near it when we emerged on the other side, because we could not transport invisibly.

Morning light streamed through a line of windows, catching stilled dust in the air. I took a quick breath, and whispered, *"Shahtabi."*

A second later, Firuz said the same wish and we stood still, allowing the beam of light to pass through us.

Where should we go first? Firuz's question felt like someone had poured icy water inside my mind, and I shivered, suddenly alert. Did he mean to let *me* make the decisions this time?

Yes, came his reply.

I wish there was a way to block some of my thoughts.

There is, but we don't have time to teach you that right now. Trust that I am trying to filter out only the most important ones. I do not wish to be weighed down by everything you notice. So where do we go?

Ibrahim's room. I have a feeling that's where we should go.

Actually, you feel as though you should head to Kamal's room.

I blushed and was glad he couldn't see me then. *Let's go to Ibrahim's room.*

We found Ibrahim's room not long before he entered it, followed by four men. It was identical to Kamal's room, except for a wall of hooks upon which every sort of weapon imaginable was hung. Even though our *shahtabi* wishes were at full strength, we hid in the garden behind a folding screen. I was grateful for the screen, because even with Firuz beside me, I didn't feel safe around Ibrahim. The solid, dark barrier would slow Ibrahim down should he happen to notice me.

Badr al-Din and Zakariyya Hadrami were two of the men who had entered behind Ibrahim. Another man, carrying the helmet of the army beneath his arm, sat down on a divan beside Badr al-Din. He dropped the helmet on the table before them and leaned back against the wall, scowling. The fourth man was Toqto'a, the mercenary from the east.

Ibrahim did not sit. He paced, traveling from the door to the screen and back. His brows were unusually calm, and his jaw was tight.

"You asked us to come here," said the man with the helmet. "What is this about?"

Ibrahim paused. "Is the army still on the road north?"

"Yes," answered the soldier. "They should arrive by tomorrow evening."

"Good," said Ibrahim. He resumed pacing, coming a little too close to the screen. "Zakariyya, when will the reeds arrive?"

"They are already there, being held downstream," said Zakariyya.

I tapped Firuz on his wrist. *What are the reeds for?*

They have made bridges.

How can a reed hold the weight of a man?

I have a feeling we will find out soon.

Badr turned to the soldier. "Saif, I must congratulate you on the design. It's unprecedented."

Saif, the soldier, nodded. "It is not my design. It is Kamal's. Although, as usual, we aren't using it as he intended."

"My brother has his uses," Ibrahim said with a smirk. "Although I'm not sure of his intentions now. How did the meeting with the jinni go?"

Badr and Zakariyya exchanged glances. Then Badr cleared his throat. "The girl insulted the army, Kamal was so flustered he couldn't speak, and Jafar knocked over his tea."

Ibrahim smiled. "So it went well, then." A flush spread up the back of my neck and across my cheeks. I gritted my teeth and forced my hands to stay calm, because the last thing I needed was for the screen to fall.

Ibrahim and his friends had planned for the meeting to fail. They had used me. Why hadn't Firuz noticed? Or had he? He had been very quiet after we'd returned, and had gone straight to the House of the Law. Something had troubled him, but he had not stopped to explain it to me.

I had felt a strange presence. It didn't fit with the men who were with us.

"We leave this afternoon. Saif, have our horses ready. We will catch up with the army by nightfall." Ibrahim slapped his hands together and nodded at the men. "We have surprise and technology on our side. This will be no Basra. The jinni guards in Samarra have never been many in number, and with Kamal's 'help,' it'll be over by noon."

We have to warn them, I said, and I tugged on Firuz's sleeve.

He pulled it out of my grasp. *Wait. There is something more.*

Saif picked up his helmet. "Yes, sir. The tunnel of Samarra will fall in two days' time."

Zakariyya tugged on the end of his beard. "I will stay and keep your brother . . . preoccupied."

Toqto'a stirred on his cushion. I was about to look away when something about him caught my eye. His braid had fallen forward and settled on his shoulder, and the tip was dipped in silver, curved and sharp as a talon. It was odd to see a jinni hairstyle on a human.

Firuz gripped my forearm. *That man is not from Mongolia. He is a jinni.* I nearly gasped from the pressure of his words in my mind. *How was I so blind? We need to return.* Now.

A *jinni* was in the room. Another jinni. He had to be a descendant of the Forgotten.

A shiver spread down my arms, and I backed into the garden, suddenly nauseated and dizzy. It didn't matter that I still had more to listen to. There was another jinni in the room, talking to Ibrahim and his men. Clearly, no one there knew what he truly was.

Did the Forgotten support Ibrahim, or were they planning something more sinister?

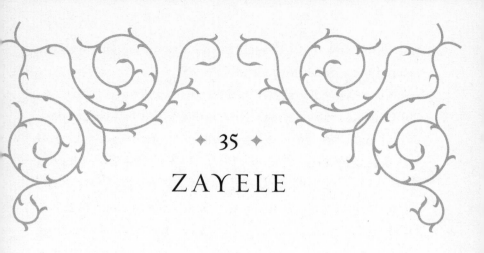

✦ 35 ✦

ZAYELE

IT WAS THE middle of the night, and there was a hand pressing against my mouth. I struggled against it, pulling away.

"Shh," came the voice, "I've come to get you, but you have to be quiet."

I blinked away the darkness and saw Taja. She was kneeling over me, holding a small wishlight orb that glowed faintly. She looked more excited than murderous, so I nodded and she took away her hand.

"Where are you taking me?" I whispered.

She pulled me off the bed. "Come. You can wear that," she whispered, pointing at my gown. It was the same dress I'd worn during the day. I had been too tired to change it before falling asleep.

"Where are we going?" I repeated.

Her eyes sparkled. "It's a secret. Keep quiet till we get out of the house."

"Is this part of my training?" It had to be. The only times I'd ever seen her were when there was something to learn or be tested on. Now that I thought of it, I'd never seen her walking around the Cavern without Melchior.

She shrugged, and gestured for me to follow, so I did.

Outside the house, the Cavern was dusky. It wasn't as dark as real night, but the wishlights lining the streets and lake wall had been dimmed. The only bright lights came from the orb Taja carried and the flickering surface of the lake, where the flames danced all day and night. Shadows stretched between buildings, flowing over the ground like a black fog. The ceiling was lost in blackness, and I could almost pretend it was the sky, the *real* sky, but one without any stars or moon.

Taja would not slow down, so I hurried to keep up with her. "Now can you tell me where we're going?"

"To the Lake of Fire." The mystery of her words seeped into me like a warm cinnamon bath. "The rest you'll see for yourself."

Together, we trotted over the cobblestones, climbed the stairs to the lake wall, and stopped at the boatkeeper's hut. Gal, a stout woman with a voice that carried, waved us over to the dock. She held a long pole with a lantern attached to the other end, and used it to point us to a boat.

"That one down there!" she called out while we passed her by. "Get the one on the end." Then she handed Taja the pole with the lantern. Gal stayed at her hut while Taja and I climbed down to the dock and made our way to the boat. After we climbed in, Taja set the pole into a hole at the front and picked up the oars.

The Lake of Fire was a different monster at night. The

flames darted across the surface in a flickering, glaring dance. It was pretty, but it left spots in my eyes when I blinked. I was glad Taja was in charge of getting us to our destination, although she still didn't tell me where we were headed.

Taja rowed in silence, with her back to the lake. At first, I thought she was taking me out to Devil's Island, where Atish and Shirin had taken me when I'd first come to the Cavern. But that was toward Iblis's Palace, and she headed in the other direction, to the far side of the lake.

There were no other islands. There weren't any platforms. There weren't any other docks. But there were, I remembered, dark arches cut into the wall of the Cavern itself, just above the waterline. I cleared my throat, because it had suddenly turned sticky.

Taja was taking me to a tunnel. At night.

"This isn't another test, is it? I don't have to run in a tunnel again, do I?"

Taja looked over her shoulder. I followed her gaze and saw that not too far ahead, another lantern bobbed on the lake. I hadn't noticed it before, because the flames sprouting from the lake had hidden it, but this light was constant, and was attached to a boat like ours. In fact, there wasn't just one boat. There was a *line* of boats, almost reaching to the opposite wall.

She rowed and rowed, and I sat on the edge of the bench and gripped the sides until my knuckles ached. Finally, we reached the far side. The other boats were tied to a series of rings screwed into long spears of gypsum, their lanterns swinging while the boats rocked at the waves of our approach. Beside the crystals was the entrance to a tunnel. A portion of the Cavern had been wiped free of crystals, and in its place was an arch, a scar of blackest black, and whoever had been in the other boats had already gone through.

Taja found another ring on the other side of the entrance and tied up the boat. Then she climbed into the hole, careful not to fall into the lake, and reached out her hand to me. From where I sat in the boat, her arm looked disconnected, her body lost in the rim. But I took her hand and let her pull me in.

I landed on a smooth, clean floor. Instinctively, I reached out around me, feeling for the walls, but I could not find them.

"Come with me," Taja said. Her voice echoed.

We walked slowly until we saw a faint reddish glow. Then Taja grabbed my wrist and pulled me along at a quicker pace. We emerged in another geode, much like the Cavern but far, far smaller. Its crystals had been filed down until only smooth, reflective disks remained. The spaces between the disks were filled in with silver, and I had the impression I had shrunk in size and had crawled into the setting of a giant ring.

The jinn filled every standing space in the room, dozens of them. They circled a pedestal with a large stone bowl filled with water, but none of them were looking at the bowl. They all turned to face us, and one by one, I recognized a few. Atish, Samir, Arzada, Rashid, and Saam stood together on one side, and on the other were Melchior and Aga. The rest I didn't recognize, but they smiled at me as though they'd known me my whole life. Maybe they had.

This was not going to be a test of endurance. Judging by the way Atish was fidgeting, this was when they'd choose between the final three.

"Welcome, Zayele," Melchior said. Taja entered the circle and then beckoned for me to join them.

My throat had tightened and gone dry. I stepped up and joined the circle. And then I felt it. A soft vibration coursed around us, in a ring.

Melchior raised his brows. "This is the Bonding, as I'm sure you've surmised. What you're feeling is the power of the Dyad, which courses through us all when we're together." He looked at Aga, who pressed her lips together and nodded back at him. "As a magus, you can do anything any other jinni can do. You can fight like the Shaitan. You can slip into places unseen, like your sister. You can heal, like the physicians. But you cannot do any of these as strongly, or in your case as *clearly,* as they can. The one thing you can do, however, is protect those around you. Each magus has a special talent, and yours, it appears, is your strength of will. This is why you were able to make the Fire Wish without knowing how to make a wish in the first place. This is why you were able to change your cousin's sight. A long time ago, the magi were set above all other jinn for their special qualities. Unfortunately, a few magi went too far, so a decision was made to bind a magus with someone in the Shaitan. The magi needed jinn who were both physically and mentally strong, to keep them from going too far once again." Melchior paused, just long enough to look each jinni in the eye. Then he stopped at me again. "But first, we must mark you, so that everyone will know you are one of us."

Suddenly, half of them slipped off their shawls and revealed a red flame marked into the divot of their collarbones. *That* was where the magi were marked.

My heart thumped against my chest like it wanted to get out. I pressed a hand against it, but it did nothing to calm it down.

Melchior broke away from the ring of Dyads and stepped up to the bowl of water, reached in, and pulled out a ruby spear. It was narrow, long, and sharp as a knife at one end. Then he walked around the bowl and came to me. He stopped an arm's length from me and held up the ruby.

"This will mark you into the magi," he said.

Without giving me a chance to hesitate, he pointed the ruby at the hollow of my throat and pressed it into the skin. It stung, but I did not move. I did not even swallow. I inhaled through my nose, deeply and slowly, and blinked away the bright red light emanating from the ruby.

The chamber filled with the reddish light, and Melchior's cheeks turned sharper, the shadows beneath his eyes a dark, bloody red.

Then the pain released, and he pulled back the ruby.

I brushed my fingers over my throat, but felt nothing. The skin was intact, and only faintly warmer than usual.

"Did it work?" I spoke too soon. A second later, a rush of fire overtook my body and spread through my arms, over and down my scalp, and down to my toes. It burned, hotter than anything I'd ever felt before, and I could not hold back an ear-splitting scream.

My scream echoed, ricocheting off the flattened crystals

on the ceiling. I fell to my knees and wrapped my arms around myself. I was burning. I was aflame. I breathed, and fire erupted from my nostrils. My hair fell down, freed now from its veil. And my dress fell to the ground in a dusting of ash.

The fire burned the bones in my body. I screamed once more, and the fire flew out from my mouth and finally, finally, left me cold.

I fell to my side, naked and singed, and felt hands upon me, lifting me up to my feet. But surely I could not stand? Surely I wasn't alive?

A cloth was wrapped around me, and two jinn held me on my feet. Taja, and someone else on the other side. They were whispering, Taja saying "What happened?" and the other one, "Was that because she's half-human?"

"Open your eyes," Melchior instructed.

I blinked, and saw that the room was less red. Melchior had returned the ruby to the water, and the light now came from a ring of wishlight orbs set into the wall above our heads. Blue—soft, cool, blue light. Not the light of fire.

Atish was on the other side, held back by Rashid and Saam. His eyes were dark pools, and I shook my head at him. I was not dead.

"What happened to me?" I croaked. My throat felt like I was rubbing two sunburned parts together.

"That is what it's like to get the mark of the magi," Taja said. "It's not the most comfortable, and it looked worse for you than it was for us."

"I almost died," I whispered.

"On the contrary. You have just been born," Melchior said. His voice was too loud, and I winced. "The mark of the magi cannot shine on human flesh. Now you are truly jinni."

The mark of the magi cannot shine on human flesh.

Melchior had burned away all that had been human.

"No," I cried, pulling away from the older woman on my right. "You can't do that. It isn't possible. It isn't *right.*"

"Shh," Taja whispered in my ear. "We'll talk about this later."

"No! We talk about it now. Melchior, you never said *anything* about this." I didn't care if my throat was falling to pieces, like burned sheets of paper. "What have you done to me?"

"I have brought you into the magi."

I was one of them now. I had burned away all the human blood in my body. I could not see it now, but I had a mark on my collarbone that flickered, garnet red and pulsating, in the shape of a flame. Was it worth losing my humanity to protect my *Dyad*?

My grandfather, ever hateful of the human blood his daughter had married, had found a way to cleanse me of it. Would my sister be next?

One glance in his eyes showed me he had won. But only in this. He had burned away all traces of a father I had never known. I did not have time to cry, so I pulled myself out of Taja's arms and stood tall.

"And now we choose which Shaitan I'm partnered with?" I asked.

Atish's eyebrows were bent in concern. "Are you sure you want this now?"

"It does not matter what she wants," Aga said. "She is a magus, and a magus cannot be without the Shaitan. The three of you, go stand before her."

When Atish reached me, he grasped my hand and squeezed it softly. "I didn't know," he whispered.

Aga gently pushed him away from me and held up a spool of thread. When she began to unwind it, I recognized it. It was the pale and luminescent silk of the glowworms. She wound it around my wrists, and then covered my hands with hers.

"Close your eyes," she instructed. When my eyes were shut, she said, "We will place the Shaitan around you. When your mind is calm, you will find your dyad."

The sounds of footsteps encircled me and then stopped. The room was quiet except for everyone's quickened breathing. I needed to find my dyad blindly. As frightening as it was to choose in the dark, it was a relief to make the final choice.

Taking in a deep, slow breath, I tried to focus my mind. I imagined a flame flickering outward from my chest like a beacon. It twisted left, then right, and then around me, searching for the man I should choose. Finally, it stopped swirling and shone straight and true, then brighter. I turned to my left and opened my eyes.

He and I both laughed in relief. Atish's face was as bright at the flame had been.

"Thank Iblis," he sighed, and he pulled me close.

Aga cleared her throat behind us. "Now that you've made your choice, we must finish the Bonding." She took his wrists and wrapped the end of the thread around them. Then she gestured for everyone to back away.

"*Dyathi.*" All the Dyads said this wish together.

The silk tightened, and then sank into our skin painlessly and disappeared. When it was gone, Atish and I both studied our wrists.

"That didn't feel like I'd expected," I said. I rubbed at the soft skin. There were no marks. "How do people know if you're in a Dyad if the mark is invisible?"

Taja shrugged. "You're a magus. You can't be a marked magus if you aren't in a Dyad."

"I don't feel any different," Atish said. "I thought I'd feel . . . stronger." Suddenly, the tension eased, and a few jinn laughed.

"You *are* stronger," Rashid said, smiling. "You have a magus as your companion." Then he glanced down at the empty spot beside him, where his dyad would have been if she were still alive, and dropped the smile.

Atish took my hand again, and I found his arm was shaking.

36

NAJWA

FIRUZ AND I ran into the room with the Eye of Iblis and found Delia staring openmouthed at the image of the jinni, spread out, larger than life, across all the tiles. His cheekbones were sharp enough to cut through the crystal.

"He's a jinni!" I shouted.

She did not turn her head, and instead she held on to the table beside her. "Did he see you?"

"Not unless he has the ability to see through my *shahtabi.*"

"Then we have a chance," she said with a sigh. "He must be one of the Forgotten. He should not have been there. When Iblis died, he left behind a mess. There wasn't a system of law, there weren't any traditions, and there wasn't anyone prepared to take his place. There was a grab for his seat, which left many, many dead. The Diwan was eventually created, and they decided that each magus should be paired with someone in the Shaitan."

"But some didn't want that, did they?" I asked.

She turned away from the wall, from the giant image of

the Forgotten jinni, and looked down at the sheets and charts scattered across the table. "Rather than be in a Dyad, they fled. Twenty-two magi left, along with their sympathizers."

Why is he working for Ibrahim? And what is Ibrahim planning? I wondered.

"Delia, there's more information than just that image." I looked at Firuz.

He nodded. "Ibrahim is planning an attack on us for tomorrow."

She blinked rapidly and stood up, straightening her body. It was like watching a wilted plant take on water. "Where?"

We told her everything, and she called for the rest of the Corps to join us. I waited in the corner while a ball of iron formed in my stomach, heavy and unmoving. The Corps filed in, and I watched while Delia relayed our information, gesturing at the jinni on the wall. There were several gasps and many frowns, and the mood of the room darkened until the shadow I stood in was empty of light and air.

An hour later, Delia found me leaning against the wall for support. Her hair had slipped out of the sapphire clip, but she did not care. She brushed it out of her face and looked me straight in the eye.

"You have to find him."

"The other jinni?"

"You need to find out where he has gone and what he is up to. Word has been sent to the Shaitan, and everyone will soon be heading toward Samarra."

"What about the reeds? Firuz said they're using them as a

bridge." Whatever it actually was, Kamal had designed it, and they were going to use it against us. Reeds didn't sound threatening, but neither had a simple ball of selenite until Kamal and Hashim turned it into a weapon.

Delia shook her head. "I'm sending Parviz ahead to see if he can find out anything. In the meantime, you will be tracking down Toqto'a. But be careful. He and his friends, if he is not alone, will not be pleased if they find out they've been discovered."

"Delia," I asked, pausing by the door, "can they do what the Shaitan can do?"

"I do not know, but please, do not try to find out."

"How do I find him?"

Delia called over a member of the Corps, a woman ten or fifteen years older than me. She was the smallest jinni in the Corps, and rumored to be more observant than most. She smiled weakly and handed me a thin bangle. I took it and laid it on my palm, a circle of pure, soft gold.

"It's made from the same gold as the Shaitan spear. It can track down anyone, if you know what they look like."

"What wish do I use?"

She closed my fingers over the bangle, sealing them between her warmth and the gold's cool metal. "Think only of the face you mean to find, and it will show you the way."

I waited to use the bangle until I was out of the Room of Iblis and alone beside the Lamp. Then I slipped it onto my wrist and closed my eyes. I pictured the jinni and his penetrating gaze, his sharp features, and his dark, oily braid.

My wrist started to burn, and then it pulled me out of my skin. I started to twist, to dissolve, to turn to smoke, and then the bangle yanked me right out of the Cavern and through basalt and shale, pockets of air and layers of sand.

I was a cyclone pulled by the circlet of gold. It was my compass, my light, and it delivered me from the depths onto a ridge. I was a speck in the landscape, a lone figure standing on high ground between the sky and the earth flowing out before me, and I was exposed.

I crouched to the ground and looked around me. There were no jinn, no humans, no animals at all but for a falcon. It circled over a valley of strange, dark boulders separated by thin plumes of smoke that rose to my elevation and dispersed in the air.

The jinni was somewhere nearby, but where?

I spun, holding out my wrist with the gold dangling from it, and felt a tug in the direction of the boulders. But they weren't boulders—they were tents. Hundreds of dark tents bunched up together in the hollow of the ground.

People milled between the tents, small and quick as beetles. And everywhere, as numerous as the people, stood horses in leather-and-copper armor. These horses, however, wore no bells or tassels. They were outfitted for silence and darkness.

"*Shahtabi.*" As soon as I was hidden from sight, I ran down the side of the ridge onto the packed dirt and horse droppings. They had come from this direction, then.

I reached the edge of the army, for that was clearly what this was, and lurked from tent to tent. These were all humans, not jinn, but they were not of the caliphate. Their armor was different, their horses were slung with footholds I'd never seen before, and their swords curved backward. Many wore two swords strapped to their backs, deadly mirrored moons of iron.

Somewhere in this foreign army, the Forgotten jinni walked free.

I crept to the center of the encampment. A few times, I had to leap aside in an effort to avoid being run into by a horse or man. At last, I saw the banner signifying the general's tent. The long banner was black and gold, and too heavy for the faint wind to lift it off its post.

The bangle jerked, pointing me toward the general's tent, so I went to the back entrance and pulled away the flap. My hand shook and my heart was in my throat, but I could not make it this far without setting eyes on the jinni.

The interior was dark and smelled of smoking oil, but I found him, sitting in a circle of men. They sat cross-legged, each with his hands on his knees, and listened while a man in black armor and with thick, felted plaits of hair barked out his commands. They were in a language I didn't recognize. There was a wish for this, and I whispered it to myself.

"Alefjaala." This wish was supposed to enable me to speak and understand their words, but I'd never used it before.

"We will strike while they are busy," the commander said. The wish worked! "I want to see these bridges they've constructed first," he went on.

"Master," Toqto'a said. He grabbed one of the golden cuffs on his wrists and bowed. "Where would you have my men be positioned?"

The general pursed his dry lips. "When we arrive in

Samarra, I would like your kind to be in the same formation we used in Ashgabat. And, as always, I appreciate your assistance, Toqto'a."

"As you wish."

Was he enslaved to this man? I didn't see anything binding him, and the general didn't seem like the sort of man to acknowledge a slave, much less thank him.

An army with a handful of jinn would be unstoppable. Toqto'a had heard what Ibrahim planned. It did not take much thought to piece it all together: this army was going to attack the caliph's army from behind.

A third army. A third army with far more power and numbers than Ibrahim's soldiers would be able to withstand.

Toqto'a lifted his head and his eyes traveled toward me. I almost dropped the flap, which he would not have missed. The moment the wind picked up, I let the flap go and backed away.

This army was from the northeast. They had come from beyond the mountains, light and quick on their multitude of horses. This was far worse than Delia could have imagined. She needed to know as soon as possible. And so did Kamal and his brother.

✦ 37 ✦

ZAYELE

THERE WAS NO time for celebration. The moment the boats reached the dock, Gal and Delia were waiting for Melchior, Aga, and Rashid. I had barely straightened my legs when Rashid shouted out at the congregation of Dyads, "We must get to Samarra. Ibrahim and his army are planning to attack us there!"

The boats rocked in the lake, empty, while we ran to the tunnel that led to Samarra. I stole a glance at Atish and caught him watching me.

"Will you be all right?" he asked. "You haven't had to fight anyone yet. Not really."

I grimaced. "Don't have a choice, do we?"

He laughed cynically and shook his head. I looked back at Melchior and Delia. They were out of earshot, but I could see they were arguing with each other about something.

Atish took my hand in his and pulled me with him. "Come. I won't let you fall behind."

We ran in groups of two, and when we reached the entrance

to the Samarra Tunnel, we had to slow down, because the entire Shaitan was already filing in, clogging the mouth like too many ants.

"Delia must have alerted them already," Saam said, coming up on my right. We slowed to a walk, and caught our breath. "Get to the river. Taja and I will show you what to do on the way there."

"Where are the other magi and their partners?" I asked, remembering the dozens who had been there when I was marked.

Atish looked at Saam, who frowned before he answered. "Most of them only came for that one event. They are positioned at many different tunnels, throughout the earth. There is always the possibility we will be attacked from another source when busy with battle."

"So we're on our own," I said.

"Precisely. But we don't need them," Saam teased. "We've got Taja, who can kick any army off their feet with her eyes closed." Taja snorted, and then ran ahead.

While we ran, the sound of a hundred feet echoing down the tunnel pounded against my eardrums, and no amount of covering my ears made a difference. At one point, Taja pulled my hand away and shook her head.

"You cannot unhear it. You can only ignore it. Like all the sounds in battle."

I had never fought in a war. I had never fought against anyone. I did not know how to use a dagger, or send out balls of fire. And although the women in the Cavern fought alongside the men, I had been raised amongst humans, where women never wielded any weapons. The only time I had seen real fighting had been in the Baghdad palace, when the Shaitan fought against the palace guards. And then, I had not been expected to be a part of it.

"Atish, what are we going to do?" I asked.

"I was wondering the same. I know as much about being in a Dyad as you do, you know."

"Yes, but you can fight. I can barely keep a flame going."

He grinned. "That's not true and you know it. You've blazed through magus training. I've never heard of anyone completing it so quickly. Besides, you just need to cover me."

This made everything twice as bad. I pretended to look at the heels of the jinni in front of me. "I barely passed. The only test I did well on was the last one."

He snapped his jaw shut and sucked in a deep breath. We went on like this, silent and dark, for another minute before he shook his head. "No, I don't think you failed."

"What?"

"Melchior would never have initiated the Bonding if you weren't good enough. Those tests weren't there to see if you could overcome them. If they're like the Shaitan tests, they test you, *all* of you, and the instructors are looking deeper than you think."

"So I was supposed to fail?"

"They were impossible tasks. And when we did the run, you did better than most Shaitan, Zayele. Melchior and Taja wore down your defenses. They saw what was beneath. Of course, they could have just asked me," he said slyly.

I jabbed him in the shoulder, and then Taja pushed into

mine. We were slowing down, and I had almost tripped over her. "Done?" she asked. "Good. Because it's time to transport to the other end. Atish, have you been there before?" Atish shook his head. "Then I'll take Zayele and Saam will take you. We need to get there before everyone else. It's our job to put up the barricades."

She gripped my upper arm and took me away from the middle of the earth to a place struck through with the amber light of sunrise. We landed at the edge of the tunnel and nearly fell into the swiftly rushing Tigris. She pulled me back, and we bent over, gripping our knees and breathing heavily. Atish and Saam had arrived farther back in the tunnel.

"I told you not to transport so close," Saam said, rushing up to us and frowning. "That river is faster than it looks." We all looked down at the jade-colored water, and I was taken back, remembering how I had floated past these very caves only a few weeks ago, whining about how I had to marry a prince in Baghdad. The water was the same, deep and translucent, but everything else—me, my sister, and the war—had changed.

"Come," Taja said in my ear. Her voice was urgent. "We have work to do."

38

NAJWA

NO ONE WAS inside the Eyes of Iblis Command, so I went outside and found Delia and Melchior arguing by the fountain. Yashar stood behind Melchior, looking like he wanted to say something but was too afraid.

"But what about *after* the battle?" Delia asked. She was an arm's length from Melchior, eyes blazing and mouth curled in disgust. "Have you *any* consideration for what happens next?"

Melchior, in contrast with Delia, was calm. "There will not be an 'after' if we do not take advantage of this now," Melchior said. He was about to leave when he saw me. "Najwa. What do you report?"

Delia spun around and pressed her palm to her heart. "Thank Iblis you've returned. Did you find the jinni?"

"Yes. He is with another army."

"Another army?" Melchior asked, frowning. "Whose?"

"I did not recognize them, but they came from the northeast. They are working with him and a few other jinn. The jinn will help them fight the caliph's army."

"And so the caliph's army will be caught between two armies," Delia said, her voice barely above a whisper. "They will be decimated."

Melchior nodded. "As fortunate as that would be, we cannot let this army have these jinn. They must be freed."

"But, Melchior, they're the Forgotten. They aren't . . ." Delia's lip began to tremble, and she bit it hard. A moment later, her face was hard as stone.

"You've not forgotten them, it seems," he said to Delia. "Najwa, you need to go back and release them from their bonds. What sort are they? Are they chained together? Did you see any signs of selenite or hematite?"

"No. Toqto'a wore golden cuffs, but they didn't look like shackles. I don't think they're slaves, Melchior."

"Of course they're slaves," Melchior snapped. "You must break them free, Najwa, because once they push through the caliph's army, their masters may never stop."

I opened my mouth to protest, but the only words I could come up with would just prove my youth, my inexperience, and my inabilities, so I clamped it shut. They weren't slaves, and there wasn't anything I could do about them helping the foreign army if that was what they wanted to do.

"When you finish, join us at the mouth of the Samarra Tunnel. It is where your sister will be, fighting beside her dyad."

"You mean she's—"

"Yes. She has been bonded with Atish. With any luck, they will prove themselves at tomorrow's battle."

My mind was reeling, but I did not have time to straighten

it out. I bowed at Melchior and Delia. "I will go collect some things and be on my way."

There was nothing I truly needed, but I could not return to the third army's encampment now. Too much had happened all at once, and both my body and my mind were growing weak.

When I reached the house, I found Rahela sitting on the floor in the very center of the room. She startled, backing up a little on her knees, and then regained her composure.

"I finished it," she said, and she brushed her hand across the rug beneath her. It was the brightly colored rug she'd been working on earlier. How had she finished it so quickly? She was only a human. Had Abdas helped her?

She crawled off the rug and showed it to me, pointing out the mountain peaks, the gorge and agate-blue river, the crust of the earth, and the Cavern. She had found milky-white thread for the shards in the ceiling, and strangely illuminated thread for the flames on the lake. I brushed the pile, which was thick and stiff, amazed. This was not an ordinary woven rug. The snow on the mountains was cold to touch. I ran my finger down the river, and it came away moist. The wall of the gorge was rough and filed down my nail when I scratched at it. Most amazing of all was the Lake of Fire. The flames flickered, just as they did in real life.

And that's what this was: a living, true-to-life rug.

"How did you do this?" I asked. "It's beautiful. It's *magical*. But you're not a jinni."

She smiled knowingly. "I think it was all of these things," she said, pointing at the loom and piles of glistening thread. "There is power in that loom, and in the dyes."

"But no one has ever made anything like this before. Not Laira."

"I think . . . I think it's because they've never thought to. I wanted something that would let me travel the world without having to depend on anyone else." Then she crawled back onto the center of the rug, not seeming to care that the river left a wet mark on her knee. "Watch." She motioned for me to get off the rug. Then she held her hands out, palms up, and lifted them up to the ceiling.

The rug rose off the floor and hovered waist-high in the air.

"Shards, Rahela! How did you *do* that?"

She shrugged. "I had a little help from a friend. But it was my idea."

"Where is he?" I asked.

"Abdas went to help the physicians. They called for more bandages, in preparation for this battle." She brushed off the tassels at the edge of the rug, pushing them over the edge so they hung down. The rest of the rug was surprisingly straight. It didn't bow under her weight at all. "Don't worry. I plan to help them. But in my own way."

I did not have time to find out what she meant. I wished her luck and ran to where we kept the flatbread and water. It tasted like chalk, but it settled my stomach. Then I left Rahela behind with her flying rug.

I transported straight to the center of the encampment, but the tents were gone. Two warhorses flanked me, and in the slight shadow, I wished, *"Shahtabi."*

I did it just in time, because the soldier atop the horse on my left turned and looked down at where I stood.

"Did you see that?" he asked the other soldier. I cringed, and kept myself still. The horses were probably trained to ignore strange scents and surprises, but I did not want to test them. "Something flew straight through here. Something big."

"It was probably a vulture," said the other soldier. "It knows what we're about."

The other one shrugged, and they clicked their tongues at the horses, who began to move. That was when I noticed I was in the midst of a herd of warhorses carrying soldiers gleaming in steel. They moved en masse, and if I did not move out of the way, I was going to find myself beneath their hooves.

I weaved, running around the horses and careful not to startle them. Finally, I reached the shallow slope of the valley, where the horsemen did not bother to climb. From there, I looked for Toqto'a and any other jinn.

It did not take long. In the center of the horde waved five black flags from the saddles of five heavily armored horses. Each horse was ridden by a man with gold cuffs like Toqto'a's, and they were marching away from me.

I would have to go back into the army of hooves and swords, of choking dust and whipping tails. I could feel my *shahtabi* wish was not as strong as it had been earlier. I was losing my strength, and I did not have time left. I took a breath, focused on the cloud of dust in front of the jinni horses, and transported. A moment later, a horse reared in front of me. In the shock, my *shahtabi* fell away. A man shouted, echoed by another, and I backed into the swirling dirt.

When the horse calmed down, I forced myself to go up to the first jinni. It was Toqto'a. He saw me immediately and glared at me down his nose.

"At long last, they've sent a jinni to claim us, friends," he said to the other jinn.

I swallowed. "I have come to release you from your imprisonment."

Toqto'a slowed his horse, but it was still moving quickly. I trotted beside them, trying to keep my eye on Toqto'a while not tripping over anything on the ground. "What makes you think we're imprisoned?"

"But you're being used by this army. To fight."

One of the other jinn chuckled behind me. "They've sent a little one to do a man's job. Do you think you can take us by force? All five of us, and only one of you?"

Then Toqto'a laughed. It was loud and full of pain and anger. "We are not captives here. We fight with this army willingly." My mouth was dry. I tried to swallow away the dust, but my tongue was paper. It could do nothing without any words. "Go back and tell your jinni family we are coming for them. This army intends to wipe out the caliph's army, and *we* intend to wipe out *yours*."

"Go now, and tell them," said the other jinni, and I felt something sharp press into the space between my shoulder blades. "The sooner they hear we're coming, the more the terror will build."

"Please," I pleaded.

The sword pressed harder, and the pain was immediate.

I transported away, back to the ridge I'd first arrived on,

relieved I hadn't said the secret wish home in front of them. But then, home wasn't where I needed to go, anyway. I caught my breath and cried, "*Shatamana.*"

I slipped into the dirt, and fell, faster and faster, down into the earth.

39

ZAYELE

THREE THINGS HAPPENED at once. The rest of the Shaitan arrived, we sealed up the bottom half of the tunnel with a haphazard layer of rocks and wishes, and the caliph's army appeared. I stood in the shadows behind the barricade and watched as they filed up on the opposite bank. Their horses' hooves lifted and settled. Their foot soldiers lined the edge of the bank and stood still. I watched all of this as though I were viewing it from afar, and had to grip the rock in front of me to remind myself this was real. This was what the buildup to battle looked like.

Rashid came up behind me and pulled me out of the way. He looked through the opening and sucked air in through his teeth. "We barely got here in time. Atish, I need you to get on the other side of this, up above the tunnel. Take Zayele with you."

Atish nodded and began climbing over the rocks we'd only just cemented.

"They don't know we're here yet, so use your *shahtabi*," Rashid snapped.

We complied, but even invisible, I felt exposed while we climbed the bluff. I pulled myself up the side, but it was soft and crumbled. Once, Atish reached out and grabbed my wrist. "Be careful, or they'll know what's causing the dirt to fall."

Finally, we reached the top, where we could see for miles and were eye to eye with the opposing army. But the Tigris was wide here at the bend, and impossible for them to cross.

"Why didn't they come from behind and climb down the bluff instead?" I asked Atish.

"Because all that area over there is riddled with fire. We set up clear orbs in the field, and if they're stepped on, they erupt with fire and oil. I helped set some up a few weeks ago. Sometimes, they get broken by animals and need to be replaced."

"What are those?" I asked him. Three boats were forging upriver, propelled by dozens of men at oar. None of these men were armed, but what alarmed me was what each of these boats towed behind: a long, wide raft of woven reeds. At first glance, they looked like barges, but on closer inspection, I saw they were too flat, and two wooden poles extended from each end. They were bridges! Even more alarming was that they were the width of the river.

A horn blared, and the horsemen on the bluff across the river all turned to the south. Then they began to cross down the embankment on a narrow trail that switched back and forth.

Atish ran to the edge, flopped onto his stomach, and

cupped his hands over his mouth. "Rashid!" he shouted down. "Watch out for the bridges!"

There was a moment of silence that was broken by a round of cursing. "Get rid of them!" Rashid called back. "Before they have a chance to use them."

Atish pushed himself onto his feet and pulled me to the edge. "We have to destroy those."

"How?"

"I don't know. Fire?"

The bridges were not yet in place, and were at least fifty feet away from where we stood. "Are we close enough?"

"We have to be," he said tightly. He held out his hands and wished.

His aim was true. The fire hit the center of the first bridge, blasting a few reeds into the air. Smoke swirled up from the point of impact. A moment later, an arrow shot out from behind the army's ranks and hit the scorched mark on the bridge. It had carried with it a bladder of water, which doused the fire.

Atish sent a series of fireballs, all targeted at various points on the nearest bridge, and each ball of fire was met with an arrow of water. The bridge kept moving closer to the tunnel.

If the bridges could not get close to the tunnel, they were worthless. I focused on the men in the boat, at their oars. Then I imagined the oars were nothing but fish, and I wished, pushing the idea forward.

There was a shock wave, and in an instant, each of the men held a writhing, living fish. They dropped them in shock before realizing they now had no way to navigate the river. Once the fish hit the water, they returned to their original form, and some of the men reached out, grasping at the oars as they rushed downstream.

Atish hooted and clapped me on the back. "That was my magus, Rashid!"

Orders, directed from both the boats and the army making its way down to the river's edge, were barked across the water. Someone blew a horn, and the foot soldiers ran down the sides of the bluff, stumbling and rolling over one another, until they hit the water. Some began swimming out to the first boat.

There were too many. Atish kept attacking the bridges, and was answered by the water arrows. I bent over the edge and looked at the tunnel. No one had yet come out.

"Rashid!" I shouted. "Tell me what to do!"

"Do the same thing to the other oarsmen. We will be ready in a moment."

"What are they doing in there?" I asked Atish, but he was too focused to hear.

My skin began to tingle, and I knew the *shahtabi* was wearing off. I had used up too much energy on the oars. We would soon be out in the open, there for all the army's archers to see. I pulled on his shoulder and he whirled on me.

"We have to hide," I said. He blinked, realization dawning on him.

"There's isn't anywhere to go. We have to finish off the bridges."

I watched in dismay as the soldiers positioned the first bridge, turning it against the current. The long poles at the front pushed onto the bank, and the back end was lifted until it settled. The bridge was light enough for the men to lift, but looked sturdy enough to let horses cross, two abreast.

It didn't seem to matter to the commander that several men had gone downstream, smacking their heads against the bridges. Again, I wished away the oars in another boat. But these men had been watching the first. Someone on board barked an order, and they held their fish tight, grabbing at tails and snapping jaws. When the wish faded, they had their oars again, and they pounded at the water, harder and fiercer than before.

"It's not working!" I shrieked.

The first wave of horsemen reached the bank and raced across the river, hooves cracking at the reeds. A second later, they charged the tunnel and began to pull away the rocks.

"Rashid!" Atish shouted, but there was no response. The second bridge was set onto the banks, and soon it too was covered in hooves and men with swords.

A wave of heat came over us from behind, and we turned in time to see four figures, one of azure flame and the other three of shimmering smoke, settle onto the ground. The first was Melchior, who did not wait for the others to re-form before setting up an invisibility shield around his immediate area. Then the smoke cleared.

Aga brushed off her black vest and then turned to the people beside her. One was Firuz, but I barely gave him a look because the other person that had transported to the bluff was Yashar.

I ran at Melchior. "What is he doing here!" I screamed. "Why would you bring a boy to battle?"

Melchior gestured at Yashar, whose face had gone pale. His mouth twitched, as if he was trying to keep it from peeling back in fear. "He will prove useful. He can identify the enemy's fears, Zayele. We cannot let an opportunity like that be wasted."

"But he could be hurt!"

"Zayele," Yashar croaked. He left Aga and Firuz and came to me. I turned, ready to pull him into my arms, ready to transport him as far away as I could imagine, but he shook his head and stopped a foot away, just on the other side of Melchior's invisibility shield. "I am one of them now."

"You're *what*? Melchior, what have you done to him?" Had he burned away all of Yashar's humanity just as he had done to me?

"I have done nothing but welcome him and give him something to strive for. He is not physically changed, like you. Any man willing to fight with us is part of our tribe."

"Yashar, you can't do this. There are people dying down there. You don't want to see this."

"I can see it already, Zayele. And *I* am not afraid."

I felt it well up, bitter and thick as mucus: horror. Pure, nauseating horror at what Melchior was willing to do to this boy.

Yashar blanched. "Zayele, don't feel that way. I want to be here. I want to help. At home, Father never let me do anything. I wasn't a part of anything. But here, I'm useful."

I whirled on Melchior. "When this is over, I am taking him away from you. If you're still alive." Then I felt the *shahtabi* fall away, and I stood exposed on the edge. I looked at the men waiting to come down to the bridge and caught the eyes of a soldier. He lifted his bow.

40

NAJWA

THE DUST PUFFED beneath my feet while I ran, invisible, along a path between flattened green stalks of barley. Ibrahim's army had come through here, trudging over the fields. He did not care that they had left a trail from here to the horizon. He did not care that he had destroyed the livelihood of his own people. I, in turn, did not care that I had not gone straight to Melchior. He already knew of the foreign army.

I had wished myself to Samarra. But I did not wish to be on Melchior's side of the Tigris, so I focused on finding Kamal. He, at least, would listen to me. I slipped through the ranks of dozens of soldiers before I finally found the horses with Ibrahim's colors. At the top of the bluff, the banners flapped wildly, whipping in the drying, crisp wind of midmorning. Ibrahim sat atop his gray horse in full armor. His dented helmet was blinding in the sun, and I shielded my eyes while I crept closer, scanning the surrounding area for Kamal.

Where was he? Ibrahim's captains surrounded him, taking

turns to urge on their soldiers down the bluff, down to the river.

I stood in the empty space between Ibrahim and the edge of the cliff. Ibrahim's stallion sniffed and cocked his ear at me. I froze. I was upwind, and the horse had taken notice. He knew someone was there, even if he couldn't see me.

Then I heard a cry from the opposite bluff and turned to see my sister fall. Atish was dragging her back, away from the edge. Melchior and Aga stood fast, with Yashar shielded between them. Off to the side stood Firuz, and his presence confused me the most. Why were they standing out in the open? Why weren't they in the tunnel?

I looked down and saw the Shaitan had given up on protecting the tunnel. They were pouring out of the entrance on their way to halt the advance of the soldiers who had come across the bridges. I knew in a second that those were the "reeds" Ibrahim had mentioned.

"Kamal, where are you?" I asked quietly.

I turned around just as a gloved hand wrapped around my neck. I struggled, and my *shahtabi* wish fell away.

"Did you think I wouldn't expect you to come? I've been waiting," Ibrahim said, growling in my ear. "Thank you for saying something so I knew just where to grab you."

"Let me go!"

He grabbed my wrist with a bare hand and let go of my neck. "I have you now."

"Ibrahim, *please*. I only came to warn you." Not only was I pinned between a giant of a man and the river bluff, but the man held me skin to skin. I could not get away unless he released me of his own will.

"To warn me of what? I know all there is to know about war with the Shaitan. This time, I've planned to draw them out of the tunnel. Then, when they've left it unguarded, we'll go in. All the way in."

"Ibrahim, please! There's another army coming." I pulled, but his hand was hard as marble.

"Is there? Another jinni army from some other hole in the ground?"

"Yes. Well, no. But they have jinn. They're coming to attack you. I came to tell you. Where's Kamal?"

"Prince Kamal was not invited. You, on the other hand, are welcome to help us. In fact, I don't think you'll have much choice." Then he dragged me away from the edge of the cliff. With his other hand, he motioned to someone to come. I kicked, pulled, and hit at his arm, but his armor was thick and he only laughed. "You know what I'll do now, don't you?"

"Don't. Please. They're my people."

"I thought you cared more about your human half. Isn't that why you came to the palace dressed as one? Isn't that why you chased after my brother?"

He lifted his hand, pulling me up into the air. My elbow ached, and I shouted, kicking him in the stomach. He pulled me away and lifted me in front of his soldiers. "I've caught us a jinni!" he bellowed. One by one, the soldiers spotted me and raised their weapons in salute to Ibrahim. I quit kicking, realizing it was a useless waste of energy. Ibrahim shook me once and then hissed, "I wish for you to kill every last Shaitan down on that riverbank."

"I won't."

He raised his brows so high they disappeared into his pointed helmet. "I command it."

"Even if I wanted to, I can't kill with a wish." I glared at him, wishing I could burn him with my eyes.

His grip tightened. "Can you knock them down?" I looked away. "Do it. I wish for you to knock those Shaitan into the river."

"Please, don't make me do this. Why are you attacking us? We've done *nothing*!"

"Grant my wish, *Consul*."

The wish bubbled, like the pools of acid in the cracks of the earth. It filled my body, unbidden, and a scream erupted from my mouth. *No.* I was *not* going to grant him this wish. The Shaitan would drown. The tunnel would be unguarded. The Cavern would be open to these dusty, steel-wielding soldiers and their bloodlust.

I pushed back, willing the wish to fade, to disperse, to dissolve. But like those pools of acid, they gushed from some unnamed source, filling the brim, filling my brain. I was not going to give him this. I was not going to.

Najwa, you are stronger than him. You can fight this.

Firuz! I can't—

I screamed. It shredded my throat, shook my teeth, and left me with nothing to breathe. The wish continued, seeping into my bones, into my veins, and pushed through. All I could do was take Ibrahim's wish exactly as he said it. *Those* Shaitan. Not all of them.

Fight it, Najwa. Use your human *strength. You're not as bound to his wishes as the rest of us.*

I opened my eyes wide and pulled against Ibrahim's wish. But power bolted out my fingertips. It spread outward, like a ray of killing sunlight, and blasted into the riverbank. Three Shaitan fell, one in the midst of a fight. Like magnets drawn to iron, they slipped into the Tigris. Nails scraped at the bank, but it did them no good.

They lost their hold or were hit by a human soldier. Then, like orbs of light cast into the canal, they bobbed downstream. One of them continued to send out fireballs while she floated away. None of those fireballs hit their marks.

I fell limp, held up only by Ibrahim. I knew I was dangling like a wilted flower, but I could do nothing about it. Somewhere in the back of my mind, I knew I had not been strong enough. I had not resisted enough. I had not fought him hard enough. I was not enough.

My sister would have fought him to the end. She would have burned in the wish before letting it fly.

My eyes were too heavy, and I let them fall as I heard a dozen voices cry out in victory. Then, in the midst of it all, I heard my name. Someone was calling for me, but I could not tell if the voice belonged to a jinni or a human.

+ 41 +

ZAYELE

I DROPPED TO the ground as an arrow whooshed over me. The archer pulled back again, but Atish sent out a fireball that hit him in the chest. We had long lost our invisibility and were fighting out in the open.

I started to push myself up off the ground when I saw it: a dark, churning cloud on the horizon, far behind the last lines of the caliph's army.

"Atish, look!"

He bent down and dragged me onto my feet, then pulled me back, away from the edge of the bluff. "What is that?" he asked.

"I believe I know what that is," Melchior said. I turned around to see Melchior shake his head. His eyes were focused on the bluff behind me. Yashar and Aga, however, saw the roiling darkness.

"What is it?" Atish asked.

"It's the other army," Melchior answered.

"Another army! And what's that cloud before them?" I

asked. It rolled over the terrain, ripping up all that stood in its way.

Aga reached for Yashar, who cowered from her. "That's the storm I never wanted to see," she said.

Firuz suddenly brought his hands over his ears and crouched. "Najwa's been caught by Ibrahim," he shouted at us. "She's trying to fight him off."

"Then we've all but lost," Melchior sputtered.

A handful of Shaitan fighting along the riverbank were pulled by an invisible hand into the Tigris. Aga and Melchior both shouted out a stream of wishes, but none were strong enough to counter the power that had brought them down.

The human army cried out in victory, shaking their swords in the air.

"Najwa!" Atish screamed. He pointed across the river at the opposite bluff. Ibrahim was dragging Najwa away from the edge. A moment later, she was lost behind the victorious soldiers.

I ran to Melchior and grabbed him by the sleeve. "We need to help her!"

"We can do nothing to help her now. She's a slave of the army's," he said.

"She was more defiant than you or I could ever have been," Firuz said. His eyes were bright with angry fire, and he shook his head at Melchior. "She had been commanded to kill them *all*."

Melchior's mouth twisted in pain. "She's too much like her mother."

"She was right, you know," Firuz said to Melchior. "You sent her back to free the Forgotten, but they weren't slaves. They came here to wipe us out. She is strong, and if she hadn't resisted Ibrahim's wish, all of the Shaitan would have died!"

Melchior glared at Firuz, pulled Yashar into his arms, made a wish, and slipped down to the entrance to the tunnel. I stood dumbfounded while he brought my cousin to face the onslaught of a rush of jubilant men.

When I looked around, Aga was gone. Only Atish and Firuz stood by. Firuz looked lost in his anger, but Atish was determined. His nostrils flared. "We're going over there."

"What's that storm?" I asked. It was dark as coal, but the closer it got, the more I noticed the thousands of small flying balls. Iron balls. "We have to get Najwa. Before—"

"Let's go," he said.

"Wait," Firuz said. He pulled his dagger out of its sheath and handed it to me.

"I don't know how to use that."

"It's not hard to use," he said. "Your dyad has firepower, but you've only got wishes. This is in case you can't think of any. Go save your sister."

I took the dagger and held it out. "Over there, then."

Atish and I arrived on the other side, in the very center of the caliph's army. It took them a second to realize we were there. A few men laughed when they realized only two jinn had entered their midst. One made a dash for me, hand outstretched and ready to grab hold.

I didn't have time to think of a wish. I slashed out with the dagger and cut through his forearm. He reeled back just before Atish thrust a ball of fire into him.

The crowd encircled us, inching closer with their swords outstretched.

"This wasn't the best idea," I said to Atish.

"Then think of something! You're a magus!"

There was no need, because a horn blared for a moment before being overtaken by a rumbling so loud and deep it shook the ground. I stumbled back into Atish, and we held each other up. The iron cloud was coming, and it blocked out the sun.

42

NAJWA

IT WAS THE sound of an earthquake, but coming from the wrong place. Then I saw it, smearing the sky in black and gray. Ibrahim backpedaled into me, and let go.

"What is that?" he asked.

"I told you: it's the other army." I tried to sound stronger than I felt. "They have jinn."

Ibrahim whirled on the men beside him. "Everyone, down to the river! Get into the tunnel."

"It will not help you," I said, "Their goal is to follow and finish both your army and mine. That man you hired, Toqto'a, is one of them!" I spat the words in his face. "He's a jinni. You have to stop whoever's controlling the iron storm. And you can't do that without our help."

The curtain of swirling iron continued to plow over the land, uprooting anything in its way and pummeling the air. The men ran in fear, stumbling over each other to get down to the bridges, down to the tunnel. But in their way stood the rest of the Shaitan, the ones I had managed not to kill. In the center of the Shaitan stood Dyads Taja and Saam, Melchior and Aga. And in the very middle, pointing straight at Ibrahim, was Yashar. His mouth moved quickly, whispering the fears only he could see into Melchior's ear.

Ibrahim's men could overpower the remainder of the jinn, but they could not protect themselves from a cloud of iron. I was about to tell him this when I noticed I was not being held. I had granted his wish, and he had asked no more. I was free.

Then I heard my name coming from within the thunderous sound of the cloud.

"Najwa!" I looked, and in the shrinking space between the caliph's army and the approaching iron balls, I spotted a horse at full gallop. The man on its back wore the turban of the vizier.

"Kamal!" I shouted. The cloud was too close. It would reach him in seconds.

Ibrahim's wish had drained much of my wishpower, but I was not empty. I reached forward and, without even thinking up a word to wish on, *pulled* him to me. He and the horse flew over the landscape and I barely had time to sidestep out of their way.

Kamal leaped off the horse and rushed to me, swooping me into his arms. "Thank you," he said.

"What were you *doing* there?"

He shook his head. "I was— We don't have time. We need to stop them. And this mess that Ibrahim started." He ran to Ibrahim, whose face was as dark as the oncoming storm.

Ibrahim reached out for me. "We need the jinni. She can stop them." I slipped out of his hands and stumbled into Kamal. "Kamal, she must stop their storm."

"I can't," I said. "Your wish left me with barely enough strength to bring Kamal here."

"You wished on her?" Kamal's eyes flashed.

"We will stop them," came a voice from behind us. We all turned to see Zayele, Atish, Taja, and Saam standing in a line. Taja's arms were crossed over her chest, and she looked taller than Ibrahim. She cocked her head at the storm. "The Dyads can stop those jinn. But we will not agree to it unless you call off your war on the Cavern."

Ibrahim's nostrils flared. "You expect me to take the word of a female jinni?"

Two soldiers grabbed for Taja, but she darted out of the way and marched up to Ibrahim, stopping out of arm's reach. "Prince Ibrahim, I can end your life right here, if that will convince you. That storm is controlled by a wish from the jinn in the other army. Do you want them to crush your army? Or do you want us to give you a fighting chance?"

Kamal slid up between them. "Ibrahim, do what she says. This was a never-ending war anyway."

"I *was* about to end it, until they showed up," Ibrahim said.

"Please, Ibrahim," I said. I stood across from Kamal, right beside Ibrahim. If he wanted to grab me again, so be it. "Let the Dyads help. Let us join our forces. If we do not, the army will overpower us all. There will be nothing left, and they will not stop until they reach Baghdad."

Ibrahim scanned the surrounding soldiers, his captains, and the unprotected tunnel. He had everything he'd wanted, up until this other army arrived. Snarling, he nodded. "When this is over, we will sign a pact."

"No," I said, practically spitting out the word. "You cannot expect me to take the word of a man who has just used me to kill my own. We will sign a pact *now*."

"The storm is almost here," Kamal said. He reached into his *kameez* and pulled out a scroll. "I've been carrying this around for a week. Just in case you changed your mind."

"Let me have it," Ibrahim growled. "I'll sign it now." He looked around for something to sign it with, and I shook my head.

"Here." I took a dagger out of Zayele's hand, sliced the back of my hand, and held it up to him. "This is more binding."

He nodded in respect, took the dagger, and dipped it in the welling blood. Carefully, he scraped his name onto the scroll and then handed it to me. I, in turn, signed my name to the pact. Kamal, as vizier, signed his name beneath ours.

Ibrahim cleared his throat and then shouted out for all to hear: "Our battle with the jinn is done. From now on, we will join our swords to defeat this army from the east." Then he pointed at one of his captains. "Spread the word."

"Now," Taja said, whirling on the dyads, "let's stop this monstrous thing."

WE TOOK OFF running, shoving aside the human soldiers who had frozen in fear. Taja and Saam exchanged a glance and sped up, leaping over the trodden clumps of grain on their way toward the veil of iron. They stopped just after passing the last of Ibrahim's army and settled into wide stances, ready to face the opposing jinn's power.

When Atish and I caught up to them, Taja spoke over her shoulder. "We need to put up a barrier. It's moving too fast for us to take it down before it would reach the others."

"How do we do that?"

"There's a wish that'll make a wall. But you have to be completely focused. If you can't stay focused, it'll fall."

"Just us, then?" I asked.

"The other magi aren't here, so yes. You and me."

"What do I do?" Atish shouted. The wind had picked up and was tugging us toward the iron balls.

"We make sure nothing distracts them," Saam shouted back.

Then she told me the word and together we wished:

"Qushev!"

The power came from the pit of my stomach and I lurched forward when it flew out of me. I kept my eyes focused on the whirling balls of iron. They swept across the remaining distance, faster now, closer. The wind whipped my hair toward the storm.

Somewhere between the storm and where we stood was a wall that would protect us, but I couldn't see it. How would we know if the wish worked?

"Don't doubt it!" Taja screamed. "It's there. Can't you feel it?" She pressed her palms forward, as if they alone could stop the advancing wall of destruction.

I wiped the hair out of my eyes and felt Atish's hand on my shoulder. Somehow, his presence strengthened me. I felt a jolt sink from his hand into me, all the way down to my feet. It anchored me, and I stood straighter, taller, and yelled out at the iron wall.

"Try to break through *that*!" I cried. After that, the rumbling grew too loud, and I couldn't hear my own voice above it. Balls clanged together, smacking and ringing like iron bells. It reverberated in my ears, but I could not cover them. I had to quiet my mind more than anything else.

Bits of sand and rock stung the back of my legs. The iron balls reached out, arching into the empty space before hitting the invisible wall. The balls smashed against it, but could not break through. As they whirled, they smacked into each other. The resulting sound was a thousand bells calling out death and power.

Through the dust and swirling mass of iron, we could see

the approaching army. They had come up behind their iron veil on horseback. When their advance was stopped, they tried to halt, but the momentum was too strong. The rest of the army crashed into them from behind. The horses reared, pulling back. Their riders' mouths opened, most likely screaming out commands, but they were voiceless over the roaring and clanging.

One of the jinn lifted his hand, palm outward, at the wall.

"Taja!" I screamed. I couldn't tell if she heard me, but she saw where I was pointing and nodded. Then she turned to Saam and kissed his cheek.

A second later, she was gone. Her body dissolved into a long bolt of cobalt fire that pierced through the wall like an arrow.

"Taja, no!" Saam screamed. We watched in horror as she solidified beside the jinni and pulled him off his horse.

The roaring became an echoing ringing, as if everything had gone silent at once. I watched as Saam transported to her side, and the two of them rolled on the ground, grappling with the foreign jinni. There was a flash of silver through the rust-colored cloud, and then they disappeared beneath it.

Taja had left me with the weight of the wall, the weight of protecting everyone behind me. But I was a new magus. I wasn't as strong as Taja. If it had taken two of us to hold up the wall before, how could I do it alone?

Atish squeezed my shoulder, and I remembered to focus. I could not watch for the jinni's dagger. I could not drop my eyes again.

The iron wall pushed against mine, and I held it. Painful vibrations echoed through my wrists, up to my elbows, and shook my arms, but I was not going to let it go. I was not going to let it fall.

If it hadn't been for Atish squeezing me every time my eyes drifted, every time I tried to look through the wall, I would have failed. I gritted my teeth, and pushed.

My arms were shaking. All of my wishpower was flowing through my hands, and it was thinning. There wasn't much time left.

My hair whipped into my mouth and stuck there. I was shaking so hard I could barely breathe, and then I felt it: the last of my wishpower. Like the last grains in an hourglass, it trickled out. It didn't even reach the invisible barrier. Then Atish's wishpower flooded into me. It was like being drenched in cold water, and I sucked in a deep breath, renewing my push against the iron.

At last, Atish's power waned and we slumped onto the ground, arms wrapped around each other, waiting for the wall to run over us.

Suddenly, the wind was sucked away. The iron balls dropped onto the broken field like scattered beads. The stilled air smelled of blood and grass and horses. My ears rang, echoing the ringing of the iron balls when they smacked each other.

On the other side of the band of iron balls lay a small mound of figures surrounded by a horde of men on horses. Atish pulled me onto my feet.

"Transport back," he said. *"Now."*

"I can't," I said hoarsely.

"Go," he said, and he shoved me behind him. Then he lifted his hands out to the men on horseback. A few had pulled away from inspecting the fallen, and were starting to urge their horses across the line. They would be on us in seconds.

I couldn't have transported if I'd wanted to. I took out Firuz's dagger and held it up. My wishpower was spent, but I could still use my arms.

The other army yelled, and the sound pushed through me, nearly knocking me down. Then I heard a rumbling behind me. I turned to look and saw the unbelievable. Hundreds of soldiers, men and Shaitan together, were lifting their swords and daggers in the air, shouting a response to the Mongols in one thunderous, unified voice.

The battle had begun.

✦ 44 ✦

NAJWA

WHEN THE IRON dropped to the ground like a heavy, deadly rain, the tension eased considerably. Relief rippled through the ranks. Yashar, Melchior, Aga, and Firuz had transferred across the river to stand beside me just as it fell. Yashar was shaking, but when the roaring of the storm stopped, his shoulders relaxed and he looked up at the clear sky. I caught Firuz watching me, and I nodded at him.

Thank you, I said.

I did nothing. It was all you.

Now that the veil of iron was down, the attacking soldiers kicked their heels into their horses' flanks and leaped over the newly drawn line in the ground. Zayele and Atish were at the front, and I watched Atish throw out fireball after fireball. The soldiers parted and flowed past Atish and Zayele, like a river parting at a large stone.

Kamal and Ibrahim raced forward, side by side, raising their Damascus steel swords. I did not want to watch, but I could not look away.

Yashar reached for my hand then and squeezed it. "Najwa," he said, and his voice shook.

"Melchior, he needs to leave," I said.

"We need him most now," Melchior said. "Tell me, child, what do you see?"

Yashar's lower lip was trembling and blood streamed from his nose, but he faced the coming horses. "There is a jinni there. His fear is not like the others'." We looked to where Yashar pointed. A man walked slowly between the horses. His eyes were locked on Atish.

"What is it?" asked Melchior. "Tell me!"

"He's afraid of lightning."

Instantly, Melchior lifted his hand, made a wish, and blew it at the jinni. A bolt of lightning cracked from Melchior's palm and hit the ground directly in front of the jinni. He back-pedaled and followed the trail of smoking air to look straight at Melchior. Then his eyes widened.

"He's afraid of you," Yashar told Melchior.

"He has good cause," Melchior said. Then he cast another bolt of lightning. This time, when the jinni jumped away, Aga had a fireball already on its way. It hit him squarely in the chest and he fell over, never to stand again.

"Are there any others?" I asked. As much as I disliked using Yashar, I could see we needed him. If we could find the remaining jinn, the other army would no longer have an advantage.

"Yes," Yashar said. He squeezed his eyes closed and grew very still. "There is another. I think he is the only one." He raised a hand and pointed. "There."

This jinni was dressed exactly like the soldiers, but instead of carrying a long sword, he held out a spear. "Are you sure?" I asked.

"Does it matter?" hissed Melchior.

"He is afraid of dying. And drowning."

Melchior made a noise that sounded like he was choking, and I looked at him, alarmed. He was grabbing at his throat and his eyes were wide as eggs.

"Melchior!" The last jinni was pointing the spear at him. What wish would do such a thing? I didn't know what to do. I could not kill the jinni, and I could not help Melchior.

But I could make the jinni feel like he was drowning. Quickly, I transported to his side and grabbed him by the wrist. He tried to make a wish, but I was faster, and I transported him to the only place I could think of.

We splashed into the Tigris and I let him go, shocked by the coldness of the water. He drifted downstream, screaming and grasping at the bits of straw that had come loose from the bridges. They did nothing to hold him up, and he clawed at the water. Then, as if he knew all was lost and he had nothing to lose, he narrowed his eyes and aimed his palm at me. I dove under the water and felt the fire graze the back of my neck. After it passed, I came up and grabbed on to the edge of the bridge.

The jinni was gone.

I climbed up onto the bridge, grateful now that it had remained, despite an array of scorch marks. There, I sank to my knees, heaving and trying to shake out the jitters that raked my body.

Everyone was still fighting. Yashar was still there, too young for war. Melchior might be dead. And my friends were in the thick of swords and fire. I had to return, even though every muscle in my body wanted to lie down on the bridge and give in to any darkness that might come my way.

Groaning, I wiped the water off my face and stood. After an initial rush of blood to my head, I took a deep breath.

"*Shatamana*," I said. And although the wish was weak and my voice betrayed my will, it worked.

45

ZAYELE

"ATISH, WE NEED to get to Taja," I said. He grunted in response while he knocked over an enemy soldier with the point of his elbow.

"Can you see her?" he asked, pushing against the torrent of soldiers and blades, but they were too many.

"I wish these men would get out of our way," I hissed. I hadn't meant to make a wish, but it sprouted within me, unfurling and blooming. I released a breath and the wish flowed with it, a gray, smoky tendril that reached for each man and wrapped around his neck. The smoke drifted off me, up into the air, and dragged the men by their throats into the air. They screamed and kicked, but it did them no good. They were like leaves writhing on an ironwood branch.

The wish pulled the men out of our way and across the battered fields. I watched, openmouthed, until they were nothing more than a dot in the distance, and although these men had meant to kill me, I cringed at the thought of what might happen when the wish dissolved. They would have far to fall.

Atish nudged me in the shoulder. "And you said you weren't sure you were a magus."

The soldiers who had not been within reach of my wish scattered away from us, making a wide berth on their way to the fight along the river's bluff. Atish and I ran to the three jinn.

The jinni commander lay slumped over Taja, and we pulled him off. Blood had pooled between them, making him slippery, and soon we were wet with it. Taja lay on her side atop broken stalks of barley. The leaves must have been green before they were drenched in brilliant red. The jinni had ripped Taja's chest in two, and the cut ran from her mark, over her left breast, and down to her waist. She was gone, but her eyes were still open.

She was looking at Saam, whose glazed eyes reflected back at her. He had fallen beside her, and there they lay, hand in hand. Saam had taken half a dozen arrows in the back before he fell. Atish gingerly pulled the arrows out and laid them on the ground between the Dyad.

I curled over Taja and sobbed, but my cries were dry and hollow. "Atish," I croaked, not looking up from Taja. I wiped at her hairline, brushing away the stray locks that had fallen over her eyes. I did not want her to not be able to see Saam.

Atish picked up the handful of arrows and broke them over his knees. He tossed them onto the foreign jinni's body. Then he knelt beside me and held my hand. "When we were running, Saam told me he wouldn't let her go alone. I didn't know what he meant then, but now I know. He didn't want to be left behind like Rashid." He rubbed his thumb at the thin white scar on my wrists left behind at the Bonding. "Rashid told us it feels like you're living behind a veil, unable to see the colors as they are. Everything is muted, half as bright. I don't think Taja and Saam ever wanted that. They wanted this."

"They didn't want this!" I yelled back. "They didn't want to die."

"No, but they wanted to make that last step as *one*." His voice got quieter. "And, Zayele, so do I. When our time comes."

The tears finally came. I wept, not caring that I was smearing the blood of my friend across my brow. Not caring that we were sitting in the middle of the fallen jinn and trampled grain.

Tears trickled down Atish's cheeks too, but he did not wipe at them. He looked up and surveyed the battle behind us. Then he sighed in relief. "They're retreating."

I swallowed the souring lump in my mouth and followed his gaze. It was true. They were leaving, some on horses but many by foot, limping or running or dragging one another. They skirted around us, as though we bore a plague. Or perhaps the anger and blood, so plainly exposed on our faces, frightened them.

In the distance, I saw Yashar standing tall beside Melchior, pointing at the front line. Melchior was turning the air into a series of ghostly shapes and monsters, and the Mongol soldiers were fleeing, eyes wide with terror.

Yashar was safe. After all he had seen and not seen, after a morning full of blood, screams, and thunder, Yashar was alive.

Then, as if he knew I was watching, the corners of his mouth lifted and he turned to face me. His lips formed my name, and it came to me over the cries of frightened men, the jubilation of the unified jinni and human army, in a whisper.

"Zayele . . . Zayele . . . Zayele."

✦ 46 ✦

NAJWA

WHEN THE OTHER army started running away, Kamal turned his horse and came to my side. "Climb on," he said before reaching down. "We have to go after them. We need to find out who they are, and why they attacked."

He pulled me up and I slipped in behind him on the saddle. All at once I was awash in the cinnamon smell of him, and I leaned in, not caring now if Ibrahim saw me so close to the vizier. I wrapped my arms around his waist and held on. He kicked the horse's flanks, and we leaped forward, running over the fallen, over the balls of iron, and paused by Zayele and Atish.

They were covered in blood, red and wet. "Are you hurt?" I asked, ready to climb down. Kamal held me on the horse.

"We're fine," Atish said. He glanced at Kamal for a second. "Are you going after them?"

"Yes," Kamal said. "Do you know who they were? You came the closest to their general."

"I never saw their general," Atish said. Then he stepped

over a body and picked up the top half of an arrow and wiped it against his thigh. "This is not your design. It's almost like Damascus steel, but it flares there." He handed it to Kamal.

"These were not made in the caliphate. I think they're from Persia. Thank you. I'm sorry for your friends," Kamal said.

I took a closer look. It was Saam and Taja, hands locked together in death. That was why Zayele had not said a word. She stared at me, hollow-eyed.

"She's dead," she said. "They're both dead."

"I'm so sorry, Zayele." I was unable to say any more. The battle was won, but too many lives had been taken. Greater than the feeling of relief were sadness and loss.

"When you return, tell me who these attackers were," Atish said. "And I will avenge them."

"You will not do it alone," Kamal said. "I believe my brother has a new enemy. And this time, his enemy means him *real* harm."

We said our farewells and urged the horse on again. The horse picked up speed, nearly flying over the landscape, passing stragglers and the mortally wounded. Kamal turned in his saddle to speak to me. His brows were level and serious, his cheeks streaked with dirt, but his eyes were the same as always, and my breath caught in my throat.

"When we're close enough, I need you to make us invisible."

I pulled back. "I'm not sure I can. I mean, even when I'm not tired, it's difficult to take others with me in the wish."

"You were able to transport me to the Cavern once, and this was after you used up nearly all your energy saving your sister's life. You can do this, because it needs to be done."

"The horse too?"

He grinned. "If you can. I'm sure Jasmine wants to be included."

"Your horse's name is Jasmine? After the flower?"

"Yes. If only she smelled as nice. Now, do you think you can do it?"

Was I strong enough? I closed my eyes for a moment and tried to feel for the source of power. It was in the center of my abdomen, deep within, and it pulsed. Yes. I was not empty.

"I can only make us invisible for a short time."

"How long?"

"A few minutes. Enough for us to ride in, gather the information we need, and ride back out."

"If they see us, they'll surround us."

"I know."

We rode another few minutes before we saw the tail end of the army. These weren't stragglers. They were on horseback, and they carried the black and gold banners before them, as if they had won the battle and weren't in retreat.

"Now," Kamal said.

I stilled my mind. *"Shahtabi."*

The wish rippled outward and swallowed us whole, including Jasmine. I could do nothing about the sounds we made, or the hoofprints in the dirt, but Kamal took one hand off the reins and squeezed my hand.

We slowed to match the army's pace and found our way between the ranks to the thicket of banners and burly, helmeted captains. I pinched my mark, recording image after image, and whispered, "We need to get closer."

He brought Jasmine up ahead of the officers, and I turned around on the saddle. The general was the man I'd seen in the tent, speaking with Toqto'a before the attack. He growled something at one of the officers, and the man replied, "Yes, Khan."

Khan. I had heard the name before, but I did not recognize it. Kamal, however, froze in the saddle before yanking the reins and urging Jasmine out of the ranks. When we were clear of the army, we galloped until the wish dissolved.

"Who is Khan?" I asked.

"He's the leader of the Mongols. I've only heard one reference to him before. We need to get back and let everyone know."

"With a caliphate as large as this, there are bound to be enemies on all sides," I said.

Kamal smiled. "That is why we need a friendship with the jinn. It's why we need *you*." Then he lifted my hand and kissed the back of it. "When we return to Baghdad, I'm going to have my father release the news about Hashim. Everyone deserves to know the truth, especially when word reaches them about how we fought *with* the jinn today."

I leaned forward and kissed the thin strip of skin between his jacket and his turban. He was warm, and tasted like all the spices in Baghdad.

· 47 ·

ZAYELE

THERE WERE TOO many bodies stretched across the burial ground, lying stiff and wilted on their stone tables. Twenty-three jinn died that day, and all but one were Shaitan. A few had drowned in the river, and someone had had to collect the bodies strewn along the riverbank where they'd gotten stuck in the reeds and outcroppings. Then they had to be taken to the Cavern and carried down the narrow steps of the golden dome into the shallow crypt of basalt gravel and multicolored crystal obelisks.

I had been the first to find Taja's body, but I had known her for the shortest amount of time. Since I had no claim to her, I stood behind the other magi when they laid her on the table. An older woman, possibly her mother, stood on the other side, eyes flicking between Taja and Melchior, widening in sadness and narrowing in hate. She was fortunate to have any feelings at all. The battle and all the death had left me singed. I was unable to feel anything but lost.

"Lost" wasn't fear. It wasn't hatred, or sadness, or relief. Everything around me had gone too far too quickly. I was a girl; I was a bride; I was a jinni; I was a magus. But what did any of these things mean? Who was I to take these names and stitch them into my skin?

I had these thoughts while they pulled Taja's memories into a pomegranate-colored crystal. Were we truly nothing more than a series of moments strung together and frozen in stone? Or were we the names we were given?

I left after they were finished with Taja, but I was not finished with her. I carried her with me up the stairs and into the wishlight. I let the impression of her thread itself into my mind, latching onto memories I would never forget. I had not wanted to give them up to the crystal. I would not share.

Atish found me later, sitting beside the very fountain I'd sat at when I first arrived in the Cavern. He was muted, like a lantern with dirty glass. He slumped onto the stone bench and rested his elbows on his knees. He rested his face in his hands, and shook his head. "The men and women I trained with. They're gone."

My body moved on its own, leaning into him and wrapping an arm around his shoulders. I could not imagine if I'd lost thirty Tajas. No. There could only ever be one.

"Zayele," someone said. The voice came from the other side of the fountain, and I turned to see Yashar. He stood alone, in the absence of Melchior's shadow.

I got up, leaving Atish to his grief, and went to retrieve Yashar. With each step I took, he seemed to age a year. He was no longer a child. He was a young man deposited in the scarred, thin frame of a boy. I picked up his hands in mine and brought them to my face.

He pulled them away. "I don't need to feel you to see you anymore. I know you by the fears you carry with you."

It was that sentence that crushed everything I had left. "Yashar," I croaked. "I'm sorry I did this to you. I'm afraid to try fixing you again."

"I do not need fixing, cousin."

Suddenly, I realized he was right. I had never fully looked at him. All I'd ever seen were his scars, his damages. I had not seen his determination and strength. I'd thought his poetic self had been crushed by blindness, but that wasn't something that could be taken from a person. Blindness took away a person's eyes, but it didn't take away what they were.

"I think I'm just now seeing you," I said. Tears welled in my eyes, and I let them fall. "You've done so much, Yashar. You're almost a man now, and you've found your place."

"I'm not *almost* a man," he said, and gave me a ghost of a smile. "I'm eleven and I've fought in a battle."

"Are you going to stay with the Shaitan now?" I asked.

"I will stay with them for now, as long as they need me," he said bravely. "And maybe, someday, I can turn the fears I see into words, and write them down."

"You could study at the House of Wisdom." I was so relieved, I nearly clapped. "Would they let him leave the Cavern?" I asked Atish.

"He doesn't have to ask permission," Atish said. "And I

think he has a cousin who might be able to arrange something for him in Baghdad."

"I'm going to take care of myself, Zayele. You don't have to worry anymore."

"No, I don't." I grinned at him and then pulled him into a hug. He resisted for a second before giving me a pat on the back.

The more I considered the idea that I had been blind to what Yashar really needed, the more the scars flaked off me, and I started to *feel*. I was angry Taja had been killed. I was furious with Ibrahim, and Melchior, and whoever it was that had started that storm. I was sad beyond anything I'd felt before. But there was a crack in all these feelings, splintered by the lightness of hope. Yashar had saved himself. He could have a home amongst those who did not care what sort of sight he had.

"Do you want to stay here?" I asked Yashar. "With jinn?"

"One of your fears—it's fading away," Yashar said absent-mindedly. "I don't mind staying, but maybe I can spend some of my time in the House of Wisdom, learning from the men there. Learning peace."

I wept. All of my worry concerning him had been swirling around me, and he must have known I'd feared for him. Or thought I feared him and this new sight. Crying, I held him tighter against my chest.

"Yashar, let me take you there. You don't have to see Melchior anymore. You don't have to be with jinn anymore."

"I don't mind the jinn. Everyone is afraid of exactly

the same things, so I don't see much of a difference between us."

Atish stood then and joined us. "This boy *is* a poet. We
might need him to show us the truth."

Atish and I took Yashar between us, swirling in flame and
smoke, right into the House of Wisdom. A scholar had been
placing books on a shelf and he dropped them on his feet when
we arrived. But he did not mind.

They took Yashar into their special tribe of scholars and
scribes, artisans and scientists. We did not tell the humans of
Yashar's sight, knowing that it would only cause more grief and
trouble.

The House of Wisdom gave him a scribe, and every few
days a scrap of paper would arrive through the Lamp. Each
one contained a poem, a thought, or a tale. They were all connected, and the ending never came.

One night, Atish and I had been leaning over the bridge, talking about what we planned to do next, when we heard someone clearing her throat. We turned to find Najwa standing
awkwardly in the middle of the bridge, with her hands clasped
together.

"I thought you might want to deliver this one yourself," she
said, and she pulled out a letter from her belt. "It's for Melchior, from Yashar."

Her fingertips were cold when they brushed against mine
during the handover. Something was wrong.

"What is it?"

She gave a lopsided smile. "I came to deliver this, but I also came to go . . . to see . . ."

Atish went to her and wrapped his arms around her. "It's all fine, Najwa. You can see Faisal whenever you want. You're not one of the Haunted. We won't let you get that way."

She wept into his arms for a moment before pulling away. She wiped her eyes and sniffed. "Thank you."

Before she turned away, I took her into my arms too. "Visit often," I whispered.

✦ 48 ✦

NAJWA

THE BATTLE HAD left so many dead, the funerals lasted for days, and it was hard to find a private time in which I could visit Faisal and my mother. At last, the burial ground was left only to those who didn't want to leave, or talk, or be seen by the living, and I was able to make my way to Mariam's and Faisal's crystals. My feet crunched over the black stones, but I was careful to keep quiet. I didn't want to disturb the more frequent mourners.

When I was nearly to the yellow and green crystals, I saw a figure kneeling before Mariam's. He was draped in a rough black shawl, but it did not hide his identity well. It was Melchior, and the fringe on the shawl danced by his elbows. His shoulders shook with sobs.

I stopped short, unsure whether I should head back upstairs or wait until he was done. If he was revisiting a memory, he could be there for a while. But he was crying, and no one cried when their minds weren't in their own bodies.

As silently as I could manage, I tiptoed until I was directly behind him. He was facing away from me, with his hands pressed onto the ground before Mariam's crystal.

"They are all I have left of you," he said. He curled his hands around the gravel, picking up handfuls and squeezing them through his fingers. "I was able to ignore them at first, but I see too much of myself in one and too much of you in the other to deny them. If you could see them now, you would be proud."

Melchior leaned back on his heels, dried his eyes with the shawl, and stood up. When he turned around, I was still deciding whether I should run or stay, and I knew I had a look of panic on my face. He too looked alarmed.

"Najwa?" I nodded. He had looked to my Eyes of Iblis Corps mark to see which twin I was. "I had not expected to see you." He drew up to his full height, and all the years of disdain for the weak fingered out across his face like the roots of a weed.

"I came to visit Faisal and Mariam before I return to Baghdad. I didn't expect to see you either."

"Well, it seems we have a related interest in this yellow crystal."

"Yes. I, um, saw one of your memories once." I winced as soon as I said it. It had come pouring out unbidden, and I covered my mouth.

His eyes darkened. "How is that?"

I gulped. "In the House of Wisdom, there was a shard of memory. It was of you, in the palace's dungeons."

He growled, half turning away. "I will find that crystal and crush it to powder. Tell me, what did you think of your weak grandfather, giving in to the old caliph's demands?"

"You weren't weak!" I exclaimed. "You fought him every day, and the wishes were painful, and binding. You didn't have a choice. It was pure luck you were able to escape!"

"Yes, with the help of that snake, Hashim."

That wasn't the point. "But you weren't weak. I felt the pain you experienced, and it was so much like what burned my lungs when I tried to disobey Zayele's Fire Wish. But it made you stronger. I used that knowledge, that wisdom, when Ibrahim tried to force me to drown the Shaitan. The only thing you did wrong was to deny Hashim's request to help his starving parents. You turned him into a monster."

Melchior raised a brow at me. "Perhaps I misjudged you, Najwa. Your strength is not in form, like your mother's was. Faisal must have seen your perseverance and loyalty from the start, and that is why he insisted you be trained into the Eyes." I looked away at the mention of Faisal, but he continued. "You stood your ground when I believed the Forgotten were enslaved by the Mongol army, but you returned as ordered and did what you could to help our situation. You fought off Ibrahim's wish, saving many lives. And you have convinced the caliph that we are no longer his enemy. Yes, I misjudged you, granddaughter." He sighed and turned back to the yellow crystal. "Just as I misjudged her." His voice cracked, and he sank back onto his knees.

"I'm sorry—"

"Leave me," he whispered. Before I could say any more, he

pressed his palms against Mariam's crystal and dove into her memories. His posture softened, and I knew he wasn't in the present any longer.

I decided not to revisit Mariam's and Faisal's memories that day, with a promise to return when I was ready to learn something new instead of reliving their lives in place of my own.

In the end, it didn't matter that I wasn't as powerful a jinni as my sister. Power wasn't something I wanted. After a lifetime of war, fear, and superstition, Baghdad was living up to its name as the City of Peace.

There were still many corners filled with hate, many shadows reaching for blood and nightmare, but under the bright sun of midday, the great dome radiated peace. You could not look up at the sky without feeling the city sigh in relief.

A single jinni walked alone across the Court of Honor in full view of the black-robed ministers, the peacock throne, and the three men on the dais.

My hair dripped in gemstones of all colors, and my eyes were lined in glittering mica. I had taken care to wrap a peridot hijab over it all, to mute the brightness, but the gems shone through the sheer weave, catching light and scattering the reflection across the polished floor. My gown was one that Zayele had given me. Its sleeves and neckline were bordered in the colors and weave common to my father's people. Dressed this way, I must have confused them. Was I jinni or human? Or was I both—a woman with blood of fire and water, ready to be the conduit between the races?

I lifted my chin and stopped directly in front of the caliph. He had sunk into the throne, no longer the robust man he had been the first time I spied him. But his eyes were just as alert, his mind just as calculating.

Ibrahim sat on a stool beside the peacock throne. He had taken off his armor, and with it the scowl he had always worn in my presence. Still, he would not look me in the eye. Ibrahim was no longer my enemy, but I would not call him friend.

Kamal sat opposite his brother, on the other side of the caliph. His head was heavy with the turban of vizier, and at first I thought he was disappointed I had arrived with all my jinni colors, but then he glanced up and smiled. Pride was etched in the corners of his mouth, and I smiled in return.

"Caliph al-Mansur," I said, "the People of the Lamp have accepted your request for peace."

I bowed and held out the scroll signed by every member of the Diwan. A member of the Court of Honor took it from me and presented it to the caliph. The caliph glanced over the writing, raised a brow at Kamal, and then tapped the scroll against one of the golden peacock heads beneath his arms.

"Finally, it is over with the jinn," he said with a sideways glance at Ibrahim. "But we now have enemies of our own race. We received a message today from the general of the Mongol army. He claims he will make his way into Baghdad and burn it to the ground. I have no reason not to believe he is sincere, but if we have the support of your people—your mother's people—we can save the city." He paused, brought his fingers to rest against his lips, and stared at me across the echoing space.

"You have our support," I said. Delia had already had a glimpse at this letter. She had gone to the enemy encampment in the foothills and stood behind the general while he wrote it. He tied it to the foot of a pigeon and cast it into the sky, never knowing a jinni recorded the entire event. When I had come to the Diwan for them to sign the treaty, they were ready with this news. They knew what the caliph would ask of us.

"Then I welcome any and all jinn into the city. You may pray at our mosques, you may bathe in our baths, and you may study at our House of Wisdom."

I thanked the caliph and backed out of the Court of Honor. As soon as I was clear of the ministers and their dark, heavy robes, I ran to the harem. I was not looking for the women there. I did not want their congratulations, their respect, or even their conversation.

I threw aside the red curtain, trotted over the path that traversed the harem garden, and went to the grate at the end of the stream. I plunged my hand into the cool water and spread my fingers, feeling for it. After a moment of passing panic, I found it: the remains of the jasmine blossom, slick with decay and stuck like enamel to one of the bars of the grate. Carefully, I peeled it away and pulled it out of the water.

It was a tiny thing, all gray and mottled and shriveled. Only one bit of a petal remained, but I knew without doubt it was the same jasmine blossom. The very same, because when I uncurled the edge, the tiny flame pulsed, weak and heavy with want of a place to go. I used the edge of my fingernail to scrape it off the petal, and I held it up to the light. I had tried to wish away the pain of not knowing my mother, but I no longer felt any pain. Her memories were preserved, and although I could go to them whenever I wanted, I was happy to leave them there beside Faisal's. For now anyway.

I sighed, finally content. The flame sank into my fingertip, blinked once, and was gone.

And suddenly, I remembered why I had come to Baghdad. It wasn't because I was in love with the prince, although I certainly wanted to be near him. It wasn't to watch the humans for the Eyes of Iblis Corps. It wasn't even because I wanted to end the war.

I came because Baghdad promised me sunlight and stars.

ACKNOWLEDGMENTS

THEY SAY WRITING the second novel is harder than the first. They also say every novel is equally difficult. Whether "they" are right or not doesn't matter, because I didn't write this story by myself. I have been deeply fortunate to have amazing support, and I cannot thank you all enough. You've touched my heart.

Thank you to my writing group for coaching me not only in the writing of a sequel but also in the Art of Debuting. Laurie Halse Anderson, MJ Auch, Suzanne Bloom, Bruce Coville, and Ellen Yeomans, you're an inspiration and a wealth of love. Bruce, I'm coming back to haunt Clarke Street. Ellen, you've nourished me with more than just good food. Hugs to you all.

My writing partner, friend, and life coach Emma Kress has done more than her fair share in helping me get this book written, revised, and polished. Thank you!

Thank you to the Fourteenery for the laughs, mischief, and morale, and the Hanging Gardens Tumblr group for keeping me on my toes. Thank you to the OneFourKidLit group too, for making my debut year both fun and supportive.

Marieke Nijikamp, thank you for your in-depth critiques and frighteningly fast reading. Kaye, thank you for your support, guidance, and heart. شكرا and *dank je wel*!

A warm thank-you to Alison Kolani and the entire copy-editing team. I apologize for the headaches. Sincerest gratitude goes to Nicole de las Heras for the beautiful, jaw-dropping design of both this book and *The Fire Wish*. Thank you, Lydia Finn, for being my publicity champion and helping to bring these books to the light. Random House Children's Books has been a dream come true. I am privileged to work with you all.

Diane Landolf, I would not have written this without your support, your creative genius, or your editorial talent. You are the best combination of cheerleader and slave driver a writer could ask for, and I'm grateful to call you my friend as well.

My agent, Laura Rennert, deserves more thanks than I have space to mention. Thank you a thousandfold! I can't wait to share my next book with you—I have a feeling you're going to like it.

Mom and Dad, thank you for taking care of the kids and me while I was finishing up the first draft. Mary Lough, thank you for the many, many hours you've spent taking care of the family while I was writing. I love all of you.

Henry and Elizabeth, thank you for your unconditional enthusiasm for my books. I cannot wait till you can read them.

Finally, Jim, this book is for you, for uncountable reasons. We made it through five years of graduate school (with children!) while I was writing these books. We're a good team, you and me.

ABOUT THE AUTHOR

AMBER LOUGH is a lover of foreign words and cultures, nearly forgotten folktales, and groups of three. She spent half her childhood outside the U.S. and speaks Japanese, some Russian, and not enough Arabic, and hopes to add German to her list. She lives in Germany with her scientist husband, two impish children, and a cat named Popcorn. For a pronunciation guide, cast of characters, and more, please visit amberlough.com. Follow her on Twitter at @amberlough.